ALL WE NEVER KNEW

ELENA AITKEN

For every woman who has ever forgotten who they are—even for a moment.

Maren

MAREN BENNETT WASN'T STUPID. Not that it would take a private investigator to know that they were up to something behind her back.

No.

It definitely didn't take a genius to notice the whispering between the two of them when they thought she was out of the room, the furtive glances at their cell phones when they thought she was busy with other things.

It's not that they didn't try to hide it. They did.

But there was nothing that her husband and best friend could keep from her. She knew them better than anyone else in the world. And they knew her. Which was why they should have known that she'd find out the truth that they'd tried so desperately to hide.

With the days getting longer, the sun wasn't quite down yet by the time Maren pulled into the driveway and the house was eerily quiet. If she'd needed a clue, that would have been it. By seven on a Friday night, the house she and Davis had made a home in for the last fourteen years was usually lit up with life. In the living room, the television with whatever show Davis was currently binging on Netflix would be flashing on the screen. Upstairs, Rylee's room and every single light switch she'd passed to get there, would be flicked on as she figured out her teenage life and her plans for the weekend.

Despite the quiet, the house still felt full of life—the way it always did—as Maren made her way up the walkway to the front door. She hesitated before turning the handle, which was ridiculous.

Should I ring the bell? It was a stupid question. It was her house, after all. Every inch of it was a part of her from the moment she'd fallen in love with it when Rylee was only two years old. They hadn't even been looking for a new house when Maren first drove past the white clapboard two-story with the manicured lawn and carefully tended gardens and the For Sale sign out front. It was a family house. A *home*. She could picture Rylee running through the sprinkler on hot summer days and hosting family dinners in the formal dining room on holidays. It would be their forever home.

She'd gone straight back to their two-bedroom split-level with the patchy brown front lawn and told Davis about the big white house. It had taken some convincing, and more than a little bit of sacrifice in those early days before Davis's career in finance had really started to take off, but they'd bought it and ever since, the house had become a part of her.

She straightened her shoulders, gave them one more moment to pull themselves together inside—as surely they'd heard her car in the drive—and then finally put her hand on the brass knob and twisted.

"Hello? Anyone home?" She called out—injecting just the right amount of cheer into her voice—as she pushed the oak door open and stepped into the entryway.

There was no sound at first and then, just as she'd predicted, the lights flicked on and her husband and best friend were both in front of her, wearing matching guilty expressions.

A second later, someone in the shadows behind them yelled, "*Surprise!*"

Not wanting to completely ruin the effect, Maren pressed her hand to her chest and feigned shock. "A surprise party? For me?" She glanced at Davis, who shook his head as he walked over to kiss her cheek in greeting.

"You knew."

It wasn't a question, so she didn't bother answering as she slipped her hand into his and accepted a hug from her oldest and closest friend, Sabrina Miller.

"I knew you knew." Sabrina sounded somewhat disappointed.

A twinge of guilt flickered in Maren's gut. Maybe she shouldn't have tried so hard to figure out their secret.

"Of course, I knew." Maren winked and blew her a kiss. "But it doesn't matter. I'm still so surprised to see everyone and it's super sweet. Thank you." She looked between them both. "Really. This is amazing."

Maren didn't like to lie, but she could and she would when the situation called for it. And because she'd made a habit of not wanting anyone to ever feel bad, particularly on her account, she smiled broadly and told them again how happy she was that they'd gone to so much trouble.

The truth was, the last thing Maren had wanted was a party to celebrate her fortieth year. Not even a small one. But if she'd learned one thing over the years, it was it seldom mattered what she wanted as long as her family was happy. After a while, her own wants and desires had more or less merged with those of her family's, so most of the time it was hard to tell what it was that she wanted.

"Come on." Sabrina took her hand in hers. "You should make your rounds, birthday girl. Let's go say hi to everyone and get you a drink."

They left Davis by the door in case more guests arrived,

and together they walked through to the living room so Maren could greet the gathering of her friends and neighbors. The more hugs, kisses, and well wishes she received, the more relaxed she became until she found herself enjoying the small party. She'd been hoping for something a bit more laid-back to celebrate, and had even done her best to drop a few hints for a quiet dinner at one of the fancier restaurants downtown or maybe even just some takeout. Something where no one had to go to a lot of fuss. But now that she was there and the house was full, maybe it wasn't so bad. After all, it was nice to see everyone all together and they were there for—

"Happy birthday, Mom." Rylee pushed through the crowd and to Maren's delight, let her mother squeeze her in a bear hug the way she used to when she was little. It happened less and less frequently and Maren would take it where she could. "I bet you're really surprised, right?" She rolled her eyes in the way she'd recently perfected and laughed.

"Of course I am." Maren laughed with her daughter.

"I told them not to." Rylee grabbed a mini quiche from a tray. "But you know Auntie Sabrina. Once she decides to do something…"

"There's no stopping her." Maren finished for her.

"Like a bulldozer," they said together. It wasn't the first time.

Next to her, Sabrina pretended to be offended. "Hey." She shrugged. "I may be a bulldozer, but I'm a dozer who knows what she wants and I always get it. Don't I?"

"I wouldn't have it any other way."

"Good. Because I might not be good at a lot of things, but throwing a party for my best friend is definitely one of the areas where I shine."

Maren laughed. Sabrina had been on the end of more than one joke about her flightiness over the years, but she was right: partying had always been her strong suit.

"You're good at lots of things."

Sabrina gave Maren a kiss on the cheek. "Getting better," she corrected as she rubbed her growing belly. "And right now, I'm going to be good at getting this baby some chocolate."

Maren tried her best not to roll her eyes. It may have been almost sixteen years since she'd given birth herself, and maybe she'd forgotten a few things, but as far as Maren was concerned, her best friend was definitely milking the whole cravings part of the process.

Rylee waited until Sabrina left before she whispered to her mom, "I really did tell them not to have a party." She took a bite of pastry and, with a mouth full, kept talking. "But Dad said he owed you something good after totally dropping the ball for, like, ever."

Maren laughed again. Davis *had* dropped the ball for like ever. He had a lot of strengths, but making a big deal over birthdays or anniversaries wasn't one of them. Not that she minded. Not really.

Special occasions were her area. Just four months earlier, she'd hosted a huge blow-out with all Davis's buddies from work, some of the parents from Rylee's swim club who they'd become friendly with, and all of their old friends from high school all packed into the local sports pub to celebrate his fortieth. It was no small miracle that she'd pulled it all off. But she had.

Because that's what Maren did. Organizer of parties, holidays, and...just life in general.

"It was really nice of them to do this." Maren couldn't be sure whether she was trying to convince her daughter or herself. She took a quiche of her own but hesitated before putting it in her mouth. "And thank you for being here, kiddo." She kissed her on the forehead. "It means a lot. I'm sure you'd rather be anywhere else." Rylee distanced herself a little more from them every day in favor of her friends. Even though it hurt Maren's feelings every time her daughter chose a night watching YouTube with her friends instead of time with her, she just kept telling herself it was normal developmental behavior. Even if that was true, it didn't make it sting any less.

"Happy birthday, Mom." She shrugged and looked at her feet. "Shouldn't you go find Auntie Sabrina before she eats all the chocolate?"

Even though it made her blush, Maren gave her daughter another kiss before going in search of her friend and getting herself a drink. After all, it was a party.

Not surprisingly, most of the women had found their way into the kitchen and there was a good crowd picking away at the food trays Davis must have ordered from the Italian market she favored. Or more likely, that Sabrina had ordered. Davis wasn't one for details.

"Happy birthday, Maren." Jessica Grant, Maren's next-door neighbor, gave her a big hug before pressing a glass of wine in her hand. "How surprised did you pretend to be?"

Maren winked and took a grateful sip of the much-needed drink. Jessica had lived next door for the last ten years and even though they'd had proximity, their friendship had never grown the way Maren once thought it would. Even so, Jessica knew her well enough to know when she needed wine and lots of it.

"I'm sure Davis knew you knew. How could he not? I mean, men aren't the sharpest—"

"It was nice of him to throw the party." Maren cut off the rant before it could get started. Ever since Jessica had discovered her husband cheating on her a few months earlier and kicked him out, she'd become just a shade too bitter than any of them felt was healthy.

"It was," she said quickly. "Especially because he invited some very handsome, and if I'm lucky, very single men."

Maren almost choked on her wine. "Don't tell me you're finally ready to start dating?"

She secretly, or maybe not so secretly, hoped she would.

"I was thinking about it." She shrugged, but Maren could see the glimmer of excitement in her eyes. "After all, there are definitely things I miss about having a man around."

"Is that right?" She wiggled her eyebrows as she waited for the details that, knowing Jessica, would surely follow.

"Yes." She grinned wickedly and nudged Maren with her elbow. "Like throwing me a birthday party."

She couldn't help but laugh. "Right. Don't give the man too much credit," she said, unable to defend him completely. "Davis had help. I'm sure Sabrina did most of the work."

"You got that right." Sabrina sidled up next to her and gave Maren a gentle hip bump. "Good, you got a glass of wine." She moved back a little and leaned against the sink. "God, I miss wine." Her hand went to her stomach that, at almost six months pregnant, was starting to resemble a basketball.

Not for the first time, Maren couldn't help but feel a twinge of self-satisfaction that finally after years of struggling to get back to a body that was lost to her forever—while her best friend strutted around in her little bikinis with nary a stretch mark in sight—Sabrina finally knew what it was like to have her body stretched and distorted by a tiny human.

The moment she thought it, though, Maren felt bad for allowing herself to think something so petty. After all, it wasn't Sabrina's fault that trying to regain a pre-baby body was like pouring rain back into a cloud. Besides, in only a few months she'd figure it out on her own soon enough.

"Don't worry," Maren told her. "Wine isn't going anywhere. And until that little peanut is born, I'll gladly handle your share." She raised her glass in a mini toast before taking a generous sip.

"You're such a good friend." Sabrina shook her head, but it was true.

Maren really couldn't be happier that her best friend was finally having a baby of her own. Even if she couldn't quite wrap her head around how at forty you would actively choose to become a single mother by going through all the trouble of finding a donor. But then again, it wasn't Maren's story to understand. If Sabrina was happy, she was happy.

With her fortieth birthday looming, Maren had spent a lot of time thinking about what she wanted this new era of life to look like, and becoming a new mother was definitely not on that list. Quite the opposite. With Rylee almost sixteen, and growing more and more independent every day, she was looking to this next year as a fresh start—one that didn't necessarily revolve around her little family, but maybe, a little bit more on her. After all, it was long past time.

The best thing about turning forty was knowing that she was finally right on the cusp of getting her life back. Forty was going to be her year. Hell, maybe even her decade. She took a deep drink of the wine and let the richness roll down the back of her throat as she relished the thought.

Maren didn't need a party to know that these next few years were going to be incredible. Besides finally focusing on herself, her career, and maybe some as of yet undiscovered passions, she was ready to reconnect with Davis, too. They'd always had a spark, but it was time to fan the flames of their relationship back into the roaring fire it once was. In a few years, Rylee would be gone to college and they could finally start taking all of those long vacations they'd always talked about. And they'd be able to afford them, too, because she was finally going to go after that promotion she'd been passing over for years in favor of focusing on her family.

Oh yes. Maren had big plans. And for the first time in her adult life, those plans weren't going to be defined by motherhood.

Rylee

RYLEE MINGLED and drifted around the living room, trying her best not to look too bored, but not really wanting to engage any of the just tipsy enough to be annoying adults in any real conversation. She ducked around the giant potted palm tree thing her mom kept in the living room just in time to avoid an awkward conversation with Mrs. Bingham. She'd been her Girl Scout leader a million years ago, and for whatever reason thought that meant they were friends. The last thing Rylee needed was to get sucked into small talk about what she'd been up to in the eight years since she'd spent Wednesday nights in a gymnasium making tissue paper flowers with the woman.

It was ridiculous that she had to spend an entire Friday night at home because of the stupid party anyway. Especially considering Rylee knew her mom hadn't even wanted it. Not that her dad cared. Or Auntie Sabrina. She'd tried to tell them both. More than once. But they'd insisted that throwing the party was the right thing to do. And maybe they'd been right. After all, her mom hadn't look *too* bothered by it. She'd smiled and laughed and she had seemed really happy that Rylee was there, too.

And that's why she'd given up a Friday night hanging out with her best friend. Because if she hadn't been there, her mom would have been devastated, as if she were her friend and not her daughter. Sometimes her mother's attachment to her was super annoying. Most of the time, really. None of her other friends had a mother who was always in their faces and knew everything about what they were doing and where they were going, and worse…wanted to hang out with them like they were best friends. She was going to be sixteen next month, which meant Rylee really needed her mom to get a life that didn't involve her.

She ignored the little flicker of guilt she felt every time she got annoyed by her mother's involvement. It wasn't all bad.

Besides, it didn't take much for Rylee just to humor her. Mostly because it made her mom happy and of course she really did love her. But also, because her dad was constantly telling her to, "Humor your mother."

It's probably the advice he gave her most. Way more than study and get good grades or be nice to strangers or any of those other bullshit things that parents say. And it seemed to work for him, so why mess with it?

At any rate, Rylee had done her job as the dutiful good daughter, nodding and smiling and most importantly, totally ignoring the constant beeping of her cell phone in her back pocket, which was extra hard to do especially because she knew the whole time that she was downstairs playing good daughter that it was Brice texting.

Just thinking about his wavy, floppy hair that always fell just perfectly over one eye and the casual way he would lift two fingers in a wave every time he saw her—just her; he didn't do that for anyone else—made her want to scream.

In a good way. An out-of-control—*ohmyGod he likes me*—kind of pillow scream.

Because he did. Sienna Wright told her so and she was

Rylee's best friend, so she'd never lie about something so serious. Especially considering Rylee knew that Sienna couldn't even stand Brice. She would always roll her eyes when Rylee mentioned his name and try to change the subject whenever Rylee brought him up. But Rylee didn't care.

Which was why the second she escaped the party to get upstairs and out of sight, she pulled her phone out and...yes. Brice *was* texting her. She knew it.

What ya doing?

I'm bored.

Want to hang? Park in ten?

Did she want to hang? Umm, yes. Hell yes. A million times...yes.

Still standing in the upstairs hallway, she cocked an ear to the party going on downstairs.

Dammit.

Her mom would lose her shit if she asked to go out.

With a sigh, Rylee texted back.

Can't. Mom's party.

A second later—a response.

. . .

So? It's not your party, is it?

He made a good point. It was definitely not her party. A moment later—another beep.

Grab some booze.

There was no way. Her parents would ground her for the rest of her natural life if she took alcohol out of the house. Or at all. She ignored Brice's request and focused on the one thing she might actually be able to do something about.

As quietly as she could, not that it mattered with all the noise coming from downstairs, she crept to the edge of the stairs and peered down. Rylee's mom was nowhere in sight, but her dad was still in the corner with a few of the neighbors. Rylee recognized most of them. The fat bald one was new and she didn't like him. Last summer at the block party, he spent a little too long looking at her chest.

She rolled her eyes and focused on her dad.

There really was no reason her parents shouldn't let her go out. Especially if she told them she was going to hang out with Sienna. They'd been friends since the second grade and they practically lived at each other's houses. Her parents loved her. And if it wasn't for the ridiculous party that her mom didn't even really want, she'd probably already be at Sienna's house. But...

Well?

. . .

Brice's text prodded her. He liked her and he wanted to hang out. How could she not go?

Maybe Tia is free.

Oh hell no! He was not going to call Tia. Not if Rylee had anything to say about it.

Coming. Give me 10.

She looked down the stairs again. Mom still wasn't anywhere to be seen. She must be in the kitchen, which meant if Rylee was quick, she could pull it off.

Moving quickly, Rylee ran back to her room, grabbed her jean jacket and her big slouchy purse before slipping down the stairs. She put her biggest, brightest smile on and walked straight over to her dad.

"Hey, Dad?"

"What's up, Ry? Having fun?"

"That's the thing." She shifted from foot to foot, purposely avoiding the gaze of the fat bald guy. "I'm kind of in the way here and Sienna asked if I wanted to come watch a movie."

"Go for it." He agreed the way she knew he would. Her dad always wanted Rylee to be happy. Especially when he'd had a beer or two and by the looks of the table behind him, he'd had a few more than that.

"Really? I'll only be a few hours."

"Of course. You were here for the surprise. That's the important part. Go have fun but be home by ten."

Victorious, she gave him a quick hug and took off before he could change his mind or more likely, her mom appeared.

She slipped her shoes on at the front door and was almost safely outside when she spotted a gift bag with a bottle of wine in it.

Grab some booze.

Brice's request flashed in her mind. She hesitated, but only for a second. A little wine wouldn't hurt. Her parents let her have a small glass at Christmas last year, and it's not like she got drunk or anything. Besides, no doubt her mom got a ton of wine for her birthday. She wouldn't miss one bottle.

Rylee grabbed the gift bag and shoved it in her purse before slipping out the door to meet Brice.

Sabrina

IT WAS ALMOST midnight when Sabrina Miller pulled her car into the parking space out front of her condo. She put the car into park and stared out across the shared front lawn at the two-bedroom, semi-detached home she'd bought ten years earlier, on a dare. She could remember the exact moment she'd signed the papers. It had been the single biggest commitment she'd ever made in her life. She'd been thirty years old, had never had a relationship that lasted more than three years—although one came close—had bounced between careers since college, and had never owned anything except the very first car her parents had given her as a graduation present almost eight years earlier.

And then there was the condo.

It started out innocently enough at a New Year's party at Maren and Davis's house. There'd only been a few of them drinking and toasting 2008. They'd been going around the room, talking about their accomplishments for the last year and their goals. The same as every year, Sabrina didn't have any. At least not anything of substance compared to the rest of the *grown-ups*. It was Davis who'd teased her that night: "I bet it'll be another ten years before you make any real commitment. Unless you count committing to paying too much rent for that grubby little apartment of yours."

Sabrina was used to the ribbing and normally she was able to brush it off, but for whatever the reason, that night the remark hit home. Maybe it was seeing Maren and Davis and all of their friends with their *real jobs*, their mortgages that had them constantly complaining of interest rates and ongoing repayments, their children and all of their millions of activities, their stressful schedules and *commitments* that all of their lives seemed to revolve around and for a hot minute she was actually jealous of their chaos.

It didn't happen often, but every once in a while, Sabrina looked away from her easy-going life of freedom and no-strings sex and picking up to go on vacation at a minute's notice, and looked into someone else's and felt that annoying twinge of…desire.

That's exactly what had happened in the wee hours of 2008. Something in her snapped and without even thinking about it, she'd said, "Well, I guess you'd be surprised to hear that one of the first things I'm going to do this year is buy my very own home."

She had *no* idea where that had come from, or what had made her say it, but as soon as she did, she found herself actually *wanting* to buy a home. She'd managed to put some money aside over the years, and she'd recently received a small inheritance when her grandmother had died. Maybe she actually *could* buy a house.

And that's exactly what she'd done five weeks later.

The little condo wasn't much, but it was hers and more than that, it proved to everyone that she could actually make a commitment and put down roots.

Or something like that.

As it turned out, it had been a good decision to buy when

she did. Shortly after she signed, the city had experienced a boom, and her little condo development had become *inner city* and *close to the core*, which meant the location was very desirable to young professionals working downtown who didn't want a big commute. And more importantly, it meant the value of her little property had skyrocketed.

Not that it mattered to Sabrina. She didn't work in the core, nor was she planning on selling.

Her hand fell to rest on her growing stomach.

No, she was definitely not planning to sell. The little condo that started out as something to prove was very soon going to become a *family* home.

"Family of two," she said out loud. "Me and you, kiddo."

Suddenly exhausted, Sabrina hauled herself out of the car, bringing the Tupperware container full of leftovers Maren had sent her home with. She couldn't remember the last time she'd come home from an event at their house without a care package. As if she couldn't take care of herself. Deep down, she knew that wasn't the reason Maren always sent her home with food. It was because she cared and she wanted to make sure Sabrina was taken care of. It's what she did. Maren didn't mean anything by it, and Sabrina always felt a little guilty when she let herself think otherwise.

Maren wasn't perfect. But she was damn close. She'd dedicated her entire adult life to being the best mother and wife she could. And friend. She was an amazing friend. The best friend, in fact.

She opened the door with a click, dropped her keys and purse on the hall table, and locked the door behind her before popping the leftovers in the fridge and heading upstairs to bed.

She'd been exhausted when she'd left the party, but by the time she was ready for bed and tucked under the covers, she was wide awake, her mind spinning with thoughts. Maybe it was a symptom of pregnancy, but for the last few months, she'd had a terrible time sleeping and she just couldn't seem to shut her brain off.

Tonight, her thoughts circled around Maren. Likely because she'd just celebrated her fortieth year. She and Davis had planned for months. Well, mostly she'd planned and Davis had taken care of the details she'd instructed him on. But it had all come together perfectly, and even though Maren had insisted she hadn't wanted a party, she really did look as if she'd had fun. By the time Sabrina had left, Maren was definitely tipsy from one too many glasses of wine. Just the way a fortieth birthday should be.

She'd celebrated her own months earlier. Even though they'd all gone to school together, Sabrina was a bit older. Her mother had called her a *bubble baby*, being born right on the edge of the cutoff for school. Her parents could have put her in school a year earlier, but her mom had wanted her to stay home with her. As the baby of the family, her mother had wanted to hang onto her as long as possible, she'd said.

Sabrina's thoughts flipped to her mom and predictably, tears welled up in her eyes. Julie Miller had been full of life. She exuded so much vibrance and color that sometimes it hurt to look at her. When she'd died, the world seemed to leech all of its color. The once brilliant oranges and yellows of a sunset were pastel. The bright blue of the sky where it met the greenest of the summer grass, dull. Everything just…muted. The rest of the family had felt it too. Julie had been the glue that held them all together, and without her, they all drifted apart. Sabrina saw her older brother and sister maybe once a year. And even then, it was awkward and strained, as if they didn't know each other anymore. Which, she guessed, they didn't.

She did make a point to reach out to her dad. In the five years since her mom died, he'd become more and more reclusive. Choosing to spend his days alone, reading or puttering in his garden as if when Julie died, she took the part of him that burned the brightest, too.

Sabrina shuffled herself around in bed until she was on her right side. She let her hand rub the swell of her belly as the tears dripped from her eyes. Her mother would never meet her grandchild. But it wasn't that thought that made her the saddest. It was that her mother hadn't lived to see her own baby girl as a mother in her own right.

It wasn't often that Sabrina felt lonely. For the most part, she loved her life of independence. But there were some nights when the quiet crept up on her, and memories of how things used to be smothered her.

Would things be different if her mother was still alive? Would *she* be different?

It didn't matter.

Sabrina squeezed her eyes shut against the past and focused on the future. On the life growing inside her. That's all that mattered now. Not what could have been—but what will be.

Maren

"THERE'S THE BIRTHDAY GIRL." Davis rolled to his side, the bedsheet slipping a little off his hip as Maren walked into their bedroom.

"It's not my birthday yet." He wasn't drunk, but just buzzed enough to be extra flirty. She grinned at him. "Technically, there's still three days until I'm actually forty, not that I'm counting."

"Close enough." He propped himself up on one arm and used his finger to beckon her to him before she could slip past into the en suite. "Come here."

Despite the fact that she hadn't wanted it, the party had been fun and she'd enjoyed herself. Judging by the slightly spinning room, maybe a little too much. "I need to get ready for bed," she protested, but took a step toward him.

"I can't wait." Davis gave her a fake pout that made her laugh. "I need a kiss right now."

"Okay. But just one."

The second she got close enough, his arms shot out and wrapped around her before he pulled her into the bed with him. "You look ready for bed right now." He kissed her and just the way it had for the last twenty-two years, Maren's heart fluttered and she melted into his touch.

All of her protests were forgotten when her husband started kissing her. It never got old or boring the way she'd once worried it would. Every single time they kissed, it was like the first time. Well, maybe not quite like the first time. But close enough. And even though they weren't intimate as much as they once were—in fact, it had probably been a few weeks— the passion between them was far from gone.

Davis slipped around her so in an instant Maren was underneath him on the mattress. He stroked her cheek with one finger and stared into her eyes. "Did you have fun tonight? I know you weren't surprised, but I hope it was still a good night."

"Of course I had fun." She smiled in an effort to hide her disappointment that he wasn't still kissing her. "Thank you for working so hard with Sabrina to pull it off. It was perfect." It wasn't really a lie. If she had to have a party, the one they'd thrown her had been perfect.

"I'm glad you enjoyed yourself. I know forty is a big one for you."

"It is." Conflicted between wanting to cuddle up with him and deconstruct the evening the way they always did or kiss him again, Maren wiggled beneath him. Her desire won out and she reached up and wrapped her hand around the back of his head to pull him closer. "Kiss me again."

"With pleasure," he murmured against her lips before doing just that.

They'd been so busy for the last few months with Rylee's swim practices and work and just...well, life, that time had a way of slipping past and before they knew it, days turned into weeks and they hadn't been together nearly as much as she would have liked. Maren missed it. No, she missed him.

With her mouth busy, Maren moved her hands down his

back to the elastic of his pajama bottoms and slipped them underneath to press against his bare skin. She felt Davis's lips curl up into a smile against hers and knew he was in agreement with exactly what she had on her mind.

A few minutes later, they were both naked and he was once more on top of her, staring down into her eyes. "I love you, Maren." He stroked a piece of her hair off her cheek and tucked it behind her ear.

It was an exquisitely sweet moment, but Maren wasn't in the mood for sweet.

"I know." She ran her hands down his bare arms in an effort to refocus his energies. "I—"

"No." He shook his head, his eyes narrowing. "I don't say it enough." His voice was serious, his gaze intense. "But I hope you know how much I love you."

"I do."

"I love you more now than I did when we were seventeen and I saw you on your first day of school," he said, as if she hadn't spoken. "Do you remember that?"

Of course she remembered. Starting a new school as a teenager was usually a horrific experience, except Maren had been lucky enough to meet Sabrina, who had the locker next to hers, first thing on her first day. She'd introduced Maren to Davis at lunch that same day, and the rest of the year—the rest of her life—had been anything but horrific.

"Davis." Maren stared up into her husband's deep green eyes, the same eyes she'd fallen for all of those years ago. "I love you, too."

Her heart swelled as he bent to kiss her again and threatened to explode completely when finally they made love. Afterward, content and no longer feeling quite so tipsy, she cuddled in the crook of his arm, her head on his chest, and listened to his deep breathing. She snuggled into his warmth and let her fingers draw small circles on his stomach.

For a few minutes, Maren thought he might be asleep, but then his fingers traced a gentle line down her arm and she turned in his arms to look up at him.

"Thank you again for trying to keep it a surprise," she said into the silence. "But you should know by now that I hate surprises, which is why I always know what's going on." She couldn't help but laugh. "But I do appreciate the effort. Honestly."

"I'm glad." He squeezed her arm. "But I can't take all the credit. In fact, Sabrina insisted on doing most of the work."

"I'm not surprised." Sabrina had always had the tendency to completely dominate a situation. "It's probably a good thing she decided to do the whole single parent thing. I can't imagine her ever acquiescing to anyone else."

It was still strange to think that Sabrina, who'd always insisted she never wanted children of her own, was going to be a mother in only a few short months. Let alone a single mother. Maren had to admit, she'd had her doubts about Sabrina's responsibility, but during her pregnancy, she'd really settled down. She had no doubt that if anyone could navigate the waters of single parenthood, it was Sabrina. But there was still something that didn't feel right about her best friend's pregnancy. Something Maren had always questioned a little bit but had never said aloud.

"Hey," she said before she could change her mind. "Do you think maybe Sabrina isn't telling us everything?"

Davis had his eyes closed, his voice heavy with sleep. "What do you mean?"

"About the father of her baby."

That got his attention. Davis's eyes snapped open. "She used a donor."

"But maybe she didn't." It was an idea that had niggled at the back of Maren's brain for a few months, but she'd never felt right saying it out loud. After all, why would Sabrina lie? "Remember that guy she was dating?"

"You think it's Ryan's baby?"

Ryan had been Sabrina's last boyfriend. He managed a nightclub and was always out late, living a party lifestyle. Definitely not the type to settle down and have a family. She shrugged at Davis's question. "I don't know," she answered honestly. "But maybe. I mean, he wouldn't have been the best candidate for fatherhood. Maybe she just thought it was better than telling us the truth?"

"I don't know, Maren." He closed his eyes again. "It seems like a bit of a stretch."

"What about that chiropractor she works with?"

"Dr. Tommy?"

"Yeah. He seems to be pretty into her. And I know she thinks he's…"

Davis opened one eye and raised his eyebrow. "Seriously, Maren. I don't know why you're so stuck on this. If she said she used a donor, I don't understand why you're questioning it. She's your best friend. Why would she lie?"

Maren knew her husband was right. After all, why *would* she lie? She shook her head and laughed at herself. "You're right. Besides, it doesn't really matter. She's having a baby. And as far as I'm concerned, it's better her than me." Maren sat up and pulled her hair back behind her head before letting it fall again around her shoulders.

"What do you mean?" Davis turned and propped himself up on one elbow. His eyes were wide open again. He knew her well enough to know that there would be no chance for sleep while she wanted to talk.

She shook her head and stared at him. "Can you even imagine having a baby right now? Starting all over again, when we're finally almost home free."

"Home free?" He reached out and took her hand. "I

thought you loved being a mom. Don't tell me you're counting the days now?"

He was only teasing, but his words hit close to home. Her baby wasn't so little anymore and in only a few years she'd graduate and go off to college. The idea made Maren immeasurably sad, but more and more, it had also started to excite her.

"I do," she assured him. "More than anything else in the world. And I'm not counting the days." She paused for a moment. "But it certainly doesn't mean I want to do it again. Who has the energy for crying babies, endless diapers, and sleepless nights? Besides, if I get that big promotion at work, I wouldn't have time for any of that anyway."

Davis squeezed her hand and laced his fingers with hers. "Of course you're going to get it. When's the big meeting?"

"Wednesday." The day of her actual fortieth birthday, which was why she knew without a doubt she was going to get the job. Maren was not a superstitious woman, not really, but she also knew a sign when she saw one and there was no bigger sign that things were going to change than that. A new decade, a new career, a new Maren.

Maren

A FEW DAYS LATER, Maren woke up on her fortieth birthday and just as she had for the last few days, was struck with a wave of nausea that threatened to knock her down the second her feet hit the floor.

She spent the next few minutes throwing up into the toilet, willing her body to kick whatever flu bug she'd managed to pick up. There was no time to be sick. Especially not today of all days. The meeting regarding her promotion would be after lunch, and there was no way she was going to miss it.

She wiped her mouth with the back of her hand and pulled herself up to standing. With both hands locked on the bathroom sink for support, she took her time to make sure she wasn't going to throw up again. A deep breath. And then another. In the medicine cabinet, she found a package of non-drowsy anti-nausea medicine pills she'd bought a few summers ago when Davis had insisted on taking her sailing on a coworker's boat. It was probably expired and less effective, but this was no time to be concerned with details. She'd take what she could get. Anything to stop the swirling in her stomach.

She swallowed a pill with a handful of water and got into the shower.

By the time she made it downstairs, the nausea had passed, leaving Maren only slightly off-center and judging by the amount of bronzer she had to use, way paler than she would have liked.

"Good morning." Davis greeted her with a kiss on the cheek and pressed a cup of coffee into her hand. "Happy birthday, sweetie."

"Happy birthday, Mom." Rylee gave her mom a side hug, carefully avoiding the coffee. "Do you feel wiser?"

"Wiser?"

Rylee grinned. "You always ask me that on my birthday and now that you're forty, you must be pretty wise, right?"

Maren tried to laugh, but her stomach chose that moment to act up again, so instead she just shook her head and sat at the table. The strong aroma from the coffee, which normally was her favorite part of her morning ritual, was definitely the culprit. She pushed the cup away as far as she could and took a deep breath.

"I'm making you birthday pancakes," Davis announced from the stove. He glanced in the direction of the abandoned coffee cup and back at Maren with a look of question. "Are you feeling okay? You look a little pale."

"You do, Mom. Kind of goth, actually."

Maren ignored her.

"You're not still feeling sick, are you?" Davis put the spatula down and sat next to her at the table. "I was kidding when I said you couldn't recover from a few glasses of wine the way you used to."

When she'd woken up the morning after the party not feeling well, both of them had chalked it up to too much wine the night before. But hangovers didn't last five days. Not even when you were forty. And especially considering she'd only had a few glasses of wine. "No." She shook her head. "It must be a little bug or something, but I'm feeling a little bit better every day, so hopefully it will pass soon."

It was a lie. She wasn't feeling any better, but the last thing she wanted was anyone to fuss over her and there was no way she was going to miss her meeting.

"Really, I am feeling a lot better. But maybe I should just stick to toast this morning?"

Davis rubbed her forearm and hopped up from his chair. "One piece of birthday toast, coming up. I hope you're feeling better in time for dinner tonight. I'm going to pick up Indian from Spices on my way home."

Indian was her favorite, but the thought of butter chicken and vegetable korma was not helping her stomach at the moment.

"And don't forget your mom's coming by," Davis reminded her.

As if she could forget. Mother-daughter relationships could be tricky and Maren's was no exception. Of course, she loved her mom and of course, her mother meant well. At least she thought she did. But Barbara's way of showing her love was to pick apart everything Maren did before proceeding to tell her exactly how she could do it better. It was exhausting. And the last thing Maren was in the mood for.

Davis gave her a sympathetic smile as he put a glass of water in front of her a moment later. "Are you going to give your mom her birthday present?" he asked Rylee, who sat on the other side of the table, staring at her cell phone as if it contained the secrets of the universe. She didn't blink or make any indication that she'd heard her dad.

"Rylee?"

Still nothing.

Maren extended her leg and gave Rylee's knee a nudge under the table with her foot. Her daughter's head flew up, her eyes narrowed slightly until she saw the way Maren was looking at her. She gestured with her head to Davis, who was still waiting Rylee's acknowledgment.

"What?"

"I asked you if you were going to give your mom her birthday present?"

Her face colored briefly but she jumped up and retrieved a gift bag from the counter by the back door. "Here you go, Mom." She tried to deposit the bag on the table in front of her mother, but before she could escape, Maren grabbed her arm and pulled her in for a quick hug. She was slipping away too easily these days. And despite knowing it was all part of growing up, Maren still missed the way she used to stop whatever she was doing to give her mom a hug.

Maren held her as long as she could before Rylee wiggled and tried to pull away. "Mom, you're going to make me sick."

"Thank you," she whispered in her ear, ignoring her concerns about sharing germs. Rylee shrugged as she moved away, but there was a glimmer of a smile on her lips as she returned to the opposite end of the table.

Teenagers were tricky, and Rylee was no exception. She was almost impossible to read these days. One moment, she was the sweet girl she'd always been, laughing and smiling, and the next, she was moody and sullen.

Hormones.

Maren could remember exactly what it was like to be her age and this too would pass.

"Come on, Maren. We're waiting."

Brought back to the moment, she turned her attention to the gift bag and pulled the colored tissue paper out with a flourish. She stopped short of throwing it to the floor behind her, and tossed it to the table instead before reaching her hand inside. Her fingers slipped over buttery soft leather and when she pulled the portfolio out of the bag, her eyes filled with tears. She held it in front of her, letting one hand stroke the soft brown surface. "It's beautiful."

"It's for your new job," Rylee blurted.

She shook her head slightly and a tear slipped down her cheek. "I don't have the job yet."

"Mom! Don't cry." Rylee's mouth fell open in mortification. Maren wasn't a crier, never had been. "It's just a thing to hold your papers, Mom. Seriously. Don't cry."

"It's not just a thing," she insisted, thoroughly touched over the gift. "It's beautiful. And so thoughtful."

"And you are going to get the job." Davis put the piece of toast on the table and kissed the top of her head. "There's no doubt about that. They're lucky to have you, and I know you're going to design the best playgrounds any kid has ever seen."

PlayTime, the playground equipment company Maren worked for, designed and created state-of-the-art playground equipment for schools, community centers, and pretty much anywhere else kids played. After five years of doing mostly administration work, she was more than ready to take over her own accounts and design some playgrounds on her own. The gift was absolutely perfect.

"Thank you." She swiped at the unexpected tears. "I don't know why I'm crying."

"Maybe it's an age thing?" Davis neatly ducked Maren's hand as it flung out toward him and laughed as there was a knock at the back door. "Three guesses who that is."

Nobody bothered to answer the door and a moment later, Jessica walked in with a bouquet of early flowers from her garden. "Happy birthday!"

Maren stood to accept the flowers and give her friend a hug. "Thank you. These are beautiful."

"You deserve them." She looked around Maren's shoulder. "Pancakes?" Jessica raised her eyebrows in Davis's direction.

"You really are the perfect husband. Too bad it didn't rub off on Brent."

"Hungry?" Davis didn't wait for an answer before fixing Jessica a plate. He did his best to ignore the comments and ever so slight digs against men that had become part of Jessica's natural way of conversation. Especially because her ex-husband Brent was a good friend of his. She took the plate with a thank-you and sat down at the table.

"You're not eating?" Jessica gestured to Maren's piece of plain toast that she still hadn't managed to take a bite of. "I probably don't have to tell you that breakfast is the most important meal of the day." She winked and took a bite of her own pancake.

"I think I'm just nervous."

"Oh! Today is the big day. I'm sorry, I totally forgot," she said with a mouthful.

"It's all good." Maren took her untouched toast to the counter. "I think I've gotten myself all worked up about it, though. My stomach is a little off today."

"And every day this week." Rylee raised her eyebrow. "Mom, if it were me, you'd make me go to the doctor."

It was true, but she wasn't about to say so.

"It's just nerves," Maren insisted. "Or a little virus or something."

"Or you're pregnant."

Maren froze, her mouth open and her eyes locked on her friend.

"Excuse me?"

Jessica shrugged. "I was only kidding." She looked between Maren and Davis. "Seriously. You should see your faces. Would it really be so terrible?"

Yes! Maren wanted to scream. It would be terrible. Not ten years ago, or even five years ago. But now? It would be beyond terrible. Aware that her daughter was watching her, Maren somehow managed to swallow the words down and instead said, "I'm not pregnant."

Jessica turned back to her pancake. "Stranger things have happened."

Not to her. Those types of things did not happen to Maren Bennett.

She'd been on birth control since Rylee was born. After a particularly hard pregnancy and even harder delivery, Maren and Davis both agreed that one healthy baby was enough for the time being. They'd agreed to revisit it when Rylee was a few years older, but somehow they'd never gotten around to it. If they were going to have another child, they would have done it.

No.

She was definitely not pregnant.

The idea would have been laughable, too, if it didn't scare the hell out of her.

Rylee

"YOU'RE LATE."

Rylee peeked around her locker to see her best friend, Sienna, leaning against the wall with her arms crossed and the same concerned look on her face she'd been seeing way too much of lately.

Rylee ignored it the way she always did. It was easier that way. Besides, she wasn't late for school, just a few minutes later than she usually was. But there was still plenty of time before the first bell rang.

"It's Mom's birthday. We had pancakes." Rylee don't know why, but she felt the need to explain herself to her. She was her best friend and all, but even though they'd been friends forever, it didn't mean she had to tell her everything.

Even though it wasn't long ago that she used to.

"Oh right. I forgot."

Rylee gave her a look. There was no way she knew it was her mom's birthday, but she didn't feel like getting into it. Rylee went back to digging around her locker in search of her calculator.

"I was thinking we could hang out later," Sienna said. "We haven't really spent much time together lately."

Glad that her head was hidden in her locker, Rylee flinched and felt a flash of guilt.

"Yeah. It's been awhile." Her calculator found, she pulled her head out of her locker and looked at her friend.

"So maybe you can come over after school and we can do our homework and check out YouTube. I saw a hilarious video of cats versus dogs the other day and I know you'd love it."

Rylee couldn't help but smile. No doubt, she probably would love it. It didn't matter who you were; anyone who didn't laugh at a cat versus dog YouTube compilation was probably a little bit dead inside. They were so freakin' funny.

"I mean, if you're not busy…" Sienna looked down at her sparkly blue fingernails. "Or doing something with Brice."

And there it was.

The whole reason Rylee had been spending less time with her best friend lately. It was exhausting.

Sienna hated the fact that Rylee had a boyfriend. Well, not really a boyfriend….but a boy who she hung out with.

Whatever.

She hated it.

And she hated Brice.

And Rylee hated hearing about it.

It had just been easier to avoid Sienna's calls than listen to her talk about why Brice wasn't a good guy. On some level, Rylee knew she was just jealous. Maybe not of Brice, but definitely that she had a boyfriend.

They'd been talking about it ever since they were eight years old. What would it be like to hold hands with a guy? Go on a date? Have a first kiss?

And ever since Friday night, when she'd snuck out from her mom's party, Rylee knew the answers to all of those what-if questions. But as much as she'd been dying to tell

Sienna and lay on her bed, hugging a pillow while she spilled all of the details, she hadn't. Because Rylee knew without a doubt that Sienna would get that pinched look on her face. Especially if she told her about the wine she'd taken. Even though they hadn't gotten drunk. Not really. Brice had drank most of it. Rylee only had a few sips. Okay, more than a few. But not enough to be a big deal. Still, Sienna would not approve. She might even try to hide it, but Rylee would be able to see it. The disapproval that would take away from how exciting it had been to hold his hand, have him pull her closer and—

Nope. It wasn't worth risking the awesomeness of it all. So she'd kept it to herself.

"So?" Sienna's voice reminded Rylee she was still waiting for an answer. "Can you come over or are you busy with—"

"Hey."

Rylee's heart did the little flip-flop it always did when she saw Brice. When she turned around and saw him leaning against the locker next to her, looking effortlessly casual, and oh so cute with his hair flopping over one eye, her mouth stretched into a grin that she prayed wasn't too goofy.

"Hey."

Behind her, she heard Sienna sigh but Rylee ignored her and leaned in to meet Brice's kiss. They'd done it a few times since Friday night, but it still gave her all the feels.

His lips were soft and he tasted a little like cinnamon hearts. Rylee had never liked cinnamon hearts until that first kiss. Now she couldn't get enough.

"Oh?"

On some level, Rylee vaguely registered Sienna's surprise behind her and again felt that stupid guilt gnaw at her.

Dammit. She should have told Sienna about her first kiss.

The last thing Rylee wanted to do was stop kissing Brice, but it was a little hard to focus with her best friend's glare burning a hole in her back. Reluctantly, she pulled back and touched her fingers to her lips before turning to face her friend.

"So, maybe later…"

"Forget it," Sienna snapped. The hurt was all over her face and she wouldn't meet Rylee's eyes. "I didn't realize…" She waved her hand aimlessly between Rylee and Brice and dropped it limply to her side. "I'll see you later."

Despite her frustration with Sienna, when she turned and started to walk away, Rylee wanted nothing more than for her to come back. "Sienna," she called after her. "Wait."

She didn't even pause.

"Forget her." Brice put his hand on her shoulder and reflexively Rylee leaned back into his touch.

The bell warning them that class was about to start rang and she slammed her locker shut. "I have math." She adjusted the pile of books in her arms and noticed for the first time that Brice didn't have any. "I should go."

He shook his head and his smile twisted into a wicked little grin. "Nah. Let's cut."

"Cut?"

"Yeah. Let's go. Math sucks anyway."

Her parents would kill her dead if she cut class. They would absolutely lose their shit. Rylee shook her head. "No way. I have a quiz."

"What's the big deal? It's not a test, is it? Besides, aren't you like getting a hundred in that class, brains?"

More than anything, Rylee hated it when he called her brains. It wasn't true, anyway. She was only getting a ninety-five.

Maybe missing one quiz wouldn't hurt too badly.

She glanced down the hall that was quickly emptying out as kids popped into their classrooms, then back at Brice. The idea of spending the next sixty minutes with Brice's arms around her, his lips on hers, was way more appealing than trigonometry.

"Come on," he urged.

"I can't." She bit her bottom lip to keep from changing her mind and responsibility won out. "Not math. But I have Spanish next. I can leave then." She *was* getting a hundred in Spanish.

His lips twitched up at the corners. "Deal. I'll meet you in the parking lot."

He gave her a kiss on the forehead and disappeared in the opposite direction as Rylee watched him until the next bell rang, startling her into action. She sprinted to her class only moments before Mr. Sheppard closed the door and started handing out the quiz papers.

Maren

PLAYTIME STRUCTURES WASN'T a small company, but with only about forty employees, it wasn't one of those giant corporations where employees became just a number on a list somewhere. It was small enough that you could learn everyone's name, but big enough that there was always something going on. Maren had taken immediately to the family-like atmosphere at the office and they'd treated her well through the years as she'd taken on more and more tasks in her role of an assistant account representative, and had quickly become an integral part of the team, but stopping just shy of taking on any real responsibility.

Eileen Sands, Maren's direct boss, never could understand why, despite her desire to learn about the company, Maren continually turned down Eileen's repeated offers to recommend her for the position of account manager. She'd been pushing Maren for years to take on the role.

Maren's days of saying no were over because this year was different. When Leslie retired, and the position opened up, and Eileen once again asked her whether she was interested, Maren wasn't sure who'd been more surprised when her answer had been yes.

It hadn't been planned, and Maren hadn't even given it any real thought, but something had just clicked at that moment and she'd agreed to put her hat in the ring for the position.

That had been over a month ago and finally the day of the meeting was here. Eileen assured her it was just a formality and she was a shoo-in for the position, but still, nothing was a sure thing until the offer was on the table. She was nervous and her tumbling tummy wasn't helping matters at all.

She'd made it through most of the morning without throwing up again, but there were a few moments that were definitely touch-and-go. More than one of her coworkers had made a comment about how pale she was when they came by to wish her happy birthday and good luck on the promotion, and more than once she'd gone to the restroom to splash water on her face and try in vain to cover up the distinct pallor on her cheeks with a compact she'd found in her purse.

It didn't seem to make any difference.

"Are you sure you're okay?"

Maren jumped when Eileen came up behind her at the sink. She handed Maren a paper towel and she blotted her face dry.

"I think I'm just a little nervous is all. This is going to be a big change." She quickly caught herself. "I mean, *if* I get the job." She shook her head. "I wasn't trying to say that—"

"It's okay." Eileen chuckled. "I know what you mean. And yes, it will be a big change for you, but you're ready. Hell, you've been ready for years. I know you had your reasons for waiting, but you do know it's possible for women to have careers and families, don't you?"

Maren nodded. It was the same discussion they'd been having for years, but Eileen wasn't a mother and she didn't understand the demands and pressures of it all, so Maren just smiled the way she always did.

"No matter. You're ready now." She patted her arm and her forehead creased in concern. "Are you feeling well enough? If you need to go home—"

"No!" She caught herself and said it again, softer. "No. I really am fine. In fact..." Maren took a moment to assess the older woman who'd been more than just a boss to her for the last five years and decided it would be not only safe to confide in her, but it could also be helpful. She took a breath. "I actually think it might be menopause, Eileen. After all, I am forty now and..." She stared at the other woman as she burst out into laughter.

"I'm sorry," she said after a moment. "I don't mean to laugh, Maren. And while menopause isn't the death sentence so many women treat it as, I really don't think you have to worry about that for a few years yet."

Taken aback, Maren tried not to let Eileen's obvious humor get to her. She was grasping at straws because it couldn't just be a flu bug, but without any other options...

"It must be a bug then," Maren said. "I just can't seem to shake it." She turned back to the mirror and once again started to apply makeup in an effort to give herself some color.

"It might be a bug."

Something in the way she said it made Maren turn around. "What do you mean?"

Her boss and mentor grinned. "I'm not saying anything." She raised her eyebrows. "Except your symptoms are more like the opposite of menopause."

"Puberty?" Maren tried to make a joke, but Eileen was starting to sound dangerously similar to Jessica earlier.

"Okay," she conceded with a smile. "Maybe not quite the opposite. But I think you know what I mean." She walked to the door of the restroom but hesitated. "If I didn't know better, I'd think you were pregnant, Maren."

Eileen didn't wait for her to answer before she slipped out, not that Maren would have been able to form anything logical to say.

There was no way.

People needed to stop saying that. It was getting annoying and more than a little concerning.

She was on birth control. There was simply no way it could happen.

Stranger things…

Maren did a quick calculation in her head. It had been almost three months since her last period, but it wasn't unusual for her to skip some now and then. After over seven years of dealing with birth control pills, her doctor had recommended an IUD, and no periods was a common side effect of the IUD. She hadn't had a regular menstrual cycle in years. Besides, if that's really what it was, she would have been sick ages ago, right?

It couldn't be…

In her pocket, Maren's phone vibrated with a message.

Meet you in 5?

She glanced at the time. It was almost noon. Sabrina was meeting her for a birthday lunch at the cafe down the street from the office. She'd said it would give her luck before the big meeting. And maybe it would. If Maren could keep anything down.

She took one more look in the mirror and in a last-ditch effort, pinched her cheeks for a little color.

Maybe she'd better make a quick stop at the pharmacy, too.

Sabrina was waiting at the cafe when Maren got there almost ten minutes late.

"You're late."

"Sorry." She took the seat across from her friend and reached for the menu. "I got held up with a few things at the office." She tucked her purse under the table and tried not to glance at it or the shopping bag tucked just inside—the real reason she was late.

"But you're here now. I ordered you a glass of wine." She gestured to the glass in front of her. "After all, it is your birthday."

Maren glanced at the glass but there was no way she could drink it. "Thanks. But I'm still not feeling perfectly after the party. I don't know if I'll ever drink wine again."

Maybe not for nine months or so anyway.

The thought came out of nowhere and was so mortifying, a strange garbled sound escaped her throat.

If her friend noticed Maren's discomfort, she didn't say anything. Instead, Sabrina shook her head and gazed at the glass longingly before dropping a napkin over it. "I didn't think you'd had that much to drink," she said when she looked up. "But then again, you are getting older. We just can't drink the way we used to." Her hands went to her stomach. "Or at all right now. Less than three more months. Not that I'm counting."

"Right." Eager to talk about anything else, Maren jumped at the opportunity to change the subject. "How are you feeling, anyway? Is the baby starting to kick the crap out of your bladder?"

"And everything else." Sabrina put her menu down and

laughed. "I swear, this little guy is going to be the next David Beckham."

"Little guy?" Maren couldn't have hidden her surprise if she'd tried. And she didn't. Sabrina had gone back and forth in her decision to find out the sex of the baby. But the last time she'd checked, it was a hard no. Something about there being so few surprises in life and how we should take them where we could get them. Considering she'd found out that Rylee was a girl long before she was born, Maren obviously didn't share the sentiment and apparently, neither did Sabrina. "Seriously? You found out? I thought you didn't want to know."

Across the table, Sabrina nodded and shrugged at the same time. "I changed my mind and once I did, I couldn't wait."

"I totally understand." Maren reached across the table and squeezed her friend's hand. "I don't know how you held out so long. And…a little boy? That's awesome."

"It is, isn't?" Sabrina didn't look so sure. "I mean, I don't know the first thing about boys, not that I know anything about babies at all really. But if I'm being totally honest, I was kind of hoping it would be a little girl. I mean…" Tears sprang to her eyes and she swiped at them with her free hand. "Little boys should have fathers, right? And I'm going to be doing this on my own and…"

"Hey." Maren reached for her other hand and squeezed them both together until she looked her in the eyes. Seeing the distress on Sabrina's face broke her heart a little bit. She'd never known her best friend to be unsure about anything. *Was it because she wasn't telling Maren the truth about the father?* "You know, Sabrina…" Maren hadn't planned to say anything because of course Davis was right—Sabrina would have told her already if there was anything to tell. But she couldn't shake the feeling that there was something more. "There's nothing you can't talk to me about, you know that. I mean, if you want to talk about the father…"

Sabrina pulled her hands away and stared at Maren before blinking slowly. "What do you mean? I used a donor."

"Right," Maren said quickly. Maybe she'd been way off base. "I guess I just had this silly thought that maybe the baby was Ryan's, or…it doesn't matter." She waved one hand to dismiss the ridiculous thought before she upset Sabrina. "And none of that matters anyway. The most important thing is that you are going to be an amazing mom."

Sabrina looked as though she were going to say something, but finally she shook her head and chuckled a little. "Thank you."

"Honestly, Sabrina." Maren took Sabrina's hands again and once more squeezed them in an effort to impress upon her friend just how serious she was. "You're a strong, sensitive, awesome person. You're my best friend, an amazing auntie to Rylee, and you're going to make the best mother to that little boy. And I have no idea why I said that other stuff. Besides, you're not alone. Davis and I are here for you every step of the way, you know that, right?"

Sabrina's eyes dropped to the table but she nodded and after a moment, looked up with a small smile on her face. "Thank you, Maren."

"Of course." Maren released her hands and reached for her glass of water. "That's what I'm here for."

While Sabrina pulled herself together, the waitress came over and the women placed their orders. By the time they'd ordered their lunch and got some refills on their water, Sabrina was once again in control of herself.

Maren reached for the glass of wine out of reflex, but stopped herself when she remembered the little box that was hiding in her purse, just under the table. "Anyway." She once more reached for her water and steered the conversation. "I'm really glad you know it's a boy." It was easier to focus on her best friend's baby. The one she wanted and was excited about, rather than her own unknown situation. Especially because Maren knew deep down she was just being ridiculous and completely overreacting. "I can send out an update to your shower invitations so you don't end up with a bunch of yellow stuff. And the decorations, oh, the decorations. I'm going to have so much fun looking for just the right things, in blue. It's going to be great."

Sabrina shook her head with a laugh. "The shower isn't for another few months, Maren. You don't have to go totally crazy."

"Have you met me?" She laughed. "I love it. Besides, you totally spoiled me when Rylee was born. It's finally my turn to return the favor. I'm not going to lie—I wasn't sure I'd ever get the chance."

It wasn't a stretch to say that at all. Maren had completely given up on the idea of Sabrina having children.

As much as she loved Davis and their life, there were times Maren couldn't help but envy her best friend's carefree lifestyle. Still, she couldn't be happier for her that she was finally settling down a little and Maren was thrilled to finally get the chance to be an auntie to Sabrina's baby.

While being a mommy to my own.

For the second time since breakfast, her eyes inexplicably filled with tears. But she couldn't let herself go down that train of thought. There was no way she was pregnant. She was just being ridiculous and letting people like Eileen and Jessica get in her head. The only baby was going to be Sabrina's.

End of story.

"Maren?"

She shook her head and dabbed at her eyes. "I'm fine."

"You're not upset with me, are you? I mean, I wasn't even going to find out the sex of the—"

"No. Sabrina, it's fine. Really."

She tried to force a smile and even laugh about how crazy

she was being, but to Maren's horror, the tears kept coming, which only seemed to fuel Sabrina's need to apologize for everything.

"Please don't be upset. It really was a last-minute decision. I was just lying there and they asked and…"

Sabrina herself sounded as if she were on the verge of tears, and that would really set Maren off. Especially because her friend really and truly had nothing to do with why she was crying.

In fact, she had no idea why she was crying.

"Sabrina. I'm totally okay." Maren tried once again to pull herself together and the young waitress chose that moment to arrive with Sabrina's sandwich and her bowl of soup. She gave each of them a look and quickly backed away. "It must be a birthday thing." Maren gestured to her tears and tried to laugh it off. "I've been a bit of a mess today."

"I thought you were excited about forty?"

"I really am."

"So, what's with the tears? What's going on?"

She shrugged, took a deep breath and when she was sure the tears had stopped—at least for the moment—stirred her soup. "It's probably just nerves about my meeting today. Which is stupid because Eileen says this job is a sure thing."

"It's totally a sure thing." Sabrina took a bite of her sandwich. "You've been busting your ass there. This is your job and everyone knows it. You said it yourself—forty is going to be your year. Everything you've been working for is finally going to happen. You have nothing to worry about."

She looked at her friend, and more than anything wished Sabrina was right and that she really didn't have anything to worry about. And maybe she didn't. But either way, there was nothing she could do about the unknown at that very moment, so Maren smiled broadly and made a decision. "You're right," she said to her friend. "Now tell me, what names have you picked out?"

They spent the rest of their short lunch chatting about Sabrina's baby, veering off into other subjects and catching each other up on the details of their lives the way they always did. By the time Maren returned to the office and walked down the hall toward her desk, she'd almost forgotten about the contents of her purse.

Almost.

On the spur of the moment, she took a last-minute detour and ducked into the bathroom. She might as well get it over with. At least then she could laugh about how ridiculous she'd been and properly relax in time for the meeting.

Less than ten minutes later—Maren wasn't laughing.

Sabrina

"SABRINA...YOU'RE LATE."

She did her best not to roll her eyes as she slipped her jacket off and hung it on the hook in the storeroom. Before she even turned, she knew Dr. Tommy would be leaning against the doorframe of his office, the way he always was when she came in.

Sure enough, he had his arms crossed over his chest, but the smile on his face told her he wasn't mad. He was never mad. Not at her.

"It's only two minutes past one," she said with just enough of a teasing tone in her voice that it couldn't be considered flirty. "Besides, I didn't leave until five after and didn't you tell me that I got a full sixty minutes for lunch?" She smiled as brightly as she could. Sabrina was always careful to walk a fine line between friendly and too far. Especially considering their history. She liked her job and didn't want anything screwing that up. "So I guess I'm actually back early."

She took her place at the front desk. She'd worked for Straight Spines Chiropractic Clinic and Dr. Tommy—as he insisted on being called because, *it makes me more relatable to the patients*—for the last two years. She loved everything about the job, a lot. And she was good at it, too. Which was why she was determined to keep Dr. Tommy himself at arm's length. It didn't matter that he was gorgeous, fit, incredibly successful, and obviously interested in her. Okay, it *did* matter.

But Sabrina had a hard rule: Never to get involved with anyone she worked with. Especially when that person was the boss. Nothing good could come from it.

"Well, I guess I should be grateful." He winked at her and moved around to the other side of the counter. "And really, what am I going to do without you?"

"I think you'll figure something out." She shook her head, but couldn't help but smile. It felt good to be needed. "Besides, I'll find you a very competent temp to fill in while I'm gone."

"Just a temp, right? You *are* coming back?"

She laughed. "I promise. You know I love my job. Besides," she added. "I couldn't afford not to."

Dr. Tommy's smile faded. "If you need anything," he said. "You let me know, okay?"

"Of course."

For a moment, she thought he was going to say something more, but finally he nodded and said, "What's today look like?"

"You have a very busy afternoon." Sabrina shifted straight into business mode and as was their afternoon routine, started to run through the doctor's schedule, which involved three hours of routine adjustments, two new client exams, and a phone meeting with a new supplement company that wanted Straight Spines to carry their products. Soon enough, the bells over the door chimed, announcing the arrival of a patient and the business of the afternoon took over.

Years ago when they'd all been in high school together, Sabrina, Davis, and Maren had often speculated about where they'd end up when they were *old*. And if she had asked her eighteen-year-old self, fresh-faced and bright-eyed, if she could imagine herself working as an office manager in a chiropractic office, she would have laughed until she peed her pants. There was no way a younger version of Sabrina would ever have been able to imagine herself doing anything but living free. She'd had grand visions of backpacking all over Europe, living in hostels and working in cafes whenever she needed a few bucks. Of course, when her parents insisted she get a college degree first, she'd gone. Mostly to keep them happy, but also for herself, because deep down, as much of a rebel as she liked to think of herself, she really just wanted to make her parents happy. And by the time she graduated, traveling didn't seem quite as appealing.

She'd done a little bit over the years but it was never as exciting as she wanted it to be. So she came home and got a job as an office assistant in the real estate office of one of her dad's friends. Gradually, she moved from one job to another until one day she went into a local chiropractic office looking for a little relief for a sore back. An injury she'd sustained in a yoga class. Apparently the bird of paradise pose wasn't for beginners. She'd met Dr. Tommy for the first time and not only had he made her back feel better, but he'd also asked her what she did for a living, and when she told him she was answering phones for a local construction company, he'd offered her a job at his clinic because as it turned out, one of his office staff had just quit.

It didn't take long for Sabrina to fall in love with her job. She loved the patients she saw every day, getting to know them and watching them improve their health. And then as she got promoted, she loved the feeling of being important and relied on. It was kind of powerful.

Of course, the dramatic shift of who she'd wanted to be and who she'd actually become had been a source of amusement for her friends at dinner parties, especially considering Davis had grown up to do exactly what he'd always wanted to do: *"Make myself rich by making other people rich."* He'd become a successful financial advisor almost right after college. There'd been some tricky years for sure, but somehow he'd managed to ride them out. And Maren, all she'd ever wanted was to be a mother. Mission accomplished.

Sabrina used to think that her friend didn't set her sights high enough and that she was capable of so much more, but motherhood made Maren happy and she was good at it. Maybe now that she was about to be a mother of her own, Sabrina would finally understand.

Although it did seem like she and Maren were going to experience a bit of a flip. While Sabrina became a mom, Maren was finally focusing on a career and herself. Thinking of her best friend, Sabrina grabbed her phone and typed in a quick text.

Just wanted to check. How did the meeting go?

She waited a few minutes but there was no reply. *Maybe she was still in the meeting? Or maybe it hadn't gone well?* But that was silly. Maren had said that the meeting was more or less a formality and that she had the job. So maybe her text had come off wrong and Maren thought Sabrina didn't have confidence in her. She picked up her phone and typed another message.

I'm sure it went awesome so I'm going to go ahead and say congratulations now! We'll celebrate soon.

· · ·

Satisfied that Maren wouldn't take her message the wrong way, Sabrina tucked her phone away and got back to work.

It wasn't until hours later, when she was on her way home from work, that she realized with a flicker of concern that Maren had never replied.

Maren

WHEN RYLEE WAS BORN, those first few months were full of endless feedings, more diapers than Maren had ever imagined possible, and sleep deprivation at a level that must have been akin to torture. She'd existed in a sort of thick fog. More than once, she'd drive home from the Mommy & Me class just to marvel at how she'd managed to actually navigate the car through the streets because she couldn't remember a moment of actually getting there.

There would be times that entire days would pass and Maren could hardly remember who she'd spoken to, or whether she'd eaten lunch. It worried her endlessly, but Davis would just laugh and say it was her body's way of triaging what was important. That her brain and body were putting all of their resources into essential tasks, which was why she sometimes felt like she was on autopilot.

Essential tasks.

As Maren sat in her car, parked in front of her house later that day, not remembering more than snapshots of the entire afternoon that had just passed, including how she'd made her way home from the office, Davis's words from all those years ago once more flashed through her mind.

Essential tasks.

And what exactly was the essential task today?

She stared blankly at the house in front of her. The perfect home she'd made her priority for all those years, the one she'd always been so excited to return home to, and willed herself not to cry. Again. Because the last thing she wanted to do at that moment was walk through the door.

Because the essential task, of course, was processing the information that at the ripe ol' age of forty, she was dealing with an unplanned pregnancy.

Fuck.

It took her a moment but Maren managed to muster up the strength to sit up and tuck her hair behind her ears. She couldn't fall apart in her car in front of her house. Of course she couldn't fall apart inside either because her mother's white Cadillac was parked in the driveway.

Dammit. The party.

Her birthday.

The irony was too much.

A slightly manic laugh slipped out of her mouth and she quickly clamped a hand over it.

She seriously had to keep it together. At least until there'd been a little time to process everything. Just get through dinner. And then she could talk to Davis and then together they could decide what to do.

What to do.

The unspoken words echoed through her brain, as if there were actually any choices.

With one last deep breath, Maren gathered up her purse, pasted a smile on her face, and went inside. She was barely two steps in the door when a cloud of Chantilly encased her, causing a completely different type of fog to descend upon her brain.

"Happy birthday, darling." Barbara Magnus landed a delicate kiss on each of Maren's cheeks in turn before putting a hand on each of her shoulders so she could hold her daughter at arm's length. "You look tired," she assessed as she tilted her head to examine her more thoroughly. "Now that you're of a certain age, you're going to have to start using the right products or your skin will wither and before you know it, you'll really start to show your age, or..." She clicked her tongue against her teeth and Maren forced a smile that no doubt looked pained and likely slightly maniacal. "You might even start looking ten years older. In fact, you really should have started with a good anti-aging cream earlier."

Maren stayed still in her mother's critical gaze the way she always did. It was easier than confronting her about it. Besides, she meant well. At least Maren was pretty sure she did. At any rate, Barbara Magnus was who she was, and that wasn't going to change. Especially not in one night.

"Thanks, Mom." Maren finally twisted and freed herself. "Have you been here long?"

"Only about fifteen minutes. I used my key." She pursed her lips. "Davis told me dinner would be at six and I wanted to spend a few minutes with my granddaughter. Where is she?"

"Rylee?"

"Do you have another one?"

Maren flinched at her tone, but forced a smile. "No. Of course not. Is Rylee not home?" It was almost six. She should have been home by now.

Barbara trailed Maren into the kitchen. Her eyes flicked to the bottle of red Davis had opened the night before but she quickly looked away and poured a glass of water instead.

"You don't know where your daughter is?"

Maren ignored her as she gulped down the water. "I'm sure she's working on a project or something with a classmate. She knows to be home for dinner. I'm not worried." And she wasn't. Rylee was a responsible kid. She knew the rules and she'd never given either of them any reason to be distrustful of her. As far as teenagers went, Maren was pretty sure they'd won the lottery.

Would the next one be the same?

The thought hit her so suddenly, she choked on her water.

"Maren? Cover your mouth when you—"

"Did someone order a birthday feast?" Davis's voice rang out, rescuing Maren from any further critiques from her mother—at least for the moment.

Having gotten her coughing under control, Maren called out, "We're in here."

Barbara's lips pursed again. "Really, the way you two yell at each other."

"We don't…" The protest died on her lips. She just didn't have the energy to argue with her mom. Not then.

"It smells delicious," she lied to Davis when he joined them in the kitchen.

He placed two heaping bags on the counter and turned to give her a kiss. "Happy birthday again. I hope you had a good day." There was a question in his eyes, but she didn't want to talk about the meeting. She didn't want to talk about anything. "Where's Rylee?" He glanced around as if she should have been standing behind him.

Maren shrugged and started to unpack the food. "Not home yet. But I'm sure she just got caught up with something at school. Let's eat."

"Hungry?"

She nodded despite the fact that just the smell of the Indian food, normally her favorite, was making her stomach turn.

Maren would never normally think of starting dinner

without Rylee, especially not a birthday celebration. But it wasn't a normal day. Not even close. And the sooner they got dinner over with, the sooner she could go to bed and put the entire day behind her. With any luck, she'd wake up in the morning to find it had all been a very bad dream.

———

Davis had just passed the butter chicken when the front door flew open, followed by Rylee, who ran past them and up the stairs. "I'm so sorry I'm late. I'll be right there, I just need to change."

Maren exchanged glances with Davis. He raised his eyebrows but didn't say anything and a few minutes later, Rylee ran into the room and slid into her chair.

"Hi, Grandma. Sorry I'm late."

Barbara nodded with a smile and, with none of the criticism reserved for Maren, patted Rylee's hand. "I'm just happy to see you."

Even almost sixteen years later, it still amazed Maren to see her mother with Rylee. It's not that her mother had been cold and distant when Maren was growing up, but she'd never gone easy on her. Quite the opposite. Nor did the woman ever seem to have enough time for Maren. Not the way she should have. Not the way that Maren would have liked. One of the many reasons she'd vowed to be a different kind of mother to Rylee.

Over the years, Maren had heard from others in her mommy groups that their parents were much different as grandparents than they'd been as parents, but it never failed to take her off guard to think that the same woman who had a "social function" the night of the science fair when she'd won a silver ribbon had never once missed any of Rylee's swim meets or school concerts.

"Where were you?" Davis handed her the naan.

"Studying." Rylee took a piece and ripped a chunk off.

"At school?"

"Yep, at school."

"Alone?"

Maren gave Davis a look. Why was he interrogating her? Rylee was a good kid. If she said she was studying, she was. He knew that. "Davis."

He ignored her.

"No." Rylee paused, the spoon held aloft. "With Sienna."

"Really?"

"Why are you questioning the girl, Davis?" Barbara piped up. She was never one to stay quiet, particularly if she thought Rylee was subject to even the slightest injustice. "If she said she was studying, she was." She turned her attention to Rylee. "What books are you reading in English this year? I'm always so—"

"I got a call from the school today."

Maren's head whipped around and she stared at him, her mouth open. "A call?"

Davis nodded in her direction, but kept watching Rylee, whose mouth had also dropped open. She recovered quicker than her mother had and stuffed another piece of naan in her mouth.

"Where were you today?"

All eyes were on Rylee when Maren asked, "You skipped class?"

"No!"

"Why did the school call?" Davis was remarkably calm. The school never called unless it was to tell them about an award Rylee was receiving.

She shook her head, her eyes wide. "I don't know. It must have been a mistake. I was in class. I wouldn't skip."

Of course she was. Rylee would never skip a class. She didn't do things like that.

Davis must have believed her, too. After a moment, he nodded and picked up his fork again. "It must have been a glitch in that electronic student attendance program the high school got last year. That's kind of what I thought," he admitted. "But I have to do my job as a dad."

Rylee's smile was weak. "I get it."

From the other side of the table, Barbara made a clucking noise with her tongue, which meant, whether they liked it or not, they were all about to be treated to her thoughts on the situation.

"You both need to leave the girl alone. Rylee would never skip school. We all know that. She's on the honor roll, for God's sake."

Maren nodded and pushed her chicken around on her plate. It was easier to just let her run her course.

"It's okay, Grandma."

"It's not okay. You're a good kid." She nodded at Rylee. "Lord knows what some of those other kids are out there doing while you're studying and working hard. Your parents should be proud of you."

"We are proud, Barbara. Immeasurably."

"Well, you have a funny way of showing it." She huffed and sat back in her chair. An indication that she was either winding up to give them some more of her opinions, or had finished her rant.

"It really is okay, Grandma." Rylee's smile was over-the-top sweet. "Dad was just asking a question. Forget about it. It's Mom's birthday." She aimed her smile in Maren's direction. "I think we should make a toast." Rylee lifted her glass of water. "To Mom. I hope you—wait. Mom, you need some wine."

"Sorry, hon. I thought you had some."

Maren put her hand over the glass as Davis reached for the bottle. He tilted his head and gave her a look. It wasn't often she passed up a glass of wine. Particularly on special occasions.

"Not tonight."

"Still not feeling well?"

That was a very mild understatement, but Maren nodded. "It's been kind of a…crazy day."

"That's right. Your meeting." Davis put the bottle down with a clunk. "How did it go? Are we toasting the birthday girl *and* the new account manager of PlayTime?"

In an instant, the thick fog was back and she couldn't think. She couldn't answer his questions. But she couldn't just sit there silently. She needed to get up. To leave. But Maren couldn't feel her feet, and her hands felt as if they were somehow detached from her body. The fog became thicker, suffocating her. Making it hard to breathe.

If anyone noticed her distress, they didn't say anything.

"You got the job. Right, Mom? It's about time. I mean, you should have taken the promotion ages ago."

"Do you start on Monday or is there some kind of transition period?"

Their belief in her was so complete that they were talking as if the promotion was a sure thing. That she'd both been offered the job and more importantly, had accepted. They spoke as if everything was fine and Maren's whole world hadn't been completely turned upside down only a few hours earlier.

Because they didn't know. They had no idea that everything had changed.

But how could she tell them?

"Rylee's right." Davis's voice sounded tinny and small, as if he were in a tunnel and not on the other side of the table. "A toast is in order."

Out of the corner of her eye, Maren saw him raise his glass. Rylee followed suit.

Her mother's arm didn't move. "Maren?" Her voice was equal parts annoyance and concern. "Are you okay?"

"To Maren," Davis continued, as if he hadn't heard

Barbara. More likely, he had and was ignoring her. "A new decade, a new career, and a new start."

"To Mom."

The sound of their glasses clinking echoed in Maren's head, but still she couldn't move. Hoping it would give her strength to say or do something, Maren squeezed her eyes tight and when she opened them a moment later, she was staring directly at her mother's assessing gaze.

"Maren?"

She shook her head and squeezed her eyes shut again, unwilling to look at her.

"Maren. Honey?" Her voice was all concern now.

"Mom. Why aren't you—"

"I'm pregnant!" She hadn't meant to yell. Hell, she hadn't meant to say anything at all, but the pressure was too much. It needed release. But once the words were out of her mouth, not only did the pressure not abate, but she couldn't take them back. They bounced around the dining room, echoed from the walls, and finally landed in a heavy heap on the table in front of her.

The room was silent for a beat. Then another.

It was Davis who spoke first. "What?" His voice was strangled and unfamiliar. "What did you say?"

Finally Maren opened her eyes and looked at her husband, who'd aged at least five years in the past few seconds.

"We're going to have a baby." She repeated the words she'd last spoken when she'd discovered her pregnancy with Rylee. All those years ago, the words had changed their lives forever. Sixteen years later, they'd just done the same.

Only this time, no one was celebrating.

Rylee

"PREGNANT?" Rylee barely managed to swallow down the bite of vegetable korma she'd just taken. It was better than spitting it out, which was what she really wanted to do because suddenly the creamy coconut sauce seemed to curdle in her mouth. "Like, with a baby?" She barely managed to get the words out and as soon as they were, she wanted them back as she realized how stupid she sounded. But for the life of her, Rylee couldn't figure out anything else to say, except to state the obvious.

Across the table, her mom nodded and then did something she never did.

She cried.

Shit.

Rylee could probably count on one hand how many times her mom had cried in front of her, and it was never a good thing.

"At your age, Maren?" Her grandma had put her fork down and was doing that thing with her lips that made her mom crazy. But Rylee's mom wasn't looking at her, so she probably didn't notice. Instead, she was staring at Rylee's dad, who had turned a strange gray color and looked like he might pass out. "Really?" Her grandma kept talking, and her voice only seemed to make her mom cry more.

Rylee looked between all three of them and almost laughed, even though nothing about what was happening was funny. But to think that she'd been worried that everyone would be freaking out at her because she was a few minutes late because she'd been hanging out with Brice. Her infraction seemed absolutely minuscule compared to the bomb her mother just dropped.

"I know it wasn't planned." Her mother didn't even sound like herself. Instead, she was some sort of bizarre cross between her actual self and one of those perky motivational speakers they brought into the school who spouted nothing but bullshit about how studying and waking up early could change your life. "But it won't be that bad," she continued. "I mean, not that a baby would be bad. I was just…"

If Rylee hadn't been in such shock herself, she might actually have felt sorry for her mom. Clearly, she was trying to come up with something positive to say. It was painfully obvious that she was struggling. She just kept staring at Rylee's dad, who sat staring straight ahead, shaking his head as if he couldn't quite believe what he'd just heard.

It was too hot in the room. Her sweater itched around her neck and for a horrifying minute, Rylee thought she might actually throw up. And then she heard herself ask, "You're not going to keep it, are you, Mom? I mean, a baby? Now? Like at your age? That's kind of…"

She had no idea where the question came from or even why she thought getting rid of the pregnancy could possibly be an option. Not that she'd ever given it any thought before. Sure, as a young woman, she probably had some sort of civic duty to care about these things. But she couldn't honestly say she'd given it any thought before. But that was when her mother wasn't pregnant. The idea of it all turned her stomach.

"Rylee!" Her grandma's face was a frightening shade of pink.

Rylee shrank back in her seat as everyone's eyes turned to stare at her.

"Rylee." Her father finally broke his silence. "I never want to hear you talk like that again. Am I clear?"

Was he clear? Was he *kidding?*

She wasn't the one pregnant.

"Are you kidding me right now?" She knew on some level, a very *major* level, that she should just shut up. But she couldn't seem to help herself. Anger she likely had no right to feel bubbled up from somewhere deep inside. "It's a totally fair question. You obviously don't want the baby." She waved her hand around. "I mean, no one here is happy." She knew she was being mean, and even though she wouldn't turn her head to confirm it, she was pretty sure she could hear her mom crying even harder with every word that came out of her mouth. Rylee knew she should stop, but once she was started, she couldn't seem to find her off switch. "And Mom's *old*." She spat the word at her father. "She can't have a baby. It's disgusting." Her mom choked on a sob and Rylee looked up. "You're disgusting." The words felt like daggers flying off her tongue and as if she were watching through some sort of slow-motion camera, she could see as each one landed in her mother's heart.

"Rylee!" Her father's voice boomed through the room.

Dammit. She should have just kept her mouth shut. But it was too late. She couldn't take them back. Ignoring her father, she pushed back from the table so quickly the chair hit the wall behind her. It probably left a mark, but she didn't care.

Rylee threw her napkin on the table and ran out of the

room and up the stairs to her bedroom, where she slammed the door like a tantruming toddler.

As soon as she was in the sanctuary of her own space, she collapsed on the bed and let herself cry. She didn't even know why she was crying. It's not like she was upset that her parents were having a baby. Not really. Except everything would change. But hadn't she *just* been wishing that her mother would get a life beyond her?

Careful what you wish for.

A voice that sounded suspiciously like Sienna's bounced around her brain.

Sienna.

Rylee wiped her tears and reached for her cell phone. Sienna was never going to believe it.

Instinctively, Rylee pushed the button to dial her best friend's number. But it rang three times and her message came on.

Frustrated, she disconnected without leaving a message and typed a text instead.

You around?

Seconds later, the reply came.

Yup.

Rylee started to text her about what had just happened, but there was no way she could possibly get it out fast enough. She gave up and dialed Sienna's number again. Still no answer.

I thought you said you were home, she texted quickly. She was obviously near her phone. *I need to talk.*

She sent the text and waited. The little bubbles appeared on the screen that told Rylee she was replying, but no message came through. She sat up cross-legged on her bed and waited. Still, nothing.

Sienna? You there?

The bubbles disappeared, and then they were back. This time, a text came through.

I'm here.

Quickly, Rylee responded.

I really need to talk to you. It's an emergency. Worse than an exploded pen. Call me.

Sienna would call right away. Exploded pen was the code they'd used for a really huge, mega monster crisis. Ever since seventh grade when Sienna had gotten her period in the middle of art class while she was wearing white jeans. Of course, Jeff Baker noticed and started to tease her but thankfully Rylee had seen what was happening and had quickly grabbed a handful of pens and made up a story on the fly about how one of them had exploded on her seat and Sienna had sat in it. It was a total cover-up, but Jeff was dumb enough to buy it. And ever since then, when either of them had a big emergency situation, they rated it against the exploded pen measure. This was way worse than that. It was an explosion of epic proportions. Sienna would get that.

But she didn't call. And when her return text finally came through, it was clear that not only did she not understand the magnitude of the situation or how Rylee's life was about to epically explode. But there was a completely different type of crisis situation going on.

I don't want to talk to you.

Rylee's stomach twisted again and her fingers went numb. She didn't want to talk to her? Like, at all? Before she could respond, Sienna's next text came through.

Why don't you just go tell Brice?

Rylee stared at the phone and reread her words.

Once.

Twice.

Seriously? Brice? She dropped her head back and stared at the ceiling. Rylee wasn't dumb. Of course she knew Sienna was a little upset that she didn't tell her about the first kiss with

Brice but…this was important. Like, really important. There was no way she was *that* mad at her. *Was there?*

You don't understand.

Rylee started to type more. To maybe tell her what was going on, but before she could, her response came.

I understand that we're obviously not the friends I thought we were. Best friends don't ditch for a boy.

Oh my God. Rylee let out a noise that was part scream and part groan. She was going to text again, but for some reason remembered what her mom always said about important conversations happening in person. That wasn't going to happen, at least not at that moment, but at least she could make another effort to try to talk to her. Once again, Rylee pushed the button to dial Sienna.

This time, she picked up.

"I don't want to talk to you."

"You answered, didn't you?"

"That's because I—"

"Sienna." Rylee cut her off. "You're not really mad, are you? I mean, *really really* mad?" She didn't want to talk about Brice at all. It wasn't the time. Besides, it wasn't going to get them anywhere. Sienna was never going to like him. And there was a way more major crisis going on. She needed to talk to her about her mom and how insane it was that she was going to have a baby. She *needed* Sienna on her side. "It wasn't anything. And I—"

"It was something, Rylee." Sienna's voice shook the way it always did when she was nervous. Or really mad. "You've been spending all your time with him, which is…whatever. I guess. But you didn't even tell me that you guys kissed. Do you even get how major that is?"

She did. At least she thought she did. But she couldn't think about it. "Sienna, you don't understand. My mom is—"

"You just don't even care, do you?" Her voice broke. "You're supposed to be my best friend."

"I am. That's why I really need to tell—"

"No." She interrupted her. "No, you're not."

Rylee held the phone in her hand long after Sienna disconnected the call. She stared at the screen and the letters *BFF* surrounded by a selection of hearts and smiley face emojis that Rylee assigned to her contact information. It was identical to her info on Sienna's phone.

Best friends forever.

Or at least until you really needed them.

Maren

WITHOUT A DOUBT, it had been the worst night of her life. Even worse than the night when she was eight years old and her mother came to tell her that her father wouldn't be coming back from his business trip, because he hadn't gone out of town at all, but across it to another woman's house and that's where he would stay. Maren had spent that night, and most of the nights for the next few weeks, crying and wondering why her dad didn't love her enough to come and say good-bye. Those had been terrible times. But not even that compared to the hell that was the aftermath of her birthday dinner.

It felt like forever before Maren could finally get her mom to stop asking her questions about how they could possibly be pregnant—as if she really needed a lesson in sexual education —and go home. There was no answer that was going to satisfy her anyway, and she was the last person Maren wanted to discuss the situation with. But it didn't get any better when Barbara finally took the hint and left them alone. Davis just sat mutely and stared across the containers of cold food at her.

She'd never seen him that way. Stunned, angry, sad, and... confused. All at the same time.

Maren made a few efforts to try to talk, because now that she'd finally said it out loud, she no longer wanted to just go to bed and forget about what was happening. Instead, the desperate need to talk about their situation grew inside her. But Davis didn't seem to feel the same way because after a few efforts from Maren, he finally stood from the table and offered her his hand. "I think we should just go to bed and talk about this in the morning. I need some time to process."

Process. Of course. They could probably both use some time to process. Maren nodded in agreement because what else could she do? More than anything, she needed to talk to her husband, but she knew him well enough to know that if she pushed too hard, he'd shut down. So, despite the fact that it wasn't even eight o'clock yet, she'd gone up to bed with him, leaving the food untouched on the table. Part of her thought about checking on Rylee, but the idea exhausted her. And for the first time in recent memory, Maren didn't make a choice based on what she thought was best for her child.

But then again, maybe it was best. Maybe Rylee just needed some time to *process* too.

Like a robot, Maren went through the motions of getting ready for bed and when she finally slipped beneath the sheets next to her husband, she rolled over to face his back. "Davis?"

It took a minute and she'd almost given up, thinking he'd already fallen asleep, but finally Davis rolled over to face her.

She wiggled one hand out between the sheets and across the distance to rest on his. "It'll be okay."

It was probably the stupidest thing she could have said, because of course it wasn't going to be okay. Their whole lives had been tossed upside down in an instant, and as much as things could most certainly have been worse in a million different ways, at that very moment, there was nothing worse for them.

Davis didn't answer, but she hadn't expected him to. Not

really. Instead, he offered a slight nod before closing his eyes and drifting off.

His sleep had never been affected by stress or the endless thoughts that seemed to roll through Maren's head. And apparently this life-changing announcement didn't make a difference to his slumber either, because for most of the night Maren laid next to her sleeping husband, wishing she could just go back in time. The only problem was, she had no idea when she would rewind the clock to.

To the moment she'd told them?

The decision to take the test before going into her meeting?

Or maybe it was months before then, to the moment they'd had sex?

No…further. Maybe years earlier when she'd stupidly thought she was protected from an unwanted pregnancy by a tiny piece of copper that the doctor had assured her was 99% effective?

Finally, just after five in the morning, Maren gave up on the idea of sleep and slipped out of bed. She spent the next hour cleaning up the dinner dishes from the night before, alternating between throwing out the spoiled food and running to the bathroom as she succumbed to the relentless effects of what she finally acknowledged was morning sickness.

She'd never been sick like that with Rylee. Hers had been an easy pregnancy with only a few rare mornings of nausea. She'd had endless amounts of energy and everyone remarked on how Maren seemed to glow from the inside out with impending motherhood.

She caught a glimpse of her reflection in the bathroom mirror after rinsing her mouth out for the second time and immediately wanted to look away. She was decidedly *not* glowing. It was the last thing she should have done on a morning that was already so full of angst and emotion, but for a reason she couldn't understand, Maren stood in front of the mirror and examined her reflection. She pulled at the crow's feet around her once sparkling blue eyes that were now dull with age and exhaustion. She poked and prodded at the puffiness in her face and the dark circles that had appeared, it seemed, overnight. She looked tired. Exhausted even.

And it would only get worse. When the baby was born, she'd— *When the baby was born.* Maren repeated the words in her head over and over again as she stared into her own eyes. Slowly, she looked closer and closer until her nose was almost touching the mirror.

"Maren?"

Davis's voice startled her and her face smacked into the mirror.

"Are you okay?" He was behind her, his hand on her shoulder. "What are you doing?"

"I was…" Maren rubbed her nose and turned around. His hair was still damp from his shower. The familiar scent of his cedar and citrus shampoo filled her senses, grounding her to the moment. "Nothing," she said. "I wasn't doing anything."

"Are you feeling okay this morning?" He took her hand and led her out of the hall bathroom and into the kitchen. "Can I make you some toast?" His thoughtfulness and concern washed over her and wrapped her up like a cocoon. Last night, he'd been so distant. But maybe a night of *processing* had done the trick. Because whatever it was, he was now back to his loving self. Everything would be okay. They'd get through this just the way they got through everything else. Together.

"Thank you." Maren managed a small smile. "That would be nice. And maybe some peppermint tea."

She sat at the table, suddenly exhausted now that Davis was there. She let him move around the kitchen, preparing a cup of tea for her and a coffee for him.

He placed a piece of plain toast in front of her before sitting. "You never had morning sickness like this with Rylee."

She shook her head. She certainly hadn't.

"I think we should make an appointment with the doctor this morning."

Maren looked up sharply. "This morning? Today?"

He nodded. "To confirm everything," he said. "I mean, you're on birth control, Maren." He smiled and almost chuckled. "I mean, are you sure you're even pregnant?"

"Of course I'm sure." She dropped the piece of toast and crumbs scattered across the table. "How could you even say that?" Was he completely losing his mind? Did he really think that she would tell him such a thing if she wasn't completely sure of it herself?

"It's just that…well…I mean…is it even possible? I don't mean to sound insensitive, but at your—"

"Age?" she snapped. "Is that what you're trying to say, Davis? That I'm old?" She slapped her hand on the table, conveniently forgetting that it was less than twenty-four hours ago when she herself had hoped menopause was her biggest problem. "Is that what you were going to say? You're as bad as Rylee. I'm forty, Davis. I'm hardly an old hag."

"That's not at all what I'm saying." His hands came up in defense, as if she were going to throw something at him. Maybe she was. Nothing was certain.

"Then what exactly *are* you saying? Lots of women have babies at forty, Davis. You don't just dry up and shrivel when you turn forty, you know?"

"I know, I know." He eyed her warily, but didn't drop his hands. "Maren, that is not what I'm saying." He tentatively moved one hand across the table toward her. She couldn't blame him for being cautious. Not after he said stupid shit like that. "You are absolutely not old. And I'm sure you have many child-bearing years left." Maren narrowed her eyes as he dug himself an even deeper hole. "Oh shit!" He dropped his hands and pushed up from his seat. He paced the kitchen for a moment before coming to stand in front of her. His shoulders slumped in defeat. "This is coming out all wrong."

"Ya think?"

He ignored her sarcasm. "I'm just saying that you've been on birth control for years. Why now? Why all of a sudden *now* does it not work? Maybe it's something else. We should see the doctor. That's all I'm saying." His face changed as he spoke and the anger and annoyance she'd felt a moment ago melted. Despite the fact that he'd spent the night snoring next to her, she could see how tired he was. He was freaking out too.

She wasn't alone. She needed to remember that.

Even if it felt that way.

After a moment, Maren nodded slowly. "You're right. Let's see what the doctor has to say."

Four hours later, they sat in Doctor Harrison's office during his lunch break. Davis had called and told his nurse it was an emergency and they absolutely had to see the doctor as soon as possible. As much as Maren was certain that her entire life was imploding, she wasn't convinced it was an emergency worth requesting a lunchtime appointment, but it was important for Davis to get the answers he needed.

And it was him who needed them.

She already knew what the doctor was going to say.

She was definitely pregnant.

Her mind had rejected the idea completely until the moment she held the little stick in her hands, but the second the two little pink lines appeared, there was no more denying it. The proof was all her brain needed to acknowledge what her body had known long before. She definitely didn't need the doctor to tell her what she already knew.

She was going to have a baby.

She was forty years old, with an almost grown child. About to start all over again.

Diapers, midnight feedings, first words, preschool, class mom, homemade Halloween costumes, science projects, music lessons, learning how to drive...all of it. From the beginning. Right when they should have been preparing for an empty nest, it was about to fill up again.

Maren already knew all that. But Davis hadn't quite accepted it. Maybe he needed more time to *process?* It's almost as if he needed a professional to tell him that his life was about to change completely, because she wasn't qualified for the job.

"Maren. Davis." The doctor looked at them each in turn. "It's always nice to see you, although I must say, I also quite enjoy eating the lunch Mrs. Harrison makes me every day."

Maren felt a flash of guilt for interrupting his lunch break, but a quick glance at Davis told her he felt no such compunction. Maybe he was right; it would be best to get answers. Officially.

When neither of them said anything, or apologized for interrupting his day, the doctor continued, "My nurse tells me you came in for a little test."

Little? That was an understatement. But still Maren didn't say anything. Instead, she kept her face a careful mask of neutrality.

"And I have the results right here." Doctor Harrison took his time sliding the folder across his desk until it was in front of him.

Instinctively, Maren reached out for Davis's hand, needing to feel his strength. She needed to know that no matter what, he'd be okay. That *they* would be okay. His fingers curled around hers and he gave her a little squeeze.

They'd be fine. It would all be fine. A baby wasn't the end—

The doctor cleared his throat, pulling her attention back to him. He smiled and next to her, Maren felt Davis stiffen.

"Well, it looks like congratulations are in order. You're pregnant."

It shouldn't have been a surprise to hear the doctor say the words out loud. But maybe Davis had been right. Hearing it from a medical professional made it seem…real. Maren took a breath and swallowed hard before looking over at Davis, who wasn't looking at her. In fact, she couldn't be sure he was looking at anything. He stared straight ahead, not blinking, not seeing. For a moment, Maren wasn't even sure he was breathing. She squeezed his hand and gave it a little shake. "It'll be okay. It will."

Resentment bubbled up inside her as she spoke. Wasn't he supposed to be saying that to her? After all, it was her body. As much as it was happening to them, it was really happening to *her*.

"Of course it will be okay."

Maren turned her head and looked at the man who had offered her support. "It will, won't it? I mean, with Rylee it was…"

Doctor Harrison nodded and offered her another kind smile. "First things first," he continued. "We'll have to see how far along you are."

"Well, I have to be just barely pregnant." She stared at the doctor. "I mean, I *just* started feeling sick last week."

The doctor shook his head. "Not necessarily. While morning sickness is generally more common in the first trimester, it's not unusual to experience it in any stage of pregnancy."

Maren shook her head. "But I would have known if I was pregnant. I mean…" *Would she have known?* Maybe not. "But I drank wine." The horror of what she'd potentially done to her unborn baby without even knowing chilled her. "I didn't know. I never would have…"

"It's okay, Maren. I'm sure everything will be just fine." Doctor Harrison was calm. His smile steady. "I know it's been awhile since you've done this," he said. "But things haven't changed all that much." He chuckled but he was the only one in the room laughing. "There are a few different things to consider this time, however. After all, you will now be considered a high-risk pregnancy."

"High risk?" It was Davis who'd asked. For the first time, something registered on his face besides complete and total shock. "What do you mean, high risk? Is Maren in danger?"

It was his turn to squeeze her hand, but she was no longer paying any attention to him. Instead, she was staring at Doctor Harrison, who'd just dropped a different kind of bomb on her.

"Well," the doctor started. "There is Maren's advanced age." He shook his head quickly as if realizing what he just said and tried again. "I didn't mean to say… Well, what I mean is once a mother is over forty, they are automatically placed in the high-risk category. It's just terminology we use to keep a little bit of a closer eye on things."

He turned his attention back to his file and Maren breathed a sigh of relief. If it was just her age, that wasn't a big deal. She already knew about that. Sabrina told her that she, too, was considered *high risk* because of her age. Maren wasn't worried about that. Sure, she could probably take better care of herself but she was healthy, with no major concerns. She couldn't possibly be *that* high of a risk.

She snickered a bit. "Well, that's not a big deal. I mean—"

"However, there is one other complication." The doctor cut her off and Maren stared at his finger that pointed to something in her file. "There is the matter of your IUD."

"What about it?" Davis had dropped her hand and was wringing his together in his lap. "Besides the fact that it's completely useless because it obviously didn't do its job. I thought the whole point of an IUD was to prevent something like this from happening in the first place."

The last thing Maren needed or wanted was to get into a debate about the effectiveness of birth control. It wouldn't make her any less pregnant. She ignored Davis and looked at the doctor. "How is the IUD a complication?"

"It might not be," he said. "We'll have to do an ultrasound right away to see if it's still in place."

"How could it possibly still be in place?" Davis's voice got louder. "If the damn thing was still in place, we wouldn't be sitting here right now." Once again, Maren reached for his hand, but he was too worked up and she tucked her hand back under her leg.

"Are you saying the IUD might not be there anymore?" She ignored Davis again. "Is that even a thing? Could it have gone somewhere?"

Doctor Harrison nodded. "It does happen. The device may have been expelled, or even lost into the side of the uterus. Both of those things would make it less effective, obviously."

She heard Davis grunt next to her, but didn't look at him.

"So, it probably just got dislodged at some point?" She glanced quickly at her husband and back to the doctor. "I mean, that's why this happened, right?"

He nodded. "Yes. That is a possibility. As with any birth control, there is always a risk that something can go wrong."

"But how would that be a complication?" Maren was still fixated on the *high risk* label he'd assigned her. "I don't understand."

"There is a chance that the IUD is still in place," the doctor said. "It's not common, but it does happen where pregnancy can occur with the IUD exactly in place. And if that is the case, your pregnancy will definitely be considered high risk."

Maren's stomach flipped and then clenched. She vaguely remembered the pamphlet about the IUD she'd been handed all those years ago. She hadn't really read it. With a small child demanding her attention while she waited in the doctor's waiting room, her attention was definitely elsewhere. But she did remember something about the risk of pregnancy with an IUD. She didn't want to ask. She didn't want to know what it could mean, but at the same time she didn't have a choice. "What kind of high risk is that?"

"Carrying a baby to term with an IUD in place can pose a significant risk to both the baby and the mother," he said without preamble. "Spontaneous miscarriage, bleeding, placental abruption, or premature delivery are all risk factors. However," the doctor continued, his face now a mask of seriousness. "You can choose to remove the device. It's a minor surgical procedure that of course is not without risk itself." Maren held her breath as she listened. "There is a chance of a miscarriage with the procedure as well."

"So we're damned if we do, damned if we don't?" Maren didn't need to look to see that Davis was clenching his teeth. He was furious, as if it were Doctor Harrison's fault that they'd ended up pregnant in the first place.

"I'm just letting you know about all of the risks," he said. "There's also a very good chance that everything will go smoothly, with no problems at all. But I would be remiss if I didn't let you know all of the potential situations."

Maren nodded numbly. She had no idea how he managed to stay so calm, but of course he probably dealt with this type of thing every day.

"But one thing at a time." He slapped the folder shut. "Let's do a quick ultrasound to see what we're dealing with here. It will also give us a chance to see how far along you are."

Rylee

BY THE TIME Rylee got to school the next day, her anger toward her parents had diminished somewhat. Not that she was in any way ready to tell them that, though. In fact, that morning, when she'd finally waited as long as she possibly could before going downstairs to grab breakfast, she'd done her best to send them both the message that she was in fact not ready to talk to either of them. The worst part was neither of them seemed to care. They'd both said good morning to her but neither of them had asked her about the night before, or even given her shit for her totally out-of-line behavior or anything. It was as if they were both so wrapped up in their unborn child already that they no longer had time for her.

Careful what you wish for.

She moved like a robot through first period math, only partly registering that she got an eighty percent on the quiz a few days earlier. Mr. Sheppard had drawn a small question mark next to her grade. She'd never received less than a ninety on any of her assignments or tests. Not that an eighty was a bad mark. Not at all, but no doubt Mr. Sheppard was freaking out. Rylee refused to meet his gaze for the entire class and instead focused on doodling in the margins of her notebook until the bell rang.

It wasn't until second period that she had a chance to talk to Sienna. They had English together and without fail, they always sat together in the front right corner. Close enough for Mrs. Jones to think they were super keen students and madly interested in whatever poem or play they were currently pulling apart for meaning and symbolism, but far enough away that they could have their phones tucked into their textbooks without her seeing them. Whenever it was a reading period, the girls could compare notes or more likely, whisper back and forth about whatever it was that had happened since they'd last seen each other that morning.

But when Rylee got to class, Sienna wasn't in their regular spot. Hurt hit her square in the chest as she spotted her best friend five rows back. The seat next to her was already taken.

Rylee tried to catch her eye, but she stared straight ahead like a statue at Erika Penszie's long blonde ponytail in front of her.

Point taken. She was pissed.

And maybe for good reason. But she had no idea that Rylee's life was completely exploding. Without a doubt, Rylee knew that if she could only get a second to talk to her, she'd forget about whatever she was mad about. Especially when she heard about the *baby*.

Which meant Rylee *needed* to get the seat next to her. As casually as she could, she walked down the row and stopped in front of Chris Combs, a kid she only vaguely knew from the history class they'd shared last semester. "Hey, Chris." She tried her best to sound as sweet as she could. "I really need to sit here today. Would you mind switching seats with me?"

Out of the corner of her eye, she saw Sienna's head shift focus from Erika's ponytail to her.

Chris shrugged. "I don't—"

"I would really appreciate it." She tried for flirty, despite the fact that he was one of the few openly gay students in the school.

"Yeah, sure. Why not?" He moved to gather up his things but Sienna's hand shot out and grabbed his arm.

"No," she hissed. "Don't move."

Chris stared at her first, then back to Rylee. "Um…"

"It's okay, Chris." Rylee kept the smile pasted on her face, despite the fact that her face was likely beet red, and she could feel the sting of tears in her eyes. She would not cry. Not in class. Not like this. "You can move." She focused on Chris, who pushed up out of his chair, but Sienna wasn't having it.

"No."

Frozen in a half squat, Chris looked at each of the girls in turn as if they'd completely lost their minds. For a split second, Rylee thought he might actually say that, too. But before he had a chance, she heard Mrs. Jones behind her.

"Rylee, if you're ready to take your seat, we can all start today's lesson."

Chris sat back down and shook his head slightly before opening his book, which left her no choice. Her face flaming, Rylee walked up to her usual seat and slumped down in the chair as the lesson began.

When Mrs. Jones finally quit talking and instructed the class to pull out their copies of Hamlet for some quiet reading, and to find four examples of symbolism in Act Two, Rylee whipped out her phone and started texting.

I really need to talk to you. I'm sorry for not telling you about Brice. PLEASE.

She waited but Sienna didn't respond. So, switching tactics, Rylee pulled up a little GIF image of a cartoon kitten holding a heart, the words "I'm sorry" flashing underneath it. She sent it to Sienna. Followed by another GIF and then another.

Finally, a reply came in.

You don't get it.

Rylee wanted to turn around and scream at her friend that, yes, she did get it. She knew Sienna was hurt and she didn't blame her. Not a bit. But this was bigger than a little disagreement. Rylee really needed her and of course she was sorry. Really and truly sorry. She'd never not tell her best friend something again.

I do get it. I screwed up. I'm so so so so sorry. Please forgive me. You'll be the first person to hear everything from now on. I swear. I need to tell you something. You're the only one I can tell.

There was no guarantee that Sienna would ever quit being mad at her, but Rylee was counting heavily on the fact that they'd been friends for so long that she couldn't stay mad forever. Sure enough...a moment later, the text bubbles appeared and she replied.

Okay.

Her heart jumped a little and Rylee had to force herself not to turn around.

Flex?

The administration had implemented a Flex period last semester that was supposed to be a chance for students to get extra help or study for whatever they needed to during school hours. For a while, Rylee used it, too. But lately, she'd been hanging out with Brice in the cafeteria or outside on the bleachers. Doing anything but studying or doing homework.

You sure?

Of course Sienna would expect her to ditch on Flex for Brice. But not today. Rylee had meant it when she told Sienna that she was the only one she could talk to. She *needed* her best friend in a full-scale exploded pen crisis situation.

Of course. Library?

Sienna responded with the thumbs-up emoji.

With a sigh of relief she could feel all through her body, Rylee replied with a smiley face and a heart.

"I'm so sorry, Sienna." Rylee grabbed her arm the second Sienna arrived in the library and pulled her into a quiet corner that had two big chairs set up. "I know I should have—"

"Whatever."

"Whatever?" She stared at her friend, but Sienna just shrugged.

"Yeah." She dropped her bag on the floor and collapsed into one of the overstuffed chairs Rylee had secured for them by racing to the library as soon as the bell rang. "I don't want to be mad at you, Rylee. It sucks."

She had that right. "It does suck," Rylee agreed. "So you forgive me?"

Sienna looked as if she were going to say something more, but finally she nodded. "Just don't ditch me for a boy again, okay? I mean, I get it. You're all in love or whatever." She held up her fingers in quotes and rolled her eyes, making Rylee laugh.

"I don't know about that. But I do like spending time with him." Her stomach flipped a little the way it always did when she remembered what it felt like to kiss him. "And kissing him is…"

"Is that what you need to tell me so bad?" Sienna interrupted. "Because I know I was pissed when you didn't tell me about your first kiss, but I was thinking about it and I don't know if I really need to know all the nasty details."

All happy thoughts dissolved from Rylee's mind as her best friend reminded her exactly what it was that she needed to talk to her so badly about. "No." She shook her head, her long dark hair falling over one eye. She'd started wearing it down more because Brice told her it was pretty. But Rylee still wasn't used to all that hair always being in the way. "That's not it at all."

"Good." Sienna laughed a little, quiet enough that the librarian wouldn't come over and give them shit. "Then what is it?"

"My mom's pregnant." Rylee blurted it out before she could stop herself. It was the first time she'd said the words out loud, which made it both worse and not so bad all at the same time.

Sienna choked on her gum for a moment before recovering enough to speak. "She's pregnant? Like with a baby?"

"That's what I said." It didn't sound nearly as dumb when Sienna said it. "And yes. Can you even believe it? That means that—"

"Your parents had sex." Sienna giggled but Rylee did not think it was funny.

"Of course they had sex." She smacked her lightly on the arm. "I mean, I'm not an idiot. I know they do it. Well, I mean…I never thought about it or anything. But, gross. I guess they do it."

"They obviously do it." She shook her head in wonder and leaned back in the chair. "That's crazy."

"You're missing the point." Rylee pulled her hair back and wrapped an elastic roughly around it.

"I mean…your parents are getting busy on the regular." Sienna giggled again. Rylee loved her best friend, but the sound was starting to make her crazy. "I don't think my parents do it at all," Sienna continued. "My dad snores so bad that I swear the walls are going—"

"Sienna!" Rylee hiss-whispered and glared at her. "You are totally missing the point."

She pressed her lips together, taken aback, and stared. "Okay. So what exactly is the point?"

That was the whole problem. Rylee had no idea what the point was. Now that she'd told her, the whole thing didn't seem quite so crazy and disgusting and all the things she'd thought it was when her mom had first announced it at the table. But still…it wasn't okay. It wasn't okay at all. Hot tears pricked at Rylee's eyes, which was even more frustrating because she didn't know whether it was because she was upset about the baby or because she was so frustrated that she didn't know why she was upset. It was a ridiculous circle of confusion that didn't make any sense at all.

"Rylee?" Sienna was on the edge of her seat, a look of concern on her face. "What's going on?"

She shook her head and buried her face in her hands. "I have no idea." There was no way she could start crying. They only had another few minutes of Flex block and then she had Chemistry and there was no way she could go into class with mascara streaked down her cheeks. She forced herself to take a deep breath and exhaled slowly before looking up.

"I don't know what's going on," she managed to say without her voice shaking. "I really don't. Everything is such a mess right now.

Sienna nodded and then for the thousandth time in their relationship, proved why she was Rylee's best friend. Sienna got out of her chair, squeezed herself in next to Rylee and pulled her in for a tight hug. "I get it." She hugged tighter. "I totally get it."

Maybe she did. Maybe she didn't. It didn't matter. She was there.

"You're going to sleep over tomorrow," Sienna announced a moment later. "We haven't done that in forever and it will get you out of your house. Something tells me you don't really want to be there all that much right now."

She had that right.

"Do you think your mom will mind?"

Rylee almost laughed out loud at her question, remembering the total and complete indifference of both her parents earlier that morning.

"Are you kidding me?" Rylee rolled her eyes. "I'm sure she'll be happy to get rid of me right now." She didn't actually know whether that was true or not. In fact, she kind of felt bad for taking off on her the night before because it was her birthday and she'd totally freaked out.

But, whatever. Rylee shook her head, pulled her hair out of the elastic again and forced herself to stop feeling sorry for her mom. After all, it was her own fault, and she hadn't even thought about how any of it was going to affect Rylee.

"Good." Sienna gave her one last hug and hopped up. "It'll be fun. And..." She grabbed up her backpack as the warning bell rang. "You can even tell me about the kiss with Brice if you want and I promise I won't freak out."

Maren

THE DAYS that followed didn't make the news of their pregnancy any easier to accept. Once Doctor Harrison confirmed that the IUD was intact and in place, and confirmed that she was approximately nine to ten weeks along—a fact that Maren was still having trouble wrapping her head around—Maren was sent home with a prescription for prenatal vitamins and instructions to schedule a multitude of follow-up appointments and "think about their options" and that was it.

Not that they'd expected much more. After all, there was nothing the doctor would be able to say that would help them accept the news any easier. The one thing that could have helped Maren come to grips with the way her life had completely flipped upside down would be talking to Davis. But every time she tried, he told her he was still *processing*. The word was starting to make her crazy. If he didn't finish *processing*—and soon—she might come completely unhinged.

Of course, Davis wasn't the only one who needed time. Rylee was still barely talking to either of them. For whatever reason, she seemed less upset with her father, a fact that hurt Maren but she wouldn't say anything. It wouldn't help. In the few days since her birthday, Rylee had only come out of her room to eat and go to school and swim practice. But just because she was at the table with them or in the car on the way to practice didn't mean she was talking to either of them.

Maren tried to engage her in conversation. "How was school?" "Are you excited for the swim meet next week?" "How did the chemistry test go?" But besides a few short answers, it was clear that Rylee wasn't ready to talk and Maren wasn't going to push it.

She could have threatened to take away her phone or burst into her room, refusing to leave until her daughter talked to her, but what was the point? She'd never parented with a strong authoritarian hand before; she didn't need to start now. Besides, it could've been worse. Rylee could be the one who was pregnant.

Maren shuddered at the thought. That would definitely be worse. And that was saying something, since in the span of less than three days, her entire family had imploded.

Maren managed to keep herself busy at work, which wasn't hard. She'd been convinced she'd blown her chance at the promotion because she'd sat through the entire thing barely hearing what Eileen and the other managers had said. Somehow she'd managed to answer their questions and despite the fact that she must have come off like a total space cadet, they'd given her the position of account manager. Something she'd barely even had a chance to think about in the days that followed. Including what it would mean now that her situation had changed.

She'd be transitioning to her new role over the course of a week, which was fine by her because her to-do list only continued to grow. Despite the fact that she couldn't shake the niggling feeling in the back of her mind that in light of every-thing that had happened, she should probably turn down the position, she threw herself into her work. It was the one thing she could control.

Maren had decided to work through lunch on Friday when her husband's number appeared on her cell phone.

Maybe he was finally ready to talk.

They had a strong connection and they loved each other. Everything would be okay. After all, they were Davis and Maren. High school sweethearts. Voted most likely to be happy ever after.

She pressed the button to connect the call. "Hey. How's your day?"

"Not bad, not bad. But it's busy around here today. Month end is coming up and we need to tie up a few things before we can run reports." Davis had worked for a financial advising firm for most of their marriage, and Maren had grown accustomed to last-minute client meetings and month end reports keeping him away from home. "I'm afraid I'm going to be late tonight."

Even though it wasn't unusual for Davis to have to work late, she couldn't help but feel that maybe this particular occurrence had more to do with avoidance than actual work. He wasn't ready to talk at all. "Oh, that's too bad," she said instead of pushing the issue. "Not too late, I hope?"

"Probably not," he said quickly. "But I just didn't want you to rush home or anything."

"Okay. I'll pick up a roasted chicken or something easy from the store." She mentally added it to the ongoing grocery list in her head. "And Davis?"

"Yes?"

"Maybe when you get home…we can talk, okay?"

There was a beat of silence on the other end and finally he said, "Of course."

"I mean it, Davis," she said, needing to make her point. "We really need to talk about this."

"I understand. Completely. We'll talk when I get home, okay?"

"Okay." A smile crossed her face. Finally, they'd be able to get on the same page about what was happening.

"I love you, Maren."

Her heart swelled and for the first time in days, she felt at peace. "I love you, too."

It wasn't until Maren hung up that she considered what exactly she was going to do with her Friday evening. Rylee always reserved Friday evenings for hanging out with her friends, and she couldn't imagine that would be any different today.

Of course, she could just go home, maybe have a bubble bath and read a book. There was a time not all that long ago when Maren would look forward to having an empty house all to herself. It happened so rarely that she relished those moments. But after the last few days, she was antsy and the idea of being alone was more than unappealing. She'd made her point with Davis; they were going to finally talk about things when he got home. Maybe it wouldn't hurt to talk about her own feelings before then.

It was a good idea. And there was only one person in the world to have that conversation with.

Sabrina.

Next to Davis, no one knew Maren better than Sabrina. She'd be able to help Maren get her feelings straight. In fact, she should have called her ages ago to tell her about the baby. She had an instant flash of guilt. Sabrina had sent a number of text messages since their lunch together and Maren had answered vaguely and she certainly hadn't told her anything about the baby.

Why?

.   .   .

She didn't know the answer to that. Normally she would never wait to tell Sabrina something so incredibly life-changing. But there was nothing normal about this. Normal was *before*.

Would she now start thinking of her life as *before* and *after*? The thought was way too dramatic. She'd found out she was pregnant, for God's sake, not dying.

She was being stupid, and way too dramatic. Besides, she needed her best friend, so while she finished her lunch, Maren sent Sabrina a series of texts and asked her to go shopping after work and maybe grab a bite to eat. She'd been asking Maren to go with her to grab a few baby things and they hadn't been able to find a time that worked for both of them, so when Sabrina replied with an, "Absolutely!" Maren was pleased.

Sabrina would know what to say about everything. She was her best friend in the entire world. She always knew what to say and no doubt, she'd be thrilled with the news. It would be so good to have someone react positively.

When they were younger, long before Rylee was born and Sabrina had declared she was never having children of her own, they used to talk about how fun it would be to raise their babies at the same time. How their daughters would be best friends just like they were. Obviously, that hadn't happened for so many reasons. But things changed and now...maybe it could? Of course, it looked very different than they'd planned when they were young and foolish, but sometimes life just worked out that way.

They arranged for Sabrina to pick Maren up at home so she could drop off her car, and a few hours later, she was waiting for her friend on the driveway as Sabrina pulled up.

"Someone's excited to go shopping," she remarked with a grin as Maren slid into her passenger seat. "Normally it's like pulling teeth to get you to come to the mall with me."

It was true. Maren hated shopping. Even when they were

teenagers, Sabrina and all the other girls loved to hang out at the mall, but Maren would only go along begrudgingly. It hadn't gotten any better as she got older. And Sabrina knew it.

"Well, I thought it would be good to spend some time together. Besides," she added, "I know you're excited about the baby. And…" *She should just tell her.* There was no point in waiting. But something stopped her. *Not yet.* "And, I just want to spend some time with you. Everything's gonna change when this little guy comes along." That was an understatement. Because not only was everything going to change when Sabrina's son was born—a few months later, it would all change again. Nothing was ever going to be the same.

Maren squeezed her purse on her lap and forced herself to take a deep breath. She'd done a really good job controlling the panic that was just under the surface every time she thought about having a baby again. But it was a very tenuous grip she had on herself. Which was why it was so important that she kept her focus on all of the positive parts about being a mother again, and not on the reality of it.

"Maren?" Sabrina glanced her way. "Are you okay?"

"What do you mean? Of course. I'm fine."

"Really?" Sabrina looked at her sideways. "Because you've been totally MIA. Barely answering my texts and…well, I've been worried about you and now you want to go shopping? I mean, you *never* want to go to the mall." She laughed but Maren couldn't bring herself to join in. "Seriously." Sabrina's laughter died off. "Are you okay? Really?"

It was the perfect time to tell her. She just had to open her mouth and tell her best friend she was pregnant and everything would be fine. But still, she couldn't.

"Everything's great," Maren lied. "I think maybe I need a little bit more sleep. And is it so wrong to want to go shopping?" She forced a grin. "Now tell me, what are we looking for today?"

Maren sat back in the passenger seat while Sabrina rattled off a list of items she needed. Or thought she needed. Maren fought the urge to make a mental list of her own and the longer she sat and listened, the harder it got to say anything. And then when they got to the store and started shopping, Maren almost forgot about wanting to talk to her at all.

Almost.

"What do you think of this?" Sabrina held up the cutest baby-sized jean jacket Maren had ever seen. In the years since Rylee had been little, the baby clothes had become so much cuter, if it were even possible.

Maren put down the onesies she was looking at and took the jacket out of her friend's hands. "It's adorable. Like, seriously adorable. Your little guy is going to look so cute in this. Let me buy it for you. A gift from Auntie Maren." She laughed and Sabrina tried to snatch it back, but there was no way Maren was going to let that happen. She'd bought Rylee so many things over the years, and spoiled her so completely, there was no way Maren was ever going to be able to repay her properly.

"Maren, you don't have to do that."

But she had already started walking toward the till. "You know what?" Maren changed the subject. "I was just thinking about how when we were kids we would talk about how great it would be to have babies at the same time. And raise them together. Remember?" It wasn't the best bridge to the conversation, but it was the best she could come up with.

"Of course. But that ship has sailed." Sabrina laughed. "I mean, Rylee is going to be way too old for my son. In pretty much all cultures. She'll be more like an auntie than a friend. And that's okay. I guess some things don't always work out the way you think they will." She shrugged and looked away.

Maren handed the jacket to the cashier and looked at Sabrina with a nervous smile. "You're exactly right." Her heart started to race, thinking of how excited Sabrina was going to be that they were actually going to get to raise their babies together. Maybe it was the one positive thing that was going to come out of all of this. Something she could hold onto and look forward to until her brain caught up with her body. Maren took a deep breath. "Maybe Rylee won't be able to grow up with your son, but her brother or sister will be able to."

Maren said the words quickly, swallowed hard, and clenched her teeth together in a Joker-like grin. She waited for Sabrina to squeal, laugh, grab her in a big hug, or react in some way that told her she was excited. Because of course she was excited. This was what they'd always talked about. What they'd always wanted.

But she didn't. In fact, Sabrina didn't say anything at all. At least not right away.

"Sabrina? Did you hear what I said?"

After a moment, Sabrina nodded slowly and blinked. "I think so." Confusion lined her face as she looked up at Maren. "I mean, did you just say that my son will be able to grow up with Rylee's brother or sister?"

Maren nodded.

"So…" Sabrina blinked again and spoke slowly. "Are you telling me that you are pregnant too?"

She nodded again.

Sabrina sucked in her bottom lip and bit down. "You're pregnant?" The words came out extra slowly, as if she were trying to make sense of them.

"Yes," Maren finally said. "I just found out a few days ago. My birthday, actually, and—"

Sabrina's face hardened, her teeth clenched together, and in that instant, Maren's heart sunk. Moments before it shattered altogether.

"You bitch."

The words came out like knives, slashing through her.

Maren squeezed her eyes shut as a defense mechanism, but nothing more came. She opened them just in time to see Sabrina spin on her heel and stalk away.

That wasn't supposed to happen.

Maren looked from the cashier to Sabrina's retreating form, back to the cashier, who looked apologetic and just as confused as Maren felt. She quickly scanned Maren's credit card and finished the transaction. The cashier had only barely stuffed the jacket into a bag before Maren grabbed it and ran after her friend.

For a six-month pregnant woman, Sabrina was fast. She was already out in the parking lot by the time Maren caught up to her. "Sabrina! Sabrina, wait."

She spun around and glared at her, stopping Maren in her tracks. "It always has to be about you, doesn't it?"

Slightly out of breath, Maren pressed her hand to her chest. "What are you talking about? What has to be about me?"

"You're having a baby." Sabrina's hands rested on her belly protectively. "It's like you just can't stand for me to have anything. You have to have it too."

"What are you talking about? Lots of people have babies. This has nothing to do with you."

"Doesn't it?" Sabrina shook her head and made a sound of disgust before locking eyes on Maren again. "Our whole lives, it's been about you. *Your* boyfriend, *your* wedding, *your* baby, *your* perfect life. And when finally, *finally*, I get something for myself —a family of my own—you can't let me have it." She shook her head again. "It was just too much for you, wasn't it?"

It wasn't too much. Not at all. But what *was* too much for Maren was standing there listening to the cruelty her friend was spewing at her. Was she fucking kidding? "Do you really think I did this on purpose?" Maren's voice shook both from anger and the tears that threatened to spill over. "Is that really what you think of me? That I am so consumed by jealousy for you, that I would turn my entire life upside down to have a baby at forty when all I've been able to talk about was how excited I am for the next stage? Really?" She shook and was dangerously close to losing complete control, but she couldn't do anything about that.

Especially when her best friend looked her in the eye, and said with a voice as cold as a Canadian glacier, "Yes. That's exactly what I think you would do."

"Fuck you, Sabrina." Maren could only just barely control her voice. "Just... Fuck. You." She threw the bag with the jean jacket in it at her, turned around and walked away.

Sabrina

SHE WAS PREGNANT? Maren? Pregnant?

Ridiculous.

But of course she was pregnant. The selfish bitch.

The mean-spirited thought slammed into Sabrina as she pointed her car home and sped out of the parking lot way too fast. She took a breath and forced herself to slow down. The last thing she needed was to be involved in an accident. Her gaze flicked down to her belly. She needed to remember what was important.

And it was *not* Maren's baby.

Maren's baby.

Mean-spirited or not, she couldn't seem to stop the train of thought once she'd started it. Why the hell was Maren pregnant? *Now?* After so long?

Sabrina knew exactly why Maren was pregnant.

Of course.

It was because *she* was pregnant.

Ever since they were teenagers, Maren never could let her have one thing for herself. Not one.

On autopilot, Sabrina navigated her car through the streets

until she arrived in her parking space in front of her condo. She'd planned to run a few more errands before returning home, but there was no way she could be out in public when she was so mad.

Aware that she shouldn't even be behind the wheel, Sabrina grabbed her things, slammed the car door behind her and ran to her front door.

Once inside, her anger seemed to dissipate a little bit. She looked around her comfortable space. She may not have planned to be a homeowner all of those years ago, but once her little condo was hers, she'd taken pride in decorating it. It had taken years, but piece by piece, Sabrina had picked items that made her feel good, and made her feel safe and warm. *Home.*

But now, fresh off Maren's betrayal, she felt anything but safe and warm. She was agitated and restless.

For a flash, she felt guilty about leaving Maren the way she had at the mall with no ride. Of course, she probably hadn't been alone long.

"Did Davis come to your rescue?" She spat the question at the framed photo of the two of them that sat on the mantel over her gas fireplace. "He probably ran right over to rescue you, didn't he? So you could go home to your perfect house and your perfect husband and your perfect daughter and your perfect little baby."

Tears flooded her eyes until the photo of the two of them blurred and she could no longer make out her best friend's smiling face. The picture had been taken three years earlier on a summer trip they'd all taken to the beach. She and Maren had both been sunburnt, their noses pink. But a few too many vodka coolers meant they hadn't cared. Despite herself, Sabrina smiled at the memory. But just for a second before turning away and storming up the stairs to her bedroom.

She should have a bath. That would calm her down.

But hadn't she read in one of those stupid books that it wasn't safe for the baby to have a bath?

Maybe if it wasn't too hot.

She flicked on the taps and watched the steaming water fill the tub for a few minutes before wrenching the taps closed again and sitting hard on the edge of the tub.

No. If it wasn't safe, she shouldn't do it.

Maren wouldn't take the chance.

A voice in her head that sounded oddly like a petulant four-year-old version of herself spoke up.

The logical part of her brain told her she was being ridiculous. But no matter how hard it tried, that part of her brain wouldn't be heard over the noise of the completely illogical part of her brain that was screaming at her.

It was completely unfair that Maren was pregnant. And there was no doubt that she'd planned it out perfectly so her baby would have just the right due date while Sabrina's little guy was going to be born in the summer and forever be destined to have a birthday party nobody would come to because all of his friends were on school holiday.

It was a detail Sabrina might have given some consideration, if she'd given any consideration at all to getting pregnant. Which she hadn't.

Still sitting on the edge of the tub, she took another deep breath in an effort to calm herself.

Maren had it all. The great job, with a brand-new promotion. The successful, handsome husband. The beautiful, talented daughter. The perfect life. The perfect family.

The *family.*

Maren's new baby would be welcomed into that family as if he or she had always been the missing piece. Davis would get up in the middle of the night and change diapers. No doubt Rylee would babysit her younger sibling, and spoil him or her silly, entertaining the baby while Maren grabbed a nap or made a delicious dinner without interruption.

And Sabrina would be alone. There wouldn't be anyone there to help her.

But that had been her choice. She didn't have anyone else to blame for that. Not really.

She'd told everyone that she'd made the choice to use a donor because she didn't want anyone else getting in her way of raising her baby. And people believed it, too. Anyone who knew Sabrina, and how hardheaded she could be, didn't even question her reasoning.

Until recently.

She remembered the way Maren had hinted around something at lunch the other day. But no, she didn't know anything more. And even if she did suspect the truth, Sabrina couldn't tell the truth now.

And using a donor? As far as her friends and family were concerned, using a donor had been the most responsible thing she'd ever done. Much more responsible than going out and getting knocked up with a completely unsuitable candidate to be her baby daddy. No. That would be incredibly irresponsible and Sabrina knew she'd never hear the end of it.

If everyone knew the truth, it would be a cloud over her unborn baby, tainting everything, and that wasn't a fair thing to do to a baby. Lying had been a much better choice.

For everyone.

Maren

BY THE TIME Maren called a cab and got home, the last thing she wanted to do was talk to anyone. The fight with Sabrina continually played on a loop in her head. And every time, it made her cringe. They'd been friends forever. They'd been through almost everything together. And in all that time, they'd barely argued, let alone yelled at each other. And Maren had certainly never sworn at her before. Not in anger. Not like that.

Replaying it in her mind made her stomach turn, but not with the now all-too-familiar queasiness of morning sickness, but this time with the certainty that things had irrevocably changed between them. She felt terrible about yelling at Sabrina, but at the same time, she'd do it again. After all, Sabrina clearly didn't have the same compunction about saying terrible things to her.

How could Sabrina say those things? How could she think for even one second that Maren had gotten pregnant because she was jealous? It was ridiculous.

Wasn't it?

She rejected the thought the moment it entered her head. Of course it was ridiculous. She was excited about the future.

About what a little more parental freedom would bring for her. The idea that even subconsciously she was jealous of Sabrina, when having a baby was the exact opposite of what she wanted, was ludicrous.

But that didn't stop Maren from continually second-guessing herself as she made herself a peanut butter sandwich, and sent a quick text to both Rylee and Davis that she wasn't feeling well and was going to bed early.

Okay, hon. I'm going to be a bit later than I thought anyway. Feel better.

Davis's reply came in almost instantly. Maren couldn't help but think that his long work day was very convenient considering they had so much to talk about. But there was no point arguing with him over text message. She'd done enough arguing for one night. Besides, there was no way she was in any state to have a serious conversation about their future anyway.

Thanks. Don't work too hard. Love you.

She replied, adding a kissing emoji before clicking over to check Rylee's response.

K.

Really? Maren tried not to groan. Would it kill the girl to type an actual response? With a sigh, Maren tapped in another reply.

Be home by eight. Love you.

It occurred to her afterward while she laid in bed with a cool washcloth on her forehead that she probably should have asked Rylee where she was, or what she was doing. But she was almost for sure with Sienna, watching videos. It wouldn't hurt if she slacked off on her parenting for one night.

The sleeplessness that had plagued Maren earlier in the week must have finally caught up with her, because she fell into a deep sleep within minutes of lying down. She didn't hear the door slam at five to eight when Rylee got home. Nor did she hear Davis get home just after midnight and slip into the bed next to her.

But something did wake her in the early hours of the morning. Jolted awake, her eyes struggled to fixate on anything in the still dark room. Her breathing came fast and her mind raced until finally, the shadowy form of her dresser across the room with the stack of Davis's T-shirts freshly washed and folded that she hadn't gotten around to putting away yet came into focus.

Her room.

She was home.

Try as she might, Maren couldn't grab hold of the tendrils of the dream that floated just out of her reach before vanishing altogether into the abyss of consciousness. Now awake, she scrubbed a hand over her face and looked to the alarm clock on her nightstand. Ten minutes to six. It was too early to get up. Yet, her body disagreed.

Five minutes later, after staring at the shadowy pile of T-shirts just long enough to annoy her that it was she and not Davis who felt any type of obligation to put them in the drawer, Maren kicked back the blanket and resigned herself to an early start.

It was Saturday, and usually on a Saturday, she and Davis would go to the farmers' market together to pick up some fresh vegetables, maybe one of the delicious pies that the senior center liked to bring down to sell, or just do what they did best, which was to buy an overpriced coffee and wander from stall to stall, picking up produce, squeezing melons, and basically examine everything but not really buying much at all. It was one of her favorite things to do with Davis when Rylee was little, and she'd looked forward to the weekends, and time with the three of them all together where she wasn't the only one in charge of the tiny little human who'd stolen her heart, yet needed so much attention. She'd craved adult attention in those early years. Not that she hadn't loved being a mom. She had. More than anything else she'd ever done, Maren felt at home and at peace even with motherhood. But yet, the days full of talking in a high-pitched voice to a little human who only ever responded with varying types and volumes of cries, and the occasional smile, could at times drag on, leaving Maren lonely and needing time with Davis more than ever.

It had been Davis's idea to start going to the farmers' market and it had quickly turned into a weekend ritual that all three of them looked forward to. As Rylee got older, she didn't join them as often. The demands of the swim team or home-work often kept her away, but every now and then she'd ask to go with them. Those were Maren's favorite mornings. When they were all together.

She glanced at Rylee's closed bedroom door as she made her way down the hallway to the stairs. Something told her that her daughter would not be joining them at the market that morning.

Once downstairs, Maren fixed herself a cup of tea and sat at the kitchen table. She stared at her cell phone, but couldn't bring herself to pick it up and check for messages. What if Sabrina had texted her?

But what if she hadn't?

Maren had no idea what she would say to her friend if she did reach out. But worse would be checking her messages to see that she hadn't.

No. She couldn't look.

Davis would be downstairs by seven thirty. No doubt he'd be surprised to see her up. She was generally the night owl, favoring staying up late with a book or a movie instead of waking early like he did. He tried to sleep in on weekends, but seven was usually as late as he could manage before he started to get antsy.

She sat for another minute, sipping at her tea, which, to her pleasant surprise, wasn't disturbing her stomach, before making a decision.

She'd make breakfast. A big, over-the-top Saturday morning family breakfast.

Swim club was on a four-month break, so Rylee wouldn't be in a rush to get to the pool. They could all eat together. And maybe...talk.

Yes.

That's exactly what she would do. Make an irresistible breakfast that would bring her entire family together, so they could deal with the situation life had thrown at them the way they'd always dealt with everything else—together.

She set to work mixing up the batter for the waffles and putting the bacon in the oven to cook up nice and crispy. It wouldn't be long before the aroma would reach upstairs and wake Rylee up. Waffles were her favorite. She'd never be able to resist and once Rylee was sitting across from her, pouring maple syrup into each of the little golden brown pockets, she'd have to talk to Maren. And finally, they would get everything out in the open.

Buoyed by the idea, Maren set the table and put a pot of coffee on for Davis, careful not to inhale the aroma of the beans.

For a few minutes as she measured and poured and whisked the batter, losing herself in the normality of it, she even allowed herself to believe it was a normal day and her life was completely normal and her family was behaving normal and everything was just so freakin' normal that anyone looking in on their totally normal life would call it boring. Mundane even.

She didn't even notice how vigorously she was whisking

until batter splashed over the edge of the bowl. A laugh bubbled out from the back of her throat but the sound that escaped was borderline maniacal. She clamped a hand over her mouth and pressed her free hand on the counter, leaning into it. A sob replaced the laugh and just for a moment, she let the tears slip down her cheeks for the first time.

But almost as soon as the tears started, Maren wiped them away, took a deep breath and straightened her shoulders. It would be too easy to give in to the swirl of emotions smashing through her body. The release would probably even feel good. Really good. But she couldn't. Not yet. She needed to hold herself together at least until she'd had a chance to talk to Davis. They still had so much to discuss and talk over. Decisions to make, risks to consider.

Maren made herself take another deep breath and then another. She would pull herself together, because that's what she had to do. She'd handle it. She was the mom. It's what she did. Maren held things together and pushed everyone forward. This wouldn't be any different.

By the time she heard the footsteps on the stairs, Maren was ready. A stack of light and fluffy waffles sat in the center of the table next to a plate full of bacon piled high, a jug of orange juice, and Davis's coffee. She was just finishing up with a pan of eggs. Sunny side up, just the way her family liked them.

"Good morning." Maren looked up, surprised to see it was Rylee who'd beat her father down for breakfast. The smell of waffles. She knew her daughter wouldn't be able to resist. "You're up early."

Rylee grunted in response and moved to push past her mother, but with a quick step to the side, Maren blocked her passage. She didn't recognize this angst-ridden, growly version of her daughter. She used to brag to her coworkers how Rylee had seemed to skip all of the teenage drama and they'd stayed just as close as they'd ever been. In less than a week, all of that had changed.

But it was temporary, Maren told herself before her forced smile could falter. This too shall pass. She'd make sure of it.

"You must be hungry," she said to her daughter as she twisted around to grab the pan of eggs. "I made your favorites. I thought it had been too long since we'd all sat down and eaten together and since it's Saturday, maybe we could—"

"I'm not hungry."

Maren blinked hard, momentarily caught off guard by the angry tone of Rylee's voice. "You must be," she said. And then, with more force, "Sit." It wasn't a request and even through her newfound attitude, Rylee must have heard the steel in her mother's voice, because after a moment she did as she was told.

Without asking, Maren slid an egg onto Rylee's plate before plating some for Davis. When she turned back to the table, she noted with a certain sense of self-satisfaction that Rylee was buttering a waffle.

"I know you're a little bit upset and—"

"I'm not upset." She picked up the syrup bottle and poured an obscene amount onto the waffle until it practically floated like an island in a sea of maple syrup.

Maren forced herself not to remark on the sugar content of what her daughter was about to eat. "Okay." She tried again. "I'm glad to hear you're not—"

"You think everything is about you."

The sharpness of Rylee's voice caught her off guard and Maren's head twisted around to stare at her daughter. Slowly she moved to the table and was about to sit down across from her when Davis's voice saying good morning distracted her.

"Good morning." She turned to greet him and forced yet another smile to her face, but kept one eye on her daughter, who had started to attack her waffle with her knife and fork, tearing off large pieces. "I made breakfast."

He was showered, but Davis hadn't shaved, the way he often didn't on the weekends. Maren liked the scratch of his stubble and was about to reflexively reach for it when his mouth twisted down in an exaggerated frown. "Oh no." He drew out the words unnaturally. "I need to get back to the office."

Maren's stomach knotted in disappointment as a wave of nausea—which, until that moment, had stayed away—hit her.

"If he's not staying, I'm out of here." Behind her, Maren heard the scrape of Rylee's chair as she got up from the table.

She took a deep breath to steady her stomach before looking at her daughter, who shrugged and said, "I'm going to Sienna's." She was already headed for the back door, but Maren stepped to the side, blocking her.

"Wait." She held up her hand and turned back to her husband, who was pouring himself a to-go cup of coffee. "You wait, too." She held up her other hand and was vaguely aware that she must look like some sort of crazed domestic crossing guard in her robe with her hair still tossed from sleep.

"Maren, I—"

"Mom, this is—"

"I don't want to hear it." She cut them both off and pressed her lips together in an effort to control the quiver in her voice. She swallowed hard, willing her stomach to settle down before confronting her family again. "We all need to talk, and I went to all the work of making this big breakfast. The least the two of you can do is sit down and eat instead of running away again." Rylee muttered something under her breath that Maren ignored. "I understand there's a lot going on, and there's going to be a lot of feelings about it, but we're a family and we need to start acting like one. I've given you both enough space to *process*." She looked directly at Davis as she said the word. "Now it's time to talk. Sit."

It wasn't very often that Maren lost her cool. She prided

herself on being a relaxed wife and mother, who handled every situation with a calm clarity. Well, most situations. And judging by the looks on the faces of her husband and child, they were just as taken aback at her change in attitude as she was.

She dropped her hands to her side and moments later, they both sat at the table.

Once she had their attention, Maren was no longer sure what to say, so she simply sank into her own chair and, despite the fact that she was still battling an internal war to keep her nausea at bay, took a waffle off the top of the stack. "This is nice," she said with as much cheer as she could muster.

"I really do have to go this morning. I—"

"No." She interrupted Davis with a sharp look. "There's nothing more important than this. Right now."

He stared at her, but finally nodded. "You're right."

She released a small sigh of relief when after a moment he took a waffle of his own.

The tension in the room was thick, but it was a start. Davis and Maren made small talk about the weather and whatever emergency was going on at the office that had him running in on a Saturday. It didn't happen very often, and despite the unusualness of it, Maren couldn't focus on what he was saying. She continually glanced at Rylee, who swirled chunks of her waffle around in the sea of syrup, only occasionally popping one in her mouth. She looked so young with her hair tied back in a ponytail but the eyeliner rimming her eyes and the scowl on her face told a different story.

How had her baby turned into a brooding teenager in only a matter of a few days?

But she knew the answer and it had everything to do with the other baby who was about to throw their lives for a loop.

"Do you have plans today, Rylee?"

Her daughter started a little bit at the question, as if she'd been lost in her own thoughts.

"Because if you don't, maybe we——"

"I was going to sleep over at Sienna's." She looked to Davis and then back at her mother. "If it's okay?" she added after a moment.

"Of course."

Maybe Maren should have objected. Maybe she should have put up a little resistance and insisted her daughter spend some time with them to reconnect. But her instincts told her that a little time with her best friend would be good for Rylee. Besides, maybe the time alone would be good for her and Davis. In their entire relationship, she'd never felt so disconnected from him and she didn't like it. The situation needed to be nipped in the bud. And quickly.

"Sounds good to me." Davis shrugged.

"Right?" She jumped on the idea that had just formulated in her mind. "And you and I can have a quiet night together. Since you have to go back to the office today, then tonight maybe we can get some takeout and talk." She wished she hadn't seen it, but there was no mistaking the way Davis flinched when she'd suggested takeout and talking.

Had things really changed so much between them too? No. She refused to believe it. It was just a blip and after a night reconnecting and talking together about what was happening, everything would be okay. *They* would be okay.

"That'll be nice." He said the words with a smile that didn't quite reach his eyes. Eyes that Maren couldn't help but notice looked tired. The lines around his eyes seemed to have deepened in the last few days as well. Not that she was going to mention it.

"I'll go tell Sienna." Rylee jumped up from the table and was gone. What was left of her waffle looked oddly abandoned in the pool of syrup.

"I really should get going, too." Davis didn't make eye

contact as he pushed his chair back, leaving his breakfast largely untouched.

Hot and sudden tears pricked at Maren's eyes but she refused to cry. Not twice in one morning. She blinked hard and stood so she faced him. "So...later?"

Something in her voice must have caught his attention, because Davis crossed the room and stopped in front of her.

"Of course, Maren."

When he put his hands on her shoulders, her instinct was to melt into his touch. She wanted his arms to wrap around her so she could let him hold her safe. More than anything, she wanted him to tell her that she'd be okay. That they'd be okay. No matter what.

But she held herself back because if she let herself, she could and would completely fall apart.

"I know you're feeling...well, I guess I don't know what you're feeling," he finished clumsily. "But I want you to know I'm here, Maren. I know I haven't been...well...it's not easy."

His words should have comforted her but she couldn't seem to find any solace in what he said. She shook her head and looked to her feet. "No," she said. "It's not easy. That's why you can't shut down on this. You can't avoid it, Davis. We *need* to talk." She looked up into his eyes. "I need you." She hadn't planned to say something to him. Not that way. And for a moment, she almost felt bad when she saw the look in his eyes. The same look she'd seen four years earlier, when his mother passed away after a stroke. Did their unplanned pregnancy spark that level of distress in him?

She shook her head and dropped her gaze but Davis caught her chin with his fingers and lifted it gently until she was looking at him again. "I love you, Maren, and I know I could have done a better job at communicating with you about this, but I *am* here. We're going to be okay. I promise."

This time there was more confidence in his voice, or maybe

it was just that Maren so desperately wanted to hear it. *Needed* to hear it. Either way, it was enough for her to wrap her arms around him and pull herself into his chest, where she soaked in his warmth and strength. *They would be okay. Of course they would.*

Davis slipped his arms around her to pull her in tighter and for a moment, everything *was* okay.

And then it was over when Davis pulled away and pressed a kiss to her forehead. "We'll talk tonight."

All she could do was nod and smile because she was only barely hanging on. As it was, Maren managed to make it another few minutes, until just after she heard his SUV pull out of the driveway before she dropped into a chair, crumpled to the cool wood surface and let herself sob.

Sabrina

BY THE TIME Sabrina woke up the next morning, long after she should have rolled out of bed, she was feeling better.

Mostly.

The lingering anger at Maren's news was still there, but she calmed down considerably. While she stared at her reflection in the mirror as she brushed her teeth, Sabrina had almost convinced herself that her irrational outburst that night was the fault of her out-of-control hormones.

She'd *almost* managed to convince herself. But not quite.

The truth was, it wasn't the first time she'd been jealous of Maren. And it wouldn't be the last.

It wasn't easy to have a perfect best friend. Sure, Sabrina was happy for Maren most of the time. And proud of her and everything she did. But every once in a while, it was hard to be her friend. *Really* hard.

Davis had been Sabrina's friend first. Ever since the third grade when he pulled her ponytail and made her cry. Later that day, once her tears turned into a determination to get him back, she'd kicked him in the crotch.

The teacher, of course, called both sets of parents, and

they'd all ended up sitting in Mrs. LaMew's classroom, the adults with their knees bent up comically in the small child-sized seats. Of course, the adults all tripped over themselves to apologize for their children's behavior. Davis and Sabrina were ultimately made to apologize to each other, which they did begrudgingly. But it wasn't until Mrs. LaMew made the two of them hug and Davis had whispered in her ear, "I think her name should be LaPew." and they'd both dissolved in a pile of giggles because Mrs. LaMew was known for having terrible BO, that they became best friends.

As it turned out, their behavior and Mrs. LaMew ended up bringing together their parents as well, as the two families became close friends after that initial meeting. Over the years, the Miller and Bennett families hosted each other for Fourth of July barbecues, Thanksgiving dinners, and Saturday night card games. As the kids got older, the families naturally drifted apart, but by then Davis and Sabrina were so entrenched in each other's lives, they didn't need their families to keep them close.

It was Sabrina who'd introduced Maren to Davis and changed everything. She'd hit it off with the pretty new girl right away. They seemed to complement each other— Maren's quieter personality with Sabrina's more outgoing nature—and with Davis in the mix, they all just kind of went together.

She hadn't even cared when Maren started dating Davis, not really. Especially because neither of them were the type to get all relationship crazy and forget about her. Of course, there were a few times when she'd felt like a third wheel...but mostly it worked out.

And then later, when they decided to get married, Sabrina wasn't jealous at all. Not really.

Okay, maybe a little.

But that was only because Maren got to plan a big party,

and all of the attention was on her, while as usual, she simply played the supporting role. It's what she did.

And sure, things could have been different…but they weren't.

Not that any of that mattered now.

She knew the real reason she was upset with Maren, and although right or wrong, it was rooted in jealousy. It wasn't fair. It was definitely not fair. And she absolutely could not say anything.

She dressed in a new pair of maternity jeans—none of her regular clothes fit any longer—and tugged an oversized sweater over her head. The only thing that mattered now was the family she was going to have.

The family of two.

"You and me, buddy," she said aloud. Sabrina had never been one to talk to herself, thinking it was for slightly off center, lonely people. But it wasn't really talking to *yourself* if she was talking to her unborn baby, was it? She shrugged. "We've totally got this, baby."

Downstairs in the kitchen, Sabrina contemplated the stack of baby name books on the counter. She'd bought them all in a fit of excitement after finding out she was having a boy. She hadn't even really wanted to find out the sex, but lying on the table at her routine appointment, the question just popped out before she could think it through.

"Can you see the sex?" she'd asked Doctor Martinez.

"I can." She'd moved the wand around Sabrina's belly. "Did you want to know?"

She knew why the doctor was asking. At her last ultrasound appointment, Sabrina had made a big deal about not finding out and experiencing one of life's greatest surprises. But, wasn't just being pregnant a big enough surprise? "I do," she said. "Is it a boy or a girl?"

Doctor Martinez's lips twitched up into a smile. "Most definitely you're having a little boy. Congratulations."

A boy.

Her head rolled away from the screen where Doctor Martinez had been pointing out the defining feature of her baby's sex and she stared at the ceiling.

A boy?

She'd been so sure she was having a girl. And for no reason other than the fact that the only baby she'd ever really had any experience with had been Rylee.

But a boy?

"Wow. A boy."

"Definitely a boy," Doctor Martinez said. "Congratulations."

She'd gone straight to the bookstore and bought baby name books, even though she knew right away what his name would be. She couldn't bring herself to say it out loud yet, though. Somehow it didn't feel right until she was holding him.

With a whole day stretching out ahead of her, Sabrina worked hard to keep thoughts of Maren and the fight they'd had out of her head. It wouldn't do any good to dwell in it or relive it. Instead, she threw herself into the never ending list of chores she had to finish before the baby actually arrived. A date that was getting much closer.

She started with the purchases she'd made the night before. Sabrina retrieved them from the heap by the front door where she'd dropped them and took them up to the spare room that she'd recently cleared out to become the nursery. One by one, she pulled out tiny onesies and sweaters and impossibly tiny jeans out of the bags, clipped the tags and put them in a pile to wash. Eventually she got to a different bag. The one Maren had thrown at her.

Slowly, Sabrina pulled the tiny jean jacket out of the bag. It was so cute and absolutely perfect.

Sadness and regret overwhelmed her, and she slid to the carpet, still clutching the jacket. This was supposed to be her time. Maren had her baby. But even though she was so mad, Sabrina couldn't help it. She wanted her best friend. She wanted her there to help her put baby clothes away, to discuss what she was still missing, and what were absolutely *must haves* for the nursery. Sabrina's eyes slid to the box with the crib she still hadn't assembled. She wanted Maren there to help her with the crib.

But she wouldn't call. She couldn't.

Instead, she sent a different text.

Are you free today? I could really use your help.

The message changed to indicate the text had been read. She waited a few minutes, and then five more. Still no reply.

I really need to talk.

She knew she sounded needy, but despite the fact that she'd promised herself she'd *never* do this—that she'd *never* text the baby's father, making demands—she couldn't help herself. She winced as she added:

Please. I really need you.

The three little bubbles that indicated he was typing appeared for a moment before disappearing again. She waited. Still no reply.

She could get mad. She could demand he come over and help her. She could tell him that he owed her. That despite all the things she'd said about doing it on her own and not needing or wanting him, that it was his baby, too.

Instead, Sabrina put her phone to the side and reached for the massive cardboard box that had been delivered two weeks previously. The delivery men had been kind enough to take it all the way up the stairs for her. No doubt they felt sorry for her. Either that or they'd been looking for the twenty-dollar tip she'd happily given them.

A few minutes later, Sabrina sat in the middle of the floor, surrounded by pieces and a twenty-page instruction booklet that might as well have been in Greek.

Frustrated, Sabrina threw the instructions across the room and another time when she'd been frustrated with a crib flashed through her memory.

She'd been helping Maren go through her basement. She'd decided she was finally ready to get rid of Rylee's things, but she'd asked for *emotional support* so that she wouldn't cave and keep a bunch of things she didn't need. Sabrina had been there for hours and it was going well, too, until they decided to carry the large oak crib out of the basement. No matter what they tried, they couldn't get it around the bend in the staircase and it kept getting hung up. After twenty minutes of trying, they'd given it up and taken it back into the storage room for Davis to deal with later.

"Are you sure you're done?" Sabrina had asked Maren as they opened another tote full of tiny clothes. "I mean, Rylee is pretty great." She held up an impossibly tiny snowsuit she remembered Rylee wearing when she was an infant. "And this stuff is adorable."

"She is great." Maren laughed. "And that *is* cute. But I'm sure. No more kiddos for us."

"You're sure sure?"

Maren nodded. "I'm *sure* sure. Don't get me wrong, I love Rylee and she's my entire world, but she's growing up so fast and can you imagine such a big age gap? It would be like starting over and totally not fair for either of them to have a sibling so much older or younger." She shook her head a little sadly. "Nope. That ship has sailed."

That had been four years ago. Rylee had been twelve. She was about to turn sixteen.

The age difference between Maren's children struck Sabrina for the first time.

There would be more than sixteen years between her children. A *huge* age gap.

Again, Sabrina remembered the way Maren had sorted Rylee's tiny clothes, her toys, and all of the bits and bobs needed to raise a baby. She'd packed almost everything up and set it out for charity to pick up.

She hadn't planned to have more children. At all.

Which meant only one thing…

Maren hadn't meant to get pregnant. It had been an accident.

Her best friend's pregnancy had *nothing* to do with her. Which meant, she'd been a total bitch.

Sabrina heaved herself up off the floor and surveyed the wreckage that was supposed to become her baby's crib. She reached for her phone.

No unread text messages.

He hadn't responded.

With a flicker of disgust at herself for being so needy, she reread the last message she'd sent and with a cringe, looked away.

What the hell was going on with her? She didn't even recognize herself.

If Maren's pregnancy was actually unplanned, she'd be scared and upset and she'd need her best friend.

But if Sabrina's first instinct had been right, and it was planned...

Then she could go to hell.

She shook her head and looked back at her phone and the unanswered text, everything once more coming to a head. Quickly, she typed one more message.

By the way. It's a boy.

Maren

SHE DIDN'T KNOW how long she sat that way, but Maren didn't move a muscle until the tears slowed and finally stopped. And when they did, she sat back, wiped her face with the back of her hands, and let out a breath. "You got this," she said and then promptly laughed at herself for being so ridiculous. Rylee would never let her forget it if she caught her mom talking to herself.

But Rylee wasn't there.

Rylee wasn't there.

The thought of Rylee walking in on her while she lost control smacked Maren in the face. She should know better than to lose control like that when her daughter could come in at any moment. Rylee was confused enough. She didn't need her mother adding to it by being an emotional wreck.

With a fresh resolve, spurred by the need to protect her child from more distress, Maren reached for a waffle and tore a piece off. The last thing she wanted to do was eat, but like it or not, she wasn't just thinking about herself anymore.

Immediately, resentment sparked in her. How could something so small change so much?

But what if it didn't have to change everything?

The thought came so quickly, it shook her with the force of its impact and what it would mean. *Could* mean, she quickly corrected her thoughts.

Because it wasn't an option.

Was it?

After all, women ended their pregnancies all the time, for all kinds of reasons. Maybe she…if it meant keeping her family from—

"No." She said the word so softly, at first she wasn't sure she'd said it out loud.

But she had. And she meant it.

"No," she said again. "Never." The waffle forgotten, she put her hands on her stomach as if she'd possibly be able to feel the life energy inside her. She couldn't feel it yet, but it was there.

The little spark of life growing inside her was her child. Hers and Davis's.

Her eyes floated to the refrigerator and a family picture of the three of them taken only a few months before. Rylee stood sandwiched between her and Davis. A product of their love. The baby inside her was the same. How could she possibly even entertain the idea of not bringing that love into this world? She couldn't. Not even for a single second.

It might be the right choice for some women, with their own circumstances and their own beliefs. That wasn't for her to decide.

But Maren knew exactly what kind of miracle their love could create. Rylee might be going through a bit of a phase, but she was absolutely perfect. And the baby, whoever he or she turned out to be, would be the same.

Even though the timing couldn't be worse.

By the time the breakfast dishes were cleared up, and the mostly uneaten food wrapped and put in the fridge or tossed out, Maren felt as though she'd already lived an entire day but it wasn't even nine in the morning. Unsettled and unsure of what to do, she showered and dressed, her stomach finally cooperating enough that she could imagine going out in public. If she had anywhere to go. The idea of going to the farmers' market alone didn't appeal.

Restless and unsettled, her gaze landed on the stack of files she'd brought back from the office the night before. She'd had big plans of reviewing and preparing for her first official day as a project manager on Monday but she couldn't bring herself to actually open any of them. It was only a week ago that she'd been so excited about the prospect of taking on her own accounts and what the promotion would mean, not only for her but for her family as well.

She should have been diving into the files, familiarizing herself with the latest schools and community groups that had requested conceptual plans from PlayTime. She'd been dying to get her hands on an actual project. One that she could work on from the beginning. Something she could brainstorm and design, working all the components until they fit together perfectly into the space.

It sounded so simple—designing a playground—but anyone who actually thought that had no idea of the care and consideration that went into the selection of each piece of equipment. For example, you couldn't put a slide facing a swing set. And don't even think about putting monkey bars above the tilty tiles. Never mind considering the major age groups that would enjoy the playground, and what types of equipment would appeal to them as well, of course, as the budget and space restrictions.

It was all like one big jigsaw puzzle, and Maren loved fitting the pieces together.

Despite how much she loved it, and how excited she was—or had been—to take on the projects on her own, she still couldn't bring herself to look at the files. She could tell herself a story about how it was Saturday and she needed a little break to refresh and recharge, but she couldn't even muster the energy to tell herself the lie.

She couldn't look at the files because Maren knew in her heart that she was going to have to go in on Monday and turn down the promotion.

The thought made her stomach twist and it had nothing to do with morning sickness.

But there wasn't any other solution. How on earth could she take the promotion that after so many years she was finally ready for, if in only a few months, she'd be starting motherhood all over again with a brand-new baby? After all, that had been the entire reason she'd stayed on only part time at Play-Time for so many years. How could she possibly give her career her full attention with another child at home? She couldn't.

And she knew it.

A sob threatened to escape from her throat but Maren clamped a hand to her mouth to stifle it. She was done crying for the day.

The whole hormonal thing was already getting really annoying. How was she expected to get through the day if every five minutes she was bursting into tears?

She needed to get some control.

A flash of movement out the kitchen window caught her attention. Next door, Jessica was puttering in her garden along the side of her house.

Perfect.

Maren didn't hesitate before leaving the stifling quietness of her house, and the evidence of the career she'd now never have mocking her, and headed outside.

"Good morning."

Jessica jumped a little, obviously lost in her own thoughts. But when she turned and saw Maren, her smile was wide and genuine. "Hey."

"Gardening?"

It was an obvious question, but Jessica loved talking about her garden. Sure enough, her neighbor started telling Maren about the early spring flowers and what her plans were for the summer flowers she'd tend to later. After a moment, she changed topics. "Are you feeling any better?"

Maren's face flushed. She hadn't even thought to tell Jessica about the baby. They weren't really the type of friend who ran to each other first thing with any kind of news. That was Sabrina for her. At least, it *had* been Sabrina.

Maren shook her head at the thought of her best friend, but Jessica must have taken the action as an answer.

"Oh no," she said. "You're still not well?"

"Yes," Maren said quickly. "I mean, no." Flustered, Maren sighed. "Remember when you were kidding about me being pregnant?"

If it had been any other situation, Maren would have laughed watching her neighbor's face transform as she realized what Maren was saying. Finally, Jessica's mouth formed a small *O* and she dropped her hose, causing a spurt of water to shoot up in an arc over them. Fortunately, she was able to recover quick enough to grab the hose before it managed to soak either of them. With a twist, she shut off the flow of water before once more dropping it. This time, she clasped both hands to her mouth and shook her head. "No way."

"Yes way." Despite herself, Maren did laugh a little bit. Out of all the responses she'd received thus far, Jessica's was hands down the best one. And that was saying something.

"Oh my God, Maren. That's...good?" She tilted her head and raised her voice in question.

Maren only shrugged. "It's unexpected, that's for sure," she answered honestly. "But I guess, it is what it is."

A moment later, Jessica had her arms wrapped around her in a tight hug. "This is amazing. A baby? What a blessing."

"I don't know about amazing." She twisted out of her grasp. "But it certainly is something."

Her hand went reflexively to her stomach and guilt flashed through her. Was she doing the baby an injustice by not being excited for him or her? Could the baby sense the stress and anxiety so early on? When she'd found out she was pregnant with Rylee, the excitement had been intense and immediate. There could be no doubt that Maren loved her from the moment she'd been conceived. But this baby…would her negative feelings affect the baby?

Fortunately, she didn't have much time to dwell on that particular line of thought because Jessica grabbed her hand and was already leading Maren to her front porch. "Tell me everything," her friend insisted. "Have a cup of tea with me and—do you have time for a cup of tea?"

Maren nodded. She had nothing but time.

"Great. But let's sit out here, okay?" Jessica glanced quickly behind her to the house. "I'll be right back. Peppermint okay?"

"Perfect." Maren settled into one of the rockers Jessica kept on the covered porch. She'd always been envious of her neighbor's well decorated and comfortable space. Maren herself had never had an eye for putting together the eclectic thrift store finds that Jessica had, making them look chic and new among the beautifully potted flowers. Whenever Maren tried it, the results looked more like a garbage pile than something that belonged in a Pinterest post.

Maren closed her eyes and let her head rock back against the chair before opening them again. For the first time, she noticed a strange car parked on the curb out front. She laughed as she glanced back at the house and figured out why it was Jessica had wanted them to sit outside. She was still grinning and had a series of questions of her own by the time her friend reemerged with two mugs of tea.

"Is there a reason why we're sitting out here?" She wiggled her eyebrows with interest. Or more specifically, nosiness.

She laughed and waved Maren's question away. "It's not very interesting."

"Bullshit." Maren crossed her leg over her knee and leaned forward, ready to hear a story that wasn't her own. "Besides, I told you something." She conveniently ignored the fact that she'd completely forgotten to tell Jessica her news until only a few minutes ago. She wasn't being a very good friend, but at least she could redeem herself. "And please," Maren implored. "Tell me something to take my mind off...well...everything right now."

She must have seen it on Maren's face that she needed a distraction, and Maren's love for her neighbor grew a little bit more when instead of pressing her to talk about the baby, Jessica only nodded and said, "I had a date last night."

She shouldn't have been surprised, what with the strange car out front and all, but still, Maren swallowed hard to keep from choking on her tea.

"Don't look so shocked." Jessica laughed. "I told you I was going to start dating again."

"You did. But...I guess...I didn't...is he still in there?" Maren gestured to the house behind her, despite the fact it was an obvious question and she most definitely already knew the answer.

"He's still sleeping. I thought I'd take a minute to water the plants before waking him up." She winked and Maren couldn't help but laugh at her implication.

"I'm not going to lie, Jessica. I'm a little surprised."

She shrugged. "Look, I'm not going to pretend that I'm

one of those women who has a big list of rules when it comes to dating, like no kissing on the first date."

"That's fair." Maren nodded and put her tea down on a little wicker table next to a potted geranium. "But…"

"Going home on the first date?" She looked at Maren pointedly. "Because that's what you're going to ask, right? Why I would go home with a guy on the first date."

There was no point beating around the bush and Jessica didn't seem to be offended, so Maren nodded. "Yes." She sat back in her chair. "It just doesn't seem like something you'd do."

Jessica laughed again and Maren couldn't help but notice the new lightness to the sound. She looked happier. Almost carefree. "Don't I know it," Jessica said. "And I'll be honest. I was definitely not planning on things going as quickly as they did. But we've been talking for a few weeks on the phone and then when we met up last night, it was just…well, it was fun. And easy. And I actually found myself having a good time."

Maren smiled as she listened to her friend. She'd never put much thought into the so-called *rules* of dating after divorce. Of course, she'd never had to.

"And I don't know if anything will come of it," Jessica continued. "Probably not. But I'm okay with that."

"You are?"

She nodded, the smile on her face larger than Maren had seen in a really long time. "I really am. Because you know what?"

"What's that?"

She leaned forward and stage-whispered, "It was the best sex I've had in years. And let me tell you how bad I needed that."

Maren threw her head back and laughed. For the next thirty minutes, the weight of the last few days lifted as Maren laughed with her friend and neighbor and listened to more details of her date than she probably ever needed to hear.

Rylee

"I'M REALLY glad we're doing this." Sienna flopped down on her mattress so that she was almost nose-to-nose with Rylee, who'd already been at her house for over an hour. And in that time had told her at least four times how glad she was that they were having a sleepover.

"I know," Rylee said, trying not to roll her eyes. "You keep telling me." She felt like shit the second she said it and not just because the smile on Sienna's face dipped. Not much, but enough that Rylee noticed the hurt there. Filled with guilt for not being a better friend, Rylee put a bright smile on her face. "And I'm totally glad we're doing it, too."

Her smile came back but Rylee still felt like a jerk.

"I thought maybe we could do something really fun tonight." Sienna rolled over on the bed until her feet landed on the other side. Rylee propped herself up on one elbow and watched while she crossed the room and started to dig through her desk drawer.

Her interest piqued, Rylee sat all the way up and crossed her legs. "Don't tell me you snuck a bottle of your mom's vodka?"

Sienna spun around so fast, her blonde hair flicked around her face comically. "What?"

Judging by the look on her face, it was definitely not vodka that she had in her desk. Rylee chuckled. "So...not vodka then?"

"Oh my God, Rylee. Are you serious?"

"No." She wasn't. Not really. She knew Sienna was a good girl. Hell, *she* was a good girl. They weren't the type of kids who went to parties, smoked or vaped or fooled around with alcohol—of course, they knew kids who did it—but it had never been something they'd been into.

Not really.

Except...when Brice asked her to swipe that bottle of her mom's wine. There was that. And Rylee had tried it and she'd liked it. Well, not really. But she *had* liked the thrill of it. Maybe it was the fact that she'd snuck out with him and was already feeling brave. Or maybe she just didn't want him to think she was a wimpy loser if she didn't try it. Whatever it was, it didn't matter because the taste hadn't been *that* terrible. But it wasn't just the taste. It was the way the wine warmed her up from the inside and made her feel good. Kind of happy and fun. She couldn't even explain it.

"Good. Because you know I don't have any vodka in here." Sienna shook her head and laughed. "My mom would—"

"Except." Rylee interrupted her before she realized she was doing it. "Have you ever tried it? I mean...I know your mom would kill you. So would mine, but..." She wasn't really sure how to finish the statement, so she let her voice trail off as she picked at a loose thread in the comforter beneath her.

"Rylee?"

Sienna had left her desk, abandoning whatever it was she'd been looking for a moment before. "Have *you* had a drink before?" Sienna sat next to her on the bed. Rylee scooted over to make room for her. "I mean, a real drink," she clarified. "Not like a sip of your parent's."

Rylee looked at her best friend and contemplated lying to her again. She'd been her best friend forever. They told each other everything. Well, until lately. But look what happened when she didn't. She'd more than learned her lesson there.

"Will you hate me if I tell you the truth?"

"I'll hate you if you don't."

Rylee's lips twisted up in a smile. "I drank some wine," she admitted. "With Brice."

Sienna's mouth fell open, but she recovered from her shock quickly. "I can't believe—"

Rylee held up a finger. "You said you wouldn't hate me."

"I don't." She smacked her finger down. "But I'm still surprised. And a little pissed. How could you not tell me?"

"You can't be pissed about that." Rylee shook her head quickly. "Technically, it was the same night as the kiss and you already got mad at me for that. Besides, there's nothing else to tell. I promise."

"You promise?"

"I totally do."

Sienna thought about it for a minute and then her face split into a smile. "Tell me about it," she said. "All of it."

So Rylee did. For the next few minutes, in dramatic detail, she recounted every moment of the night of her mom's party when she met Brice in the park. The way they'd climbed to the top of the slide and sat side by side. Used to drinking, Brice drank most of the wine, while she'd only had a few sips. Just enough to feel warm and a little giggly. But it was the kiss that she focused on telling Sienna about. How soft his lips were when they pressed to hers. The smell of cinnamon that filled her when he was close. The way her stomach flipped upside down and twisted in on itself all at the same time.

"So basically it was pretty amazing and I should try it?" Sienna giggled, but Rylee could tell she was serious.

"Absolutely you should." Excited and filled with the best idea ever, Rylee bounced on the bed. "Brice has some really cool friends and—"

"Do not set me up." Sienna held up her hands and shook her head, but then she stopped. "I mean…do you think Cole Benson is seeing anyone?"

She couldn't help it. Rylee squealed and threw a pillow at her.

"Is that a yes or a no?"

"That's a there's only one way to find out." Before Sienna could stop her or change her mind, Rylee lunged for her phone and started texting Brice.

"What are you doing?"

She glanced over her shoulder at her best friend with a wicked grin on her face. "What do you think I'm doing?" She hit Send on the text she'd just composed. "I asked Brice what they were up to. He said he was going to be hanging out with the guys tonight."

"Oh my God." Sienna fell backward on her bed and they both collapsed in giggles.

It would be so great if Sienna started dating Cole. Then they could all hang out and Rylee wouldn't feel like she was being pulled in a million directions. It was the perfect solution. How had she never thought of it before?

A moment later, a text came in from Brice.

Hanging at Mason's. Coming?

"He wants to know if we want to go over to Mason's." Rylee didn't phrase it as a question but she really wanted Sienna to say yes. Of course, she loved her girl time with Sienna, but now that the idea of setting her friend up with one of Brice's was in her head, that was definitely a focus. Besides, she could really go for some attention from Brice, too. And really, it was still early.

"Now?" She'd sat up and looked at Rylee as if she'd gone completely crazy.

"Why not now?" Rylee shrugged. "It's only ten."

"Exactly. My mom would never let us leave the house now."

A grin spread slowly across Rylee's face and she leaned closer to her friend. "She never has to know."

Maren

"DO you want me to open a bottle of wine?" Maren put the plate of roast chicken and grilled vegetables in front of Davis. It had been awhile since she'd had the energy, or desire for that matter, to cook a full meal, but after chatting with Jessica earlier, she'd felt better than she had in a long time. And surprising Davis with a delicious home-cooked meal seemed like a nice thing to do. Besides, it would ensure she kept him in one place long enough for them to talk.

Davis looked up at her, an eyebrow cocked.

"Not for me," she added with a smile. "But for you. Just because I can't drink doesn't mean—"

"No." He shook his head. "Water is fine tonight."

He looked exhausted. Maren tried to convince herself that whatever was keeping him busy at the office was the likely culprit for his exhaustion, but she knew better. And the only thing she could do about that particular issue was talk about it.

"Well," she said as cheerfully as she could once she'd taken her seat across from him. "What are we going to do about all of this?"

Davis choked on his bite of chicken before swallowing awkwardly.

It wasn't the smoothest transition to talking about the elephant in the room but as far as Maren was concerned, there wasn't going to be any easy way to do it, so she might as well jump in.

She pushed the glass of water closer to him and waited for him to regain his composure. "You mean, the…."

"Baby," she finished for him. "Yes. I think we've avoided any real conversation for long enough."

He straightened his shoulders, his entire body tense. "I told you. I needed time to process, Maren."

There was that word again.

"I'm pregnant, Davis." The words were simple; the implication of what exactly they meant—anything but.

He nodded slowly and his lips came up in a wry grin. "Yeah," he said, the tension melting out of him. "I got that."

"And I need you to finish *processing* already and be here with me because I don't know if I can stand much more of—" To her ongoing annoyance, hot tears filled her eyes again. She swiped at her face. "I swear, I've already had enough of these hormones." She dropped her head and took a series of deep breaths in an effort to pull herself together. She'd never cried so much in such a short time. Except maybe when her father passed away years earlier. But that was different. It was grief. Unexpected, life-changing, grief.

Maybe it wasn't all that different.

"Hey." Davis had moved from his chair to crouch next to hers. He put his hand on her leg and squeezed gently. "It's going to be okay."

She wiped her eyes one more time and looked him straight in the eyes. "Is it?"

"Of course it is. Why would you say that?"

"Davis." Maren sniffed as she finally managed to get her

emotions under control. "I can say that because you've been completely catatonic since I announced it. You're acting as if this baby is the end of the world. And I get it," she added quickly. "It's not what we planned and the timing isn't awesome. But—"

"No," he interrupted her. "It isn't."

He looked as if he had more to say, so she bit her tongue and waited.

Finally, he spoke again. "I'm sorry, Maren. I really am. I shouldn't have shut down the way I did. That wasn't right and it definitely wasn't fair to you."

"No."

"There's just been a lot of changes all at once and I guess I needed a bit of time to wrap my head around it all."

"What else is changing?" It was a dumb question because the fact that they were going to have a baby was enough of a change all by itself. There really didn't need to be anything else, but something about the way he said it gave her pause. "Is everything okay, Davis? I mean, you didn't lose your job or anything, did you? Is that what's going on at the office?"

He was silent for such a long moment that real worry started to creep into her reality. "No," he finally said. "Of course not. Nothing like that. It's just…well, I guess I'm just being dramatic."

In all their years together, Maren had never not believed Davis before. As long as she could remember, he'd been her rock. Strong and dependable. He'd never given her a single reason to doubt him. Which was why Maren ignored the flutter of concern deep in her gut when he spoke. She was probably just projecting her own stress on him. After all, the situation *was* hard on everyone.

"Okay," she said after a pause. "But if there was anything else, you'd tell me, right?"

"Of course." He took her hands in his and held them to his

lips, where he pressed a kiss on them. "Babe, everything is fine. Well…" He chuckled a little and together, they smiled. "Almost everything."

"This will be fine, too," Maren said with a reassurance she didn't fully believe. This baby was happening whether they wanted it to or not, and the sooner they wrapped their heads around that fact and embraced it as their new reality, the better off everyone would be. "It will," she said more to herself than to him. "This is happening, Davis. And I need you to get on board with that." She stared straight into his eyes. "I need you. We're a team and I can't do this on my own."

He was quiet for a moment but finally he nodded and smiled again. "Babe, I promise you. I'm right here next to you. You'll never have to do this on your own." He released her hands to put one on each side of her face so she couldn't look away. "I'm on board, Maren. Totally and completely. I meant what I said. Everything is going to be okay."

This time when he told her things would be okay, she believed him. His words sent a rush of warm relief through her.

Maren leaned forward until his lips met hers in a soft, gentle kiss that grounded her.

"So…" She hesitated, almost afraid to say the words out loud. "We're going to do this?"

Davis smiled and nodded as he stood. "How could there be any other choice? We already know that we make perfect babies. This little guy or girl will be just as perfect."

Her heart swelled with her love for him and the fact that he was on exactly the same page. They hadn't planned it, that much was true, but there'd be no other option.

"That's exactly how I feel." But that wasn't the only decision they had to make. "And what about the surgery?" When they'd left Doctor Harrison's office, he'd given them a few weeks to talk it over and think about what they wanted to do when it came to the IUD that was currently sharing space with the fetus. If they chose to have it removed, they could lose the pregnancy. But if they left it alone, they risked losing the pregnancy anyway, or an infection, pre-term labor, or even the potential to put herself and her health at risk, too.

"What does your gut tell you?"

It wasn't an answer, but Maren already knew how she felt. "I think we should go ahead and have the surgery. Doctor Harrison insists that despite the risks, it's very safe, and I think we owe it to this baby to give him or her the best shot we can."

He nodded and bent down to press a soft kiss to her forehead. When he pulled away, he touched her lips gently with his fingertip. "I love you, Maren. Don't ever forget that."

Her heart was full and peace settled around Maren as she took her husband's hand. "How could I ever forget?"

Rylee

KISSING BRICE WAS EVERYTHING.

It hadn't taken long for Rylee to convince Sienna that they should sneak out and go over to Mason's place. Especially considering he only lived a few blocks away. The fact that Cole was there, and wanted to meet her, sealed the deal. And, okay, maybe Rylee lied a little bit about the last part, but she really wanted to go. And it's not like Cole wouldn't want to meet Sienna. She was cute and blonde and smart. Maybe they'd hit it off and they'd all be able to hang out more.

As soon as the girls walked down the stairs into Mason's basement, Rylee made a point to introduce Cole to Sienna. "You know each other, right?"

"Yeah," Cole grunted. "We were in the same…"

"English class last year," Sienna finished quickly.

Rylee raised her eyebrow at her friend, but if Cole had noticed her eagerness, he didn't seem to mind.

"That's it," he said. "How's it going?"

Satisfied that the introductions had been made properly, Rylee found Brice. There was a movie on, but almost at once she was way too busy with Brice's lips to pay any attention to what it was. They sat on a big overstuffed chair in the corner of the room and Brice had his arms wrapped around her, with Rylee perched on his lap.

At first she'd been a little shy making out with everyone else right there, but as soon as he started kissing her, it didn't take long before she forgot all about it. Besides, no one else seemed to care, so why should she?

"You're so damn sexy," Brice whispered in her ear before he kissed her neck.

Sexy? Rylee had been told she was pretty before, and she knew she had nice hair and a not terrible face. Her body was lean from years of swimming, but she'd certainly never thought of herself as *sexy*. But if Brice thought she was, well…that's all she needed. And the way his lips traveled down her neck as he kissed and sucked on the skin there—well, that definitely felt *very* sexy.

Rylee closed her eyes and tilted her head so he could get better access as a small moan that should have mortified her slipped from her lips.

"Get a room, you two."

Someone threw a pillow at them and it hit her back before landing with a thud on the floor.

"Okay, okay." Brice laughed and lifted Rylee off him and slipped away, leaving her sitting alone. In a love-induced daze, she touched her fingers to her lips and smiled as she watched him cross the room before she caught Sienna staring at her. She lifted her eyebrows in a *what the hell?* expression, but Rylee just laughed it off. She'd understand one day. Especially if she could successfully hook her up with Cole.

Fueled by the idea, she moved over to the couches where everyone else was sitting and tapped the boy's shoulder. "Cole, Brice told me you're playing on the school's hockey team next season."

She couldn't have cared less about hockey, and in fact,

Brice hadn't told her anything about Cole at all, but Rylee paid attention. It's not that she knew much about the guy, but she knew enough to know the one thing he liked to talk about was hockey. In fact, it was the only thing she'd ever heard him talk about.

Just like Rylee hoped, Cole looked away from the movie. "I am." A dopey grin stretched across his face. "I think I'll have a good chance at making the starting lineup, too."

Rylee smiled and pretended to look interested, but she was very aware of Brice watching her from across the room and what she really wanted to be doing involved having his lips back on her neck. "That's great. What position do you play?" Before he could answer, Rylee made her move. "Actually, I don't really know that much about hockey, but Sienna has been going to games with her dad for years and she knows *way* more than I do, don't you?"

She gave her friend a look that she hoped expressed everything she needed it to, and just as Rylee suspected, Sienna responded by shooting her a dangerous look. Cole didn't notice, though, and without missing a beat, he shifted his attention to Sienna and started chatting with her about her favorite teams, players, and other things Rylee couldn't have cared less about. But judging by the way Sienna's face shifted into a pretty shade of pink, she actually did care, or more likely, cared about who it was she was talking to.

Either way, mission accomplished.

With a satisfied grin on her face, Rylee pushed up from the chair and went to join Brice, who stood at the bar in the corner of Mason's rec room. He had his hand on a bottle of amber-colored liquid when she came to stand next to him and slid an arm casually around his waist.

"Want a drink?"

She didn't. But more than that, she didn't want him to think she was a baby. Brice had made it clear on more than one occasion that he wasn't interested in dating a little girl. He needed a woman. And Rylee might still be a few weeks shy of her sixteenth birthday, but that didn't matter. She was definitely not a baby. Besides, maybe the amber liquid would give her that same warm feeling inside and pleasant buzz that the wine had. "Of course."

He gave her that sexy slow smile that never failed to make her knees dip a bit and handed her a glass. "Cheers."

Rylee had no idea what she was holding in her hand, of course, but there was no way she was going to ask and remind him that she wasn't as mature and sophisticated as the other girls he dated. So with only the slightest hesitation, she raised the glass to her lips and took a sip.

The liquid burned the back of her throat and despite her best effort, Rylee burst into a painful coughing fit. It took everything she had to keep it down and her eyes watered from the effort.

Brice took the glass out of her hand and laughed. "Maybe you're not ready for rum yet."

Rum? On their trip to the Caribbean a few years ago, every night her parents would both have a rum and Coke around the pool. A rum and *Coke.* "I usually drink my rum with Coke," Rylee managed to say as casually as she could considering the way her throat was still burning. "It's a little strong on its own, don't you think?"

He met her eyes and took a sip for himself. Brice didn't have to say anything for Rylee to see that the rum was plenty strong for him without any mix, too. Without a word, he found a can of soda and added to first Rylee's drink, and then his own before leading her back to the chair, where they spent the rest of the evening drinking and making out.

It was the best night ever until Sienna started to tug on her arm. "Rylee! Come on!"

She blinked and tried to open her eyes but it felt as if someone had poured sand in them. Her head was pounding and it was hard to breathe. But Rylee blinked through the grit, and then again until her friend came into view. Mostly. She was blurry, as if she were underwater.

"Wake up, Rylee. We have to go."

Go? Wake up?

Rylee blinked again and tried to bring her arm up to rub at her eyes but it wouldn't move. With effort, she turned her head, which caused a lightning bolt of pain to flash through it to see Brice draped across her, which would explain why it was so hard to breathe. When had they fallen asleep?

"What time is it?"

"It's almost four. Come on. We have to go."

Rylee still couldn't focus on her, but every time she looked at Sienna, she was a little less blurry.

"Four?" She couldn't seem to clear her head and her mouth was painfully dry, as if she'd swallowed cotton.

Sienna tugged on her arm again. "You can stay if you want. But if my mom wakes up and we're not there, she's going to kill me and probably tell your mom, too."

She was right and even in her fuzzy state, Rylee knew it. She wiggled and pushed and somehow managed to get out from under Brice's body and to the floor. Except for a slight groan, he barely noticed. The second she was free, Rylee took a deep gulping breath but hardly had a chance to gather her thoughts before Sienna was pulling her up to her feet.

"Oh my God." The whole room spun and Rylee would have fallen over if Sienna hadn't have grabbed her and held her up.

"How much did you drink?"

Rylee knew it wouldn't matter what she said. Sienna was

totally disgusted with her and she knew enough to know that if she was mad now, she'd be totally pissed if they didn't get home on time. She had to pull it together.

The cool early morning air hit them with a refreshing blast and that was probably a very good thing. Rylee wanted to ask her friend if she'd talked with Cole, if they'd hit it off and how they'd all managed to fall asleep. Had Sienna been drinking too? She couldn't imagine that she had, but…

All of the questions Rylee wanted to ask were forgotten as she focused on putting one foot in front of the other, only stopping once to throw up in a shrub. To her credit, Sienna didn't get mad or say anything when Rylee got sick. Instead, she pulled her hair—messy from sleep— back from her face and wrapped an elastic around it.

Somehow they managed to make it into the house and up the stairs to Sienna's bedroom.

"Sienna? I'm really…how did…" She couldn't finish either thought because the moment Rylee's head hit the pillow, she fell into a deep sleep. Hours later, when she finally woke up, she was alone.

Maren

THE REST of the weekend went by without incident. Rylee returned home late on Sunday from her sleepover with Sienna, and claiming she was exhausted, went straight to her room to sleep most of the rest of the day. It wasn't unusual for Rylee to be tired after a sleepover, not when the two girls routinely stayed up until the wee hours of the morning watching videos and raiding the kitchen. Maren was just glad it hadn't been at their house. She never could get a good night's sleep with the two of them giggling all night.

Not that she minded. Not really. It was nice that her daughter had such a great friend. Just like she and Sabrina had been at that age. Just thinking of her best friend made her both equally sad and mad. She missed Sabrina and she hated the way they'd left things, but there was no way Maren was going to reach out. Not when it was Sabrina who'd been so terrible.

She'd thought more than once about talking to Davis about it, but in the end, Maren decided to wait and see what the new week would bring. Maybe Sabrina just needed a few days to calm down before reaching out. She'd apologize for flying off the handle and Maren would apologize for swearing at her and they'd both have a good laugh before talking about how great it would be to have babies the same age, just like they'd wanted all those years ago.

Yes. It would be okay. Everything would be fine.

And her body must have felt the same sense of peace because when she woke up on Monday morning, the nausea that had plagued her for days before was gone.

There was a lightness in her step as she walked into the kitchen forty minutes later to see Rylee already showered and ready for school. "Good morning, kiddo. Are you feeling better?"

Maren walked directly over to her and before Rylee could dodge her, pressed a hand to her forehead.

Automatically, Rylee squirmed away. "I'm fine, Mom. I was just tired."

Her voice was defensive the way it always seemed to be lately, but Maren refused to react. "Well, I'm glad you're feeling rested at least. Anything exciting happening today?"

"Same old."

Maren kept half an eye on her daughter as she poured herself a bowl of cereal and sat at the table. She claimed it as a victory, no matter how small, that Rylee hadn't simply grabbed an apple and headed straight for the door the way she had the week before. She set the coffee to brew for Davis and made herself a cup of tea before sitting at the table.

Rylee looked up at her with question but didn't say anything, so Maren watched her for a moment. She looked so grown up in her sweater and skinny jeans, her eye makeup carefully done. But at the same time, her ponytail reminded Maren that she was still a little girl. Not quite a child. Not yet a woman. Maren's heart swelled and she had to blink back a hot tear.

"What?" Rylee stared at her, the spoon full of granola raised halfway to her mouth.

"I was just thinking that I'm glad you're not still mad at me."

It wasn't something Maren knew or had even talked about. In fact, she was mostly guessing. But the night before, after spending most of the afternoon in her room, Rylee had come downstairs and sat on the couch between her and Davis as they watched an old Adam Sandler movie they'd all seen a hundred times. Rylee hadn't said much, but Maren was willing to take it as a sign that maybe she was also finished *processing* and was no longer mad at her parents for getting knocked up.

"Whatever," she said. "I'm still not totally okay with it." Rylee shrugged and the smallest making of a smile touched at her lips. "But I guess it won't be totally terrible having a little brother or sister. Besides, it's not like I'm going to be at home for much longer, so you can't really rope me into babysitting too much." Her smile was full blown then, so Maren could only shake her head and smile along with her.

It was easier to smile and make light of the fact that Rylee was right, than to actually think about it for too long. Because the reality was, she would have one child in college and one in preschool. If she let it, the idea would completely terrify her.

And that was the last thing she needed.

"Your dad is running late." Maren changed the subject. "He said he'd drive you to school if you like." She poured her tea into a thermal cup to take with her, because she was also going to be late if she didn't get moving. "I should probably get going, too. I was hoping to get into the office early today, but I don't think that's going to happen."

"Early?" It wasn't totally unheard of for Maren to go in early, but she usually only made the effort when there was a big client presentation scheduled that she could help out with, or some other equally important event.

Like the start of a new job.

"That's right." Rylee finally connected the dots. "Today's the first day of your new job."

Maren lifted her brand-new leather portfolio, now with a few papers tucked inside, and forced a smile because she was right. It was her first day. But what Rylee didn't know, and what she hadn't even discussed with Davis, was that it might be her first day, but it would also be her last.

Every morning when Maren walked in through the front doors of the PlayTime offices, Sandra, the receptionist, greeted her with a smile and a wave and without fail, every single morning she'd say the same thing: "It's a beautiful day out there today, isn't it?"

Sandra was the type of woman who saw every day for what it could be and not the way it actually was. An eternal optimist and exactly the type of woman you wanted working at a company who specialized in creating spaces for children's enjoyment.

Every day after Sandra's usual greeting, Maren would answer her with a smile and a wave of her own because no matter what else had happened that morning—an argument with Rylee about homework, too much traffic, or even a flat tire—Sandra's enthusiasm for life never failed to be contagious. Maren often wondered what she'd been like as a young mother with toddlers pulling her in every different direction, or how Sandra had dealt with the teenage years while still keeping her cool. She'd often made a mental note to ask the older woman, but never did seem to find the right time.

But that morning when Maren walked through the doors of PlayTime, Sandra wasn't behind her desk. Maren stopped and waited, unsure of how exactly to proceed. Not one time in the five years Maren had worked there had Sandra *not* been at her desk in the morning. She looked up and down the hall, as if the receptionist would appear out of thin air and tell her what a beautiful day it was. She *needed* Sandra to tell her because whatever else it was going to be that day, it wasn't going to be beautiful. It was going to be incredibly hard when she talked to Eileen, and she could really do with an injection of positive vibes.

But after waiting a few minutes, Maren decided she was being silly. Surely she couldn't stand there all day waiting for the woman who was probably in the break room putting on a pot of coffee or she'd run to the washroom or some other equally reasonable explanation. Besides, even if Sandra *did* greet her and tell her what a great day it was going to be, that wasn't going to change anything. So Maren did the only thing she could. She took a deep breath, pulled her shoulders back and pasted a smile on her face before turning to walk up the stairs that would take her to the offices of upper management. And Eileen.

She might as well get it out of the way first thing.

If there had been any other choice, Maren would have taken it. But she'd gone over it in her head all weekend, and she knew in her heart it wasn't the right thing to do. She couldn't possibly accept the offer for the promotion when she knew she wouldn't be able to give it her full attention the way she'd planned. Sure, she'd be able to work for a few more months before the baby was born, but there was sure to be dozens of appointments and ultrasounds. After all, Doctor Harrison had called the pregnancy high risk, so she couldn't rule out the chance of complications or even bed rest.

She'd be distracted and never mind what would happen after the baby was born.

Maren and Davis had made the choice for Maren to concentrate on motherhood instead of a career when Rylee was born. They'd discussed it at length, but it had never been a choice for Maren. The formative years were crucial for child development and bonding, and although many of the women she knew had returned to work and their children had all thrived in the care of others, it had never been the right choice for Maren. And with Davis making enough money to support them all, it had been an easy decision and one she'd never regretted.

Those early years filled with peek-a-boo, first steps, and first words had been priceless. And then when Rylee was a bit older, homemade playdough, finger painting, and days filled with story time and crafts until finally she started school and Maren started volunteering. She was class mom all through the younger grades and would spend her days on field trips to the zoo, reading groups, and cutting and pasting with the students while they worked on various crafts that the teachers dreamed up. They'd been some of the best years that she and Rylee had spent together. And sure, she'd sacrificed the opportunity for a career, but it had been worth it. Every moment.

Maren knew in her heart that being a stay-at-home mom when Rylee was little had been the right choice for them both. And it would be the right choice for this baby, too.

How could it not be?

She'd come to the final decision the day before. As much as she wanted the job, she just couldn't reconcile the idea of being a working mom with the new baby when she'd made a different choice for Rylee. And there were bound to be enough challenges having a child at forty. It was bound to be a very different experience. She didn't need to knowingly make it more difficult by trying to hold down a career at the same time. Just as she always had, Maren had to put the needs of her child before her own.

So, without much of a choice, she held her head high as she knocked on Eileen's open office door before stepping inside. "Good morning, Eileen. I wanted to——" She launched into her prepared speech but almost immediately cut herself off when she realized she was speaking to an empty room.

"Where the hell is everyone?"

Defeated after building herself up, and with her anxiety and concern building, Maren retreated back down the stairs, past Sandra's still empty desk and into the small office she shared with three other assistant account representatives.

And immediately wished she hadn't.

"Surprise!"

She took three quick steps backward and would have turned and run back out into the hall if she could have done so without looking like a complete lunatic. Instead, Maren somehow managed to find her voice as she looked around the room. "What is...what's all this?"

She scanned the faces of her grinning coworkers until her eyes landed on her boss. "Eileen?"

"We wanted to surprise you, Maren."

"My birthday was last week."

"Not for your birthday." She grinned. "Everyone here at PlayTime has been waiting for you to be ready for this day for a very long time. You're going to make an amazing account manager and we just wanted to say congratulations, Maren. You deserve this."

The blood drained from her face and her stomach twisted into a tight knot. She wanted desperately to sit down, but somehow she found the strength to stay on her feet. "You... this..." She had no idea what to say. Not even five minutes ago, she'd been upstairs in Eileen's office, trying to quit the very same job they were celebrating her for. Nothing made sense.

"Have a piece of cake." Sandra thrust a paper plate in her hand and for the first time, Maren noticed the cake sitting on her desk. "Congratulations, Mare——" She was holding the frosted *n* on the plate in front of her. "It's never too early for icing."

She looked into the other woman's eyes and just as she was every morning, Sandra was smiling. But as she waited for Maren to accept her offering, the corners of her lips dipped down with concern.

"No," Maren said after a moment as she picked up the plastic fork. "It's never too early for icing. Thank you."

She must have said the right thing, because Sandra's smile returned to full power and she nodded. "It's going to be a beautiful day, don't you think?"

After the cake and coffee celebration was finally over and people started to clear out and return to work, Maren was left with mounds of paperwork and two thick files that held the distinction of being the very first accounts she was going to work on all on her own. The right thing to do would be to not even look at them. After all, she couldn't actually work on them. It wasn't right. But she just couldn't bring herself to leave them alone. Curiosity got the best of her. It might have been masochistic, but she needed to know what she'd be turning down.

The first file was a pretty standard project for an elementary school. They had a few budget restraints, but the parent council had been working hard on fundraising and they were ready to proceed. They had a few specific requests so it had the potential to be a challenging project to provide everything they wanted under budget, but it shouldn't be too big of a problem.

It was the next file that really piqued Maren's interest. A special needs school with very specific requirements for equipment both for their students and for the students' family members. It would not only be a very challenging project, but a rewarding one, too. Despite the fact that she'd told herself that looking at the file was just a formality and she was only looking for general interest, almost at once, Maren began to dig into the details.

She spent the better part of the morning looking over the requirements for equipment and the specifics of the site. Her mind whirled with the possibilities for what could be done. Everything from ramps to specially equipped swings to the color palette that would work best for sensory sensitive children. She had pages of notes beginning to fill a notebook and had actually forgotten that she needed to talk to Eileen at all.

That was, until she checked her phone and listened to her voice mail.

"Maren, it's Brenda at Doctor Harrison's office. I noticed that we hadn't scheduled you in for your next appointment when you were here last week and the doctor would like to get you in for some preliminary blood work as well as another ultrasound. If you could call the office, I'll get you booked in for both of those things right away."

Any of the high she'd been feeling from working on the accounts vanished as Maren slammed right back down into her reality.

The baby.

Turning down the job.

There was no point putting it off any longer.

Reluctantly, she closed the file, gathered up the rest of the papers, and made her way up to Eileen's office.

"I can't take the job." The words sounded much more dramatic than she'd meant them to be, and Maren instantly wished she'd led with something like *hello* or *good afternoon*. "I mean." She tried again. "I...well, I can't take the job." It sounded even more terrible than she'd imagined it would. Maren shifted from foot to foot in front of Eileen's desk as she waited for her boss to look up from her computer.

Eventually she did.

"Sit down."

Maren did as she was told. She sank with some relief into the cushioned chair, thankful she didn't have to try to stay upright anymore. The files were still clutched in her hands. "It's not that—"

Eileen held up her hand to silence her. Not once while Maren had worked for her had Eileen ever been an over-bearing boss. She'd never raised her voice or gotten angry with Maren, or anyone else Maren knew of. She led with a quiet confidence that somehow just commanded respect. It was at the same time, very similar to Maren's mother and very different.

"Would you like to tell me what you're talking about?" she asked after a moment.

Maren took a deep breath and willed her baby emotions to stay in check as she tried to explain to the woman she so respected that it wasn't the right thing to do because she had in fact found herself in the middle of an unplanned pregnancy. The words sounded ludicrous coming out of her mouth. It wasn't as though she were sixteen. But still, unplanned was probably the only reasonable word Maren could use to describe the situation at hand. And it was definitely the most accurate.

Eileen sat and listened for a moment before nodding. "So it wasn't menopause after all." Her lips twitched up in a smile, but Maren didn't think it was at all funny. "I'm sorry, I don't mean to make light of a situation that is obviously very distressing to you."

That was a major understatement. Still, Maren sat and waited for her to accept her resignation.

"Well, I don't see what this has to do with you telling me that you can't accept the job that only a few hours ago was celebrated with cake," she said, as if cake made everything extra official.

Maren opened her mouth to tell her again that she was pregnant but Eileen stopped her.

"Answer one question for me, Maren. Do you want this job?"

"Yes." The answer was immediate. She looked down to the files clutched in her lap. "Very much," she answered honestly. "I know I can do an excellent job. The Fairview school especially," she continued. "It has unique challenges, but I have some ideas. For example, I think they could benefit from a muted color palette for the children who are on the autism spectrum, and—" She swallowed the rest of her words as she realized exactly what was happening. She was selling herself on a job she couldn't possibly do. "I wish I could work on it, Eileen. I really do. But I'm afraid it wouldn't be fair to the company or the client. I'm just not the type of person who is willing to take on something that I wouldn't be able to finish."

"And I respect that about you, Maren. You are a very ethical woman. Always have been. It's one of the things I admire about you."

"I'm glad you understand." She reached forward to put the files on Eileen's desk, but the other woman once again stopped her.

"I don't understand," she said. "And I don't accept your resignation. I've been waiting for far too long for you to step into this role. You've been ready for years. Almost from the moment you started with us. I respected your decision to wait then, but I will not respect it now."

Maren's mouth fell open and she was positive she looked ridiculous as she stared at her boss and mentor, but she couldn't help it. "But why not?"

"I'm sorry." Eileen shook her head and pressed her lips together. "I didn't mean to sound so harsh. And it's not that I don't respect your decision—it's more that I don't accept it. I've been telling you for years that you could be a working mother. Millions of women do it, Maren. And while I'm sure it's not easy, I'm equally sure that it could be a very rewarding pursuit." Maren opened her mouth to argue, but closed it again as Eileen continued. "Now, I understand that you didn't plan for this deviation in your life plan. But your passion for playgrounds and children is evident. Never mind the passion you have to pursue something for yourself. Something independent of your husband and children. Something that is all yours. And that won't go away because you are having another child. In fact, don't you think that perhaps your children would benefit from seeing their mother pursuing a life that she's passionate about?"

Her arguments gave Maren pause. Over the years, she'd only once or twice tried to talk her into taking a bigger role at the company despite Maren's clear feelings of working while Rylee was still in school. But in all of that time, Eileen had never expressed her feelings quite so pointedly. But then again, it was easy for her to say. Eileen wasn't a mother. She had no idea the demands of a young child. Let alone the demands of having a baby at Maren's age.

Millions of women do it.

The voice came out of nowhere but it rang through her brain. It was true. Lots of women raised happy, healthy babies and had satisfying careers.

Why couldn't she?

"I'll think about it."

Had those words come out of her mouth? Maren moved automatically as she stood and held the files to her chest.

Eileen smiled and nodded. "Good. You will be amazing at this job."

"I will."

She heard herself say the words but for the life of her couldn't figure out how or why she was saying them. She stared at Eileen for another moment while she blinked slowly and tried to figure out what the hell had just happened.

Sabrina

WHEN SABRINA PULLED up in front of the Westside Recreation Complex, ready for her very first labor and delivery class, the feeling of dread that she'd been trying to stave off all day finally caught up with her. It had been Maren's idea for her to take the class. Sabrina had tried to brush it off as "hippy dippy shit." After all, what did she need with lessons on breathing or contorting her mouth into strange shapes so that equally strange noises would come out? She was no expert, but she was pretty sure that there would be plenty of strange noises coming from her during labor. She didn't need to learn how to make new ones.

But Maren had insisted. Two months ago, sitting in her kitchen with one of her community guides in front of her. She'd pointed to the listing and suggested it.

"It's not all breathing and weird *hippy dippy shit*." She'd made the air quotes as she laughed. "It's more about what to expect."

"I can expect a baby." Sabrina rolled her eyes and grabbed the community guide that listed all of the local classes out of her friend's hand. "What else is there?"

"Oh, I don't know." Maren drew out the words in that way she did when she was just humoring Sabrina. "There's the possibility of a breech delivery, or a c-section. Have you thought about who you want in the delivery room, and what kind of interventions you may or may not want?"

"Interventions?"

"Do you want to use pain medication, or would you prefer a natural—"

"Medication." That was an easy one.

Maren chuckled. "Okay. What kind? Nitrous oxide? Or an epidural?"

"An epidural. Obviously."

"And you're good with any potential side effects?"

"What are the—" She tossed the booklet back at Maren, who laughed. "Dammit. Fine. Sign me up."

And she had. Maren always looked after her, and she'd always liked it. Even though Sabrina was more than capable of registering herself for the class, Maren grabbed her laptop, clicked over to the website and started entering Sabrina's details. "It says here you should bring your partner or another person you want to be your labor coach." She looked up but Sabrina didn't even have to think about it.

"You, obviously. I mean," she added quickly. "If you're interested."

"Of course I'm interested." Maren clapped her hands together. "I'd be honored to be there and do this with you. It's going to be awesome."

And for a minute, Sabrina had believed it would be. But that was before.

And now she was sitting in the parking lot, ready for her first class, alone.

Maybe she should have tried harder to make up with Maren. Or at all. Because going in there without Maren at her side was going to suck.

Badly.

But it's not as though she had any kind of choice, however. So, with a deep breath, she grabbed her pillow and her water bottle and made her way inside. She followed the sign with an oversized arrow that pointed to community room four and with only the slightest hesitation at the door, stepped inside. And immediately wanted to turn around and walk out.

It was a mistake. All of it. Every single part about what she was doing was a mistake.

"Hello and welcome." A voice that sounded way too much like a mashup of a cheerleader and a yoga teacher greeted her the moment Sabrina turned around, ready to make her break for it. "Did you forget something?"

There was no help for it. Sabrina turned slowly. "No." She tried to force a smile, but was positive it came off creepy or at the very least like she had some kind of disorder. "I just wanted to make sure I was in the right room." It was a ridiculous comment considering there was a circle of very visibly pregnant young women sitting on the floor in front of her. "Community room four, right?"

The instructor nodded. "My name is Ariel."

"Ariel?" she asked before she could stop herself. "Like the mermaid?"

Sabrina was sure her face had turned almost purple with mortification, but if Ariel noticed, she didn't seem to mind. "Just like the mermaid." Her voice sounded like delicate crystal wind chimes dancing in the breeze. It was the strangest thing. "You must be Sabrina."

She nodded numbly.

"And is your partner here with you?" Sabrina didn't miss the glance Ariel made to her left hand, or the way she made a point to look around her as if Sabrina's *partner* was waiting just outside.

"No." She kept her smile pasted to her face.

"Well, that's just fine." Ariel's voice rose and fell in singsong octaves. "Why don't you find a place in the circle and make yourself comfortable. The class will start soon. I think you are the last to arrive."

Of course she was. She was going to apologize or make an excuse or something, but before she could, Ariel waved her hand, causing a stack of delicate bracelets on her wrist to tinkle —much like the sound of her voice—and Sabrina had the distinct impression that she was being dismissed.

As she made her way to an open space in the circle of pregnant women, Sabrina did her best to keep her eyes averted from the couples who occupied the spaces. She was the only one alone. And judging by the quick look she allowed herself, she was also the only one even remotely over thirty-five.

This was a terrible idea.

She was also the only one who hadn't brought a blanket to spread on the floor beneath her. She groaned. The floor was filthy in the way that only a community room at a rec center could be, but everyone was starting to look at her. She was either going to have to lower her massive body down to the gross linoleum, where she'd no doubt need help getting up later, or leave. As far as she was concerned, it wasn't much of a choice.

She hitched the strap of her purse up on her shoulder and as discreetly as she could, turned to leave.

"I'm sorry I'm late." The voice froze Sabrina in her tracks. "I went to the wrong room."

Sabrina turned around just in time to see Maren shrug casually and offer an apologetic smile to everyone in the room, all of whom were now looking at her.

She watched in a sort of odd, mouth hanging open, not really sure what she was seeing kind of way as Maren made her way right through the middle of the circle to where Sabrina was still standing, lamely clutching her pillow.

She should probably say something to her.

No. Sabrina *knew* she should say something.

"You're here." It was probably the stupidest thing she could've said, but if Maren thought so, she didn't say anything.

"Of course I'm here." Her smile was kind. "I told you I would do this with you. And I will. Because that's what friends are for."

It was what friends did. More specifically, and importantly, it was what *they* did. And even though there were still things they needed to talk about, things they needed to clear up, things they both should apologize for—or at least *she* should apologize for—at that moment, none of it mattered. Because the only thing that mattered was that Maren was standing in front of her. And she was holding a blanket.

"Thank you." Sabrina whispered the words.

"Well, since we're all here now." Ariel's voice floated around the room, landing with the tiniest bit of edge that had Maren and Sabrina hustling to spread their blanket and settle onto the floor. "Let's get started. The first thing we're going to talk about is the difference between early signs of labor and false labor. Who can tell me what a Braxton Hicks contraction feels like?"

Sabrina raised her eyebrows at Maren, who shook her head in an effort not to laugh. After all, if she *knew* what a contraction felt like, she wouldn't need to be in the class.

"Thank you again for coming, Maren." Sabrina put the two paper cups of tea on the table and took the seat across from her friend at the tiny aluminum table. As soon as the class had finished, they'd retreated across the street to the little cafe. "I really don't think I could have done that on my own." She shook her head while Maren laughed.

"Yes, you could have. It wasn't that bad."

Sabrina looked at her over the rim of her cup. "Seriously? I thought you said it wasn't going to be hippy dippy shit?"

Her friend shrugged. "There was some good information in there, too."

"Like how I need to charge my crystals in the sun and rehearse my chant?"

Maren didn't even try to restrain herself. She burst out in full laughter before catching herself. "I'm sorry. But I know a lot of people who swear by that. Good energy is good energy. Don't knock it."

Sabrina shook her head. "Look, I'm not knocking anything. And I'll take all the good energy I can get. As long as it's accompanied by an epidural. When do we get to talk about that?"

"I'm sure it's coming." Maren reached for the sugar packets. She tore three open, dumped them into her cup and stirred while Sabrina watched with big eyes. Maren hadn't used sugar in over ten years. Something about it being white processed poison.

"What?" She caught Sabrina staring at her and glanced down at her drink. "I know, it's not really a good…I can't seem to help it, though. For the last few days I've been craving it."

Craving it.

Right. Maren was pregnant.

And she'd been a bitch about it.

Sabrina swallowed hard and stared down at the table in silence.

"Look, I think we need to—"

"I'm really sorry about—"

They both spoke at the same time.

"You first—"

"Sorry, you—"

This time they both laughed and for a moment, Sabrina let herself forget that they'd ever been fighting. And it was easy, too, because for the last hour, everything had been back to normal. They'd been Maren and Sabrina again. She had her best friend back and really that was all that mattered.

Except that wasn't everything that mattered. They still needed to talk about it.

"Let me go first."

She'd been out of line. And it was way past time to apologize for it. Yes, she'd been mad when she heard Maren's news. But as the days passed, and she had a little distance, she'd gained perspective and it hadn't taken long for her to realize she was in the wrong. Besides, Maren had shown up for her. And that's what friends did. Now it was time for her to show up for Maren.

"I'm sorry," she began. "I never should've freaked out at you like that. It wasn't right. I was just… I don't know. There is no excuse."

Maren reached across the table and took her hand. "It's okay."

"No, it's not." Sabrina pulled her hand away and shook her head. "It's not okay. Don't make this okay when it's not." She couldn't allow Maren to let her off the hook. Not without a proper apology at least, because the truth was they both knew Maren deserved one. They also both knew that Maren would do what she could to smooth things over and make everything fine again. She'd never liked conflict.

"Just let me apologize, okay?" She waited and finally Maren nodded slightly, so she continued. "I could lie to you, and say that I have no idea why I reacted the way I did. But I'm not going to do that." Sabrina swallowed. It wasn't easy for her to admit when she was wrong. "When you told me you were having a baby, my immediate response was jealousy and I thought maybe you just wanted what I had." She held her hand up to stop Maren's objection. "I know, it's stupid. And I was being childish. And over the last few days, the more I thought about it, the more I realized that you probably didn't even plan on having this baby."

Sabrina's suspicions were confirmed when Maren pressed her lips together and shook her head slowly.

"Which means, you're probably freaking out right now. Am I right?"

"Oh my God, yes! I'm freaking out so bad," Maren said in a rush. "This baby was totally not planned. Not at all. I mean, don't you remember? Just a few weeks ago, I couldn't stop talking about the future and what it looked like. And that future did not include a baby. And there are risks. My IUD...well, it's all a bit much." She dropped her head for a minute before looking up with a smile that didn't quite reach her eyes. "But we play the cards we're dealt and this is my hand."

"Life isn't a poker game, Maren."

She chuckled. "No. It's definitely not. The stakes are much higher."

They sat with that for a moment. After a few minutes had passed, Maren spoke. "But it does mean that our babies get to grow up together after all. Just like we used to talk about. And that's pretty cool."

That was pretty cool. Maybe their babies would be best friends, just like they were. Maybe they would share everything and tell each other all of their secrets. Just the way Maren and Sabrina always had.

But Sabrina hadn't been sharing everything, and the knowledge of that and the lies she kept ate at her like a cancer. But she'd gotten good at compartmentalizing. Maybe too good. And she couldn't focus on that at the moment. Not when things were still kind of fragile between them. There would be time to come clean with her friend that she hadn't used a donor after all. And that time was not now.

She looked at her friend, and a rush of unexpected emotions washed over her. How had she managed to work herself into such a tight corner? She should have come clean months ago. Now it was…no. It wasn't too late. She could change this. She could fix everything. She could and she would. Soon.

She would tell the truth. Because bringing a child into the world under the weight of so many lies wasn't the right thing to do. It wasn't something a good mother would do. And she may have made a lot of mistakes with her past, but she was determined to be a good mother. The best she possibly could be. And that started with telling the truth.

"Sabrina? Are you okay?"

Startled from her thoughts, Sabrina blinked and Maren came back into focus.

"You look like you're thinking about something pretty intense."

"I am." Sabrina nodded thoughtfully. "I guess I just want to make sure you forgive me."

Maren laughed. "Of course I forgive you. I totally get why you freaked out. The hormones are killer."

She knew Maren wanted her to laugh it off with her, but she just couldn't. Maybe she should have thought it through a little longer, but Sabrina was done thinking.

"Maren, I need to tell you something," she blurted.

Her friend's laughter cut out abruptly as Maren must have sensed Sabrina's seriousness. "What's going on?"

She took a breath and blew it out as she spoke. "It's about the baby's father." Once she'd said it aloud, the relief at letting out the lie was immediate. But at the same time, panic started to take over. *What would Maren think?* There was no going back now. "I didn't use a donor. I know I should have told you right away. It's a terrible secret, but—"

"I know."

What?

Sabrina blinked hard and refocused on Maren. "You know?"

Maren smiled and nodded. "Well, I guess I didn't know *know*. But I knew. Does that make sense?"

"I guess." A million thoughts flew through Sabrina's head. "But how do you—"

"Feel about it?" Maren's smile was so kind that it made Sabrina want to cry. She nodded and Maren continued. "Obviously I'm a little sad that you felt you needed to keep it from me. I'm your best friend—you can tell me anything. You know that?"

"I do," Sabrina said quickly. "But I just…"

Maren put her hand over Sabrina's. "I could never think less of you. You know that, right?"

Sabrina nodded again.

"Good. Because it doesn't matter who the father is."

"It doesn't?"

Maren laughed. "Of course not. If you've made the decision to do this on your own, I know it's for a good reason. And besides, I totally agree with you on this one. It's not like I knew him all that well, but I don't think Ryan would have been the most responsible father."

Sabrina nodded again. She was starting to feel like a bobblehead doll.

"You're going to be a fantastic mother, Sabrina. You don't need him."

"Thank you." She bit back tears. "I really mean it, Maren, and I'm so sorry."

Maren sat back and waved away her protests. "Forget it. We're too good of friends to let something like that come between us. Besides, doesn't it feel better to finally have it out in the open?"

More than anything, Sabrina wanted to agree with her but she couldn't bring herself to say anything. Fortunately, Maren didn't seem to notice as she switched gears and started talking about something else.

Maren

"MAREN! Do you know what day it is?"

Davis ran into the kitchen so quickly that he only barely missed crashing into Maren, who managed to sidestep out of his way.

"Whoa." She chuckled a little. The chaos and confusion of the last few weeks and coming to grip with their pregnancy had been like wading through a thick fog, but just that morning she'd woken up feeling lighter somehow, like they were finally coming out of it. After lengthy discussion, they'd scheduled the procedure to have her IUD removed, and making that decision had been like lifting a weight off her back. The appointment was a week away, and Maren knew that after it was done, the fog should clear completely and they could all start the process of getting ready to have another little person in their home. "What's the panic? It's not our anniversary." She quickly scanned her memory bank. No. It wasn't their anniversary. That was in August. Still months away. So what was the— "Oh shit!"

"Rylee's birthday." Davis stared at her with the panic of a

parent who'd screwed up epically. Which he had. They both had.

"Oh my God." She clamped a hand to her mouth and looked around as if a giant bouquet of helium balloons would somehow magically appear in the corner next to the very best Sweet Sixteen birthday gift that she could ever have imagined. "I can't believe we forgot."

"We've had a lot going on."

If Davis was trying to make her feel better, it most definitely was *not* working.

"That doesn't matter, Davis. She's only barely talking to us again. She'll be…no. Okay. No more talking." She glanced at the clock over the pantry. There was still time before she woke up. "I'll make pancakes. You run to the store and get… I don't know what you can get. But get something. And make it good."

Davis moved for his car keys. "What store? What's open at this time of morning?"

"The convenience store." She stared at him, as if he had suddenly lost all of his brain cells, which clearly they both had because they had never, not once, forgotten Rylee's birthday. April twelfth. It had been the best day of her life. The day she'd become a mother. "Get something," she hissed at him when he didn't move. "Go. Hurry."

Thankfully, Davis did as he was told and Maren got to work with a frantic flurry of activity. There was no time for waffles, but she could whip up pancakes if she was quick.

Ten minutes later, she finally took a breath. There were pancakes on the griddle and because they were out of bacon, she'd had to settle for some old sausage links she'd found in the bottom of the freezer. It wasn't ideal, but it would have to do. And she'd make it up to Rylee.

"Pancakes?"

Maren whipped around with the spatula in her hand to see her beautiful, now sixteen-year-old daughter in the doorway.

Her nose wrinkled as she looked at the stove. "Happy birthday!" Maren pulled her woman-child into a hug. "I can't believe you're sixteen today. Can you believe it? Sixteen?"

"You always make me waffles and bacon on my birthday." She wiggled out of Maren's arms and took another look at the griddle, where the pancakes were starting to turn a perfect golden shade.

"I thought maybe we could try something different now that you're almost all grown up." She realized she was spouting bullshit, but with any luck, Rylee wouldn't notice.

Her daughter gave her a strange look. No doubt she was on to her. But she didn't say anything as Maren flipped the pancakes to a plate, speared a sausage to rest next to them and handed it to her. "Enjoy."

"Thanks." She took one more look between the breakfast and her mother and sat down. "Where's Dad?"

"Oh, he just ran to the——"

"Happy birthday!"

She was saved from finishing the excuse as Davis burst through the back door. In his hand was three plastic-wrapped single red roses, and a plastic carry bag. *Jesus, could he not have left the bag in the car?*

"Sweet sixteen." He kissed Rylee on the cheek and handed her the roses. "I can't even believe it. Sorry about the wrapping." He handed over the shopping bag with a shrug.

At the stove, Maren just shook her head. Rylee was never going to forgive them.

"Did you guys…" Rylee looked between them before reaching into the shopping bag. "A Reese's."

"Your favorite." Davis was trying so hard, Maren almost felt sorry for him.

Rylee only lifted her eyebrows and pressed her lips together before reaching back into the bag. "Mints? Wow. Thanks, Dad."

"I know how important fresh breath is for girls your age."

Maren did her best not to groan. This was not going well. "And," she spoke up before waiting to see what else was in the bag, "we're having a big barbecue for you tomorrow night. Friday night, so make sure you tell all your friends, okay?"

Still, Rylee did not look impressed. "Okay." She shrugged.

"See what else is in the bag, kiddo."

Maren glared at Davis. *What was with him?* The convenience store birthday gift was obviously an epic fail. They should just quit while they were ahead. At least if they had the party tomorrow night, she would have time to pull together a cake and a decent gift. Maybe those new wireless noise-canceling headphones she'd been wanting. They were pretty expensive, but it was sixteen, after all. She'd be able to—

"What's this?"

Pulled from her mental planning, Maren looked over to see Rylee holding up a cord.

"It's a charging cord," Davis said. "For your phone."

"I can see that." Rylee slid her hand to the end of the cord. "But what's this?"

"It's a lighter adaptor," he answered proudly.

"A *lighter* adapter, Davis?" Maren stepped forward. "Okay, this is getting…I mean, what on earth does she need that for?"

"Really, Dad. I mean, I get that you two forgot about my birthday."

Maren was sure her heart was going to shatter into a million pieces. She'd completely failed. How could she forget something like Rylee's birthday? "I'm so sorry, sweetie. We didn't mean to—"

"It's for your brand-new car!"

Next to her, Davis grinned so widely it almost looked maniacal and Maren was pretty sure the expression on her own face was equally frightening. But for a very different reason. "Her, *what?*" she hissed.

"My car?" Rylee jumped out of her seat and clapped her hands together. "Like, *mine* mine? Really?"

"Really."

She could hear him speaking, but for the life of her, Maren could not understand what the hell he was talking about. At no point had they ever discussed getting Rylee a car. Well, except for that one time months earlier when she'd brought it up, but he'd told her no. They didn't have it in the finances at the moment, he'd insisted. Never mind the expense of insuring a new driver. And Rylee didn't even *have* her license.

"Your mother and I thought that it would be a nice surprise."

"Oh my God!" She screeched in that way that only a teenage girl could do and in a flash had flown across the kitchen and into her dad's arms. "Thank you so much. You're the best."

Maren met Davis's eyes over Rylee's shoulder and gave him a *what the fuck are you thinking* look that he wouldn't be able to mistake, right before Rylee flipped around and into her arms. Maren was able to shift her facial expression quickly enough.

"Thank you, Mom. You guys are the best."

It was Davis's turn to give her a look. His said, *what else could I do?*

"I have to go tell everyone." Rylee spun around and grabbed her school bag off the hook by the back door. "Thank you so much." And just like that, she was gone.

"I can't believe you told her we were buying her a car." Maren flipped off the stove, abandoning the rest of the uncooked pancakes. "What were you—"

Davis's cell phone chimed, interrupting her.

"Who's that so early in the morning?"

"It's just a client." He shook his head. "And the car—I just didn't think we had much of a choice. Besides, we can—"

The phone chimed again.

"Pretty demanding client." She crossed her arms over her chest. "Are you sure you don't need to check that?"

Reluctantly, Davis pulled his phone from his back pocket and glanced at the screen. "Yup." He slid the phone facedown onto the counter. "Just a client. It can wait. So do you want to come with me to buy the car? Because I was thinking I could just pop over to that dealership by my office after work and——"

Again, the phone.

"Seriously, Davis. Can you just turn it off?"

"Of course." He glanced at the screen, his face sliding into a slight frown before he silenced it and tucked it back into his pocket. "Okay, so I'm thinking about five if you want to join me."

She nodded and tried not to notice his suddenly strange behavior. He must be more stressed at the office than she thought. "I'll meet you there."

He kissed her on the cheek and was just about out the back door when she called out to him. "And Davis?"

He turned.

She held up his birthday gift and grinned. "Do they even make cars with lighters anymore?"

"I still can't believe you promised her a car." Maren looked into the window of a gray, four-door sedan. It looked like a safe, reliable automobile. Not that she knew anything at all about cars. When Davis didn't reply, she looked over to where he stood next to a bright-red, two-door with a convertible top. She frowned. There was no way. Not for a first car. She was certain she read statistics somewhere about the accident rate for teenagers who drove sporty vehicles. Especially red ones.

But Davis wasn't looking at the convertible. He was staring at his cell phone, his fingers moving rapidly along the keyboard. They'd met at the dealership over twenty minutes ago and it was the third time she'd caught him distracted by his phone. Important client or not, he needed to put it down.

"Davis." She snapped her fingers until he looked up. "Can we do this, please?"

"Of course." He finished whatever it was that he was typing and tucked his phone away. "How about—" He moved to point to the red convertible but shook his head. "Not this one."

Maren laughed. At least they were on the same page about that.

They spent a few more minutes walking around before the salesman they'd sent away earlier so they could browse in peace returned. "Do you see anything you like?" The man who'd introduced himself as Jeff Jacobs, and had what Maren would describe as an honest smile, asked as he walked up. "This is a good choice." He pointed to the blue hatchback they'd been standing in front of. It was only a few years old, and there was nothing flashy or particularly sporty about it. But it was *cute*. A word Davis said shouldn't ever be used to describe a car. "All of our used cars come with a fifty-point inspection and a three-year warranty."

"What kind of engine is under the hood?"

The two men started talking about engine sizes and warranties, and satisfied that Davis had it under control, Maren wandered around the lot while they worked out the details. She ended up in front of the red convertible and closed her eyes. How much fun would it be in the summer? Top down, hair blowing back in the breeze, not a care in the world except driving down the freeway and—the car seat in the back.

Her eyes snapped open. There would be no carefree convertible driving for her. At least not for another eighteen years.

Oh my God. She'd be almost sixty years old when this baby graduated from high school.

Maren's knees buckled with the realization.

Sixty? She should be thinking about grandchildren at sixty, not graduations.

The world tilted dangerously under her feet and she put a hand on the car's cool metal to keep herself from falling over. What was she thinking? She couldn't do it all again. Eighteen years of playdough, ballet classes, Little League, homework, skinned knees. Starting over again.

No.

She couldn't do it. It was all too much. What were they thinking, having a baby again at forty?

She shook her head from side to side with such a ferocity that her hair whipped her in the face and stung her cheeks.

"Maren?"

Davis's voice called to her and permeated the fog that had descended over her brain.

"We're going to make this official. Are you ready?"

Somehow she nodded, her mini breakdown coming to an end as the feeling once again returned to her feet and the fog cleared enough so she could see him and the salesman across the lot looking at her. She focused on the positives. The miracle of growing a baby and then cradling that little piece of perfection, counting all ten tiny fingers and toes. First words and "I love you, Mommy's." She raised her hand in a wave. "I'll be right there."

"Come on," Davis called. "We'll wait."

———

Ten minutes later, they were settled in Jeff Jacobs's office, papers of all descriptions spread across the desk. Jeff Jacobs was talking about some sort of protective treatment for the undercarriage when Davis's phone went off. Again. He pulled it out of his pocket and looked at it in what was becoming a very annoying pattern.

"Seriously, Davis." Maren glared at him. "Can you not put that away for a few minutes?"

He frowned but nodded his head. "You're right. I'm sorry." He placed the phone on the desk and turned his attention to something Jeff was pointing out on the paperwork.

"A few more signatures and we'll be all set."

Maren nodded and smiled even though nobody was talking to her. Davis was handling the purchase and Maren would handle the party. Thinking of the party, she might as well start making a list. Maybe Sabrina could pick up the cake for her from that bakery by her house? She reached for her phone, but it wasn't in her purse. She must have left it in her car.

Maren glanced at Davis's phone on the desk. He was deep in a debate with Jeff about throwing in new tires and Maren didn't want to interrupt, so she just slipped his phone off the desk and punched in the four-digit code she knew by heart. She was going to flip through his address book and pull up Sabrina's information, but there was no need because her name was open on his texting app.

It wasn't unusual for them to text with each other, but what *was* unusual was the message on the screen.

No. We're not telling her anything.

Telling her what? Who was her? Obviously they were talking about her, about Maren. Right? Her stomach flipped dangerously in that way that stomachs flip when your body knows instinctively something is very, *very* wrong. She shook her head, not wanting to believe what she might have read. And scrolled

179

up earlier in the conversation. Maybe they were talking about—

She needs to know the truth. It isn't right.

That was Sabrina. To which Davis had replied:

Absolutely not. Maren can't know. It would kill her if she knew the truth.

They weren't talking about anyone else. She looked away from the phone in her hand and stared at her husband, who was now signing something. He glanced over and saw her with the phone in her hand.

"Maren? I don't—"

"I'm just making a list for the party in your notes app." She forced a false brightness into her voice as the lie slipped easily out of her mouth. Davis smiled at her. Was it a little unsure? Was there doubt in his eyes? Did he know she was lying? Did he suspect that she'd just seen whatever it was she obviously should never have seen?

"Okay," he said. "I know you have a lot to do for the party. I can finish this up if you want to get going?"

"Yes." She tossed his phone down on the desk. "I'm going to do that. I'll see you at home."

Moments later, she sat in her car, her breath coming in hard pants. Whatever was going on between her husband and her best friend, whatever she'd seen, it hadn't been what she thought.

Of course it hadn't. She was confused. She'd taken it out

of context. There was no truth for her to know. Nothing that would *kill her*. She was being ridiculous.

Somehow she managed to convince herself of her own lies. After a few deep breaths, her breathing slowed, her heart rate returned to normal and she no longer felt as though she were going to throw up. She switched the radio station to an upbeat top forty hit, cranked the volume and started to sing along with the catchy tune as she drove out of the lot.

Sometimes life wasn't about the truth. It was only about survival.

Rylee

IT HAD BEEN a few weeks since the sleepover, and Sienna still wasn't talking to her. Rylee had tried texting her and calling her. And besides a fit in the middle of the school hallway about how "selfish and reckless" Rylee was, Sienna had totally shut her out. Even on her birthday, Sienna didn't break her silence. It was all ridiculous. Sure, Sienna was mad that Rylee drank too much and maybe she shouldn't have.

Okay, she knew she shouldn't have. But she couldn't go back and change history.

And it wasn't like Sienna didn't have a good time. According to Brice, Cole said they'd talked all night and ended up playing some video games together. He also said he thought Sienna was pretty cool and they might hang out again. So there was that. She should be thanking Rylee, not ignoring her.

Besides, they hadn't gotten caught. Sienna's mom never knew they weren't there. If they'd been busted, Rylee would know because there was no doubt that Mrs. Wright would have told her mom and then she would have been grounded for life. And not only was she not grounded, her parents were acting super weird, like she could do no wrong. Hell, they'd bought her a car.

Okay, she knew it was because they'd obviously forgotten her birthday, but whatever. She wasn't questioning it. Especially since she'd been lucky enough to score a last-minute testing appointment and earlier that morning her dad had driven her to the DMV and she'd nailed her driver's test, thanks mostly to all of his lessons over the last few months. As soon as she got the keys to her brand-new birthday gift, she was taking it out for a spin because wheels meant freedom. Even if they were a guilt gift.

Just like the party her mom insisted on throwing for her. She'd been running around all day and Rylee almost felt bad about how much work her mom was going to when she really didn't want a party at all. But it probably made her feel better about forgetting her actual birthday, and it's not as if it mattered either way. Besides, it would be kind of funny to see the look on her parents' faces when she introduced them to Brice for the first time considering they didn't even know she had a boyfriend.

"Rylee." Her mom called up the stairs as she finished putting the last coat of mascara on. "Your friends will be here soon."

When she got downstairs, her mom was running between the kitchen and the back deck where the barbecue was already going, her dad standing guard even though there was nothing on the grill. She waved at him through the window as she walked into the kitchen.

"There you are," her mom said without looking at her. "You look really pretty." There was an extra high-pitched tone to her mom's voice, almost frantic.

She looked down at the top that she'd picked out because it was blue. Brice had told her blue was his favorite color. It was a small thing, but it had seemed really important while she was getting ready.

"Thanks."

"Your friends will be—" They were cut off by the sound of the doorbell and her mom visibly jumped before smiling. But it wasn't her normal smile. "I bet that's them now. You should go let them in."

Rylee turned to do just that, but something stopped her. "Mom?" She waited for her mom to stop mixing the salad and look at her. "Are you okay? You seem a little…" She trailed off, not sure how to finish the sentence. And then the doorbell rang again, and her mother shooed her out to greet her guests, and she never did find out why her mom was being so weird.

Rylee had invited a bunch of kids from school. It was pretty last minute, and it was probably pretty lame to go to a barbecue that was hosted by parents where there would definitely be no alcohol, but she was pleasantly surprised when most of the kids she'd told about the party showed up.

With one glaringly obvious exception.

Sienna wasn't there.

Rylee tried to not let it bother her. Instead, she let Brice drape his arm around her shoulders and pull her close as they walked around the backyard together. She'd secretly been hoping that her parents would freak out a little when they met him. But her mom had only smiled and said, "It's nice to meet you." And her dad was even worse. He'd offered Brice his hand and shook it as if he were one of his clients. It was all way more awkward than she'd expected, but not at all in the way she'd thought.

"Happy birthday, kiddo."

Rylee turned to see Auntie Sabrina standing behind her with a brightly wrapped box in her hands. Despite being called by her annoyingly childish nickname, Rylee broke out into smile. At least there would be one normal adult there. "Auntie." She jumped up and gave Sabrina a hug. "You're here."

"Sorry," Sabrina said. "I guess I shouldn't call you that anymore. I mean, you're all grown up now. I can hardly even believe it. And of course I'm here. I wouldn't miss your birthday for anything."

She handed over the present and Rylee laughed. "Auntie, don't you dare cry. You can call me whatever you want."

"I'm not going to cry," she said. "Now, are you going to introduce me to this handsome guy who I assume must be your boyfriend?"

Rylee beamed. Auntie Sabrina always knew exactly what to say at the right time. So much better than her parents. She grabbed Brice's hand and hauled him up to his feet. "Brice, this is my Auntie Sabrina. She's way cooler than either of my parents."

"It's true." Sabrina grinned.

"It's nice to meet you, Aunt Sabr—"

"You can call me Sabrina." She saved him with a smile.

"It's nice to meet you, Sabrina." Next to him, Rylee was so proud. Even though she'd secretly been hoping that her parents would freak out to find out she had a boyfriend, deep down of course she wanted them to like him. Or at least not hate him. It just made things so much easier. And that went for Auntie Sabrina, too, because she was just like family. Her grandmother would have to meet him next, and there was no telling what she would say.

Across the lawn, Rylee caught a glimpse of her mom carrying a platter full of raw burgers out to her dad. She watched as her mom looked up and then quickly turned around without handing over the tray. Her dad stood with his hands out, clearly trying to say something to her as she almost ran back inside.

Something was definitely going on.

"Would you excuse me for a minute?" she said to Brice, who just shrugged and sat back down in the circle of kids while Rylee put the present down and grabbed her auntie's hand. "Do you know what's wrong with my parents?" she asked as soon as they were out of earshot. "Mom's been acting weird all day."

Sabrina glanced around, but both her parents were inside anyway. "I have no idea," she said. "I just saw your mom the other day and she seemed fine. Well...I mean..."

"I know, I know." Rylee waved her hand. "The baby thing."

"The baby thing is kind of a big thing, kiddo. Maybe that's all it is."

"Maybe." Rylee shrugged, but her intuition told her it was more. She certainly hadn't felt as close to her mom in the last few weeks, but she knew her. And even if she wasn't paying very close attention, she wasn't blind. They'd forgotten her birthday, and now...

"Rylee!" Before she could dwell on it anymore, her mother's voice cut through the noise of the backyard. "Where's the birthday girl? It's time for your present."

Her car. She still couldn't believe they'd bought her a car. It was crazy.

Rylee spun around and met Brice's eyes. He jumped up to join her. They'd already talked about how awesome it would be for them to have a car to hang out in.

"You better go," Sabrina said. "I'll be right behind you."

Sabrina

SOMETHING WAS UP WITH MAREN. And if Rylee had noticed it…

Sabrina watched as the birthday girl crossed the yard to join her parents at the front of the house. She'd seen the blue hatchback with the bright-red, oversized bow on the hood when she'd come into the house. Rylee was going to love it.

Her gaze switched from Rylee to Maren, who had a frozen smile pasted on her face as she watched her daughter.

She was making a point not to look anywhere else. Something *was* wrong.

Her stomach filled with dread. *Did she know?*

She'd texted Maren earlier that day to see whether she wanted her to pick up a cake at that bakery she liked that was close to her house, but she'd never heard back. She'd just chalked it up to her being too busy with planning the party, but now…

No. There was no way she could know.

Sabrina waited until most of the guests had funneled through the yard to the front of the house to see Rylee get her present before she made her way in through the back door to the kitchen. It was hot, the baby was kicking, and she desperately needed a glass of water.

The kitchen was empty and Sabrina leaned up against the sink as she drank deeply, quenching her thirst. *Maybe she shouldn't have come? Maybe she should just—*

"I didn't think you'd be here."

Her body reacted to the voice that was almost as familiar as her own. She turned to see Davis.

"It's Rylee's birthday. There was no way I could miss it." As she spoke the words, she knew that that was exactly why she'd come. She loved Rylee. She was family. There was no way she would have missed her sixteenth birthday. Despite the mess she'd made.

"You shouldn't be here." Davis's voice wasn't cold or hard, but sad. Almost resigned. "Not now. Not—"

"We need to tell her." Once the idea had lodged in her head, she couldn't get it out. She *had* to tell the truth. The lies were causing almost a physical pain in her chest. It was too much. She needed to come clean.

"No." Davis stepped closer. "This is not the time or the place to have this conversation."

"Then when, Davis?" She knew her voice was rising. She knew she was dangerously close to becoming hysterical, but she couldn't help it. If he didn't talk to her about this, she thought she might just explode. "We can't keep doing—"

He crossed the floor in two quick steps and put his hands on her shoulders. "Sabrina. No. We can't do this. We can't tell her."

"We have to." She burst into tears and if he hadn't been holding her, she would have crumpled to the floor. "It's killing me, Davis. It really is."

He wrapped his arms around her and Sabrina didn't know whether it was to comfort her or hold her up, but it didn't matter. She craved the contact. The feeling of not being so completely and desperately alone. She sank into his arms and let the strength of his body hold her up. Because she no longer knew if she was going to be able to stay strong.

"You have to listen to me, Sabrina." He whispered in her ear, but it was frenzied and pointed. "We are absolutely not telling her anything."

"But she needs to know, Davis. It's not right to lie about—"

"No," he hissed. "She does *not* need to know. I love Maren. She is my *wife*. You knew exactly how this was going to be when you made the decision for this baby. This was never going to be a happy family with a happily ever after ending, Sabrina. You knew that."

She did know that. And she'd thought she'd been okay with it. No, she *had* been okay with it. She'd never even thought she wanted a baby until she peed on that stick and saw the two bright-pink lines. In an instant, she wanted that baby more than anything else in the whole world and it didn't matter how it had come to be, or what it was going to look like in the future. All she knew was that she was going to be a mother. And that was the *only* thing that mattered.

But time changed things.

And it wasn't the only thing that mattered anymore.

Maren needed to know.

She *deserved* to know.

And the baby deserved to know, too.

Everyone needed to know…Davis was the father of her child.

Maren

IT COULD HAVE BEEN A RUSTED-OUT minivan and Maren knew Rylee would have been just as excited with her gift. But Maren couldn't contain the smile when her daughter let out a squeal of joy when she saw her little blue hatchback in the driveway.

It really was the perfect first car for Rylee. And she looked so cute sitting behind the wheel.

Maren snapped a few pictures with her cell phone, secretly pleased she'd found the dolphin steering wheel cover and little blue dolphin that dangled from the rearview mirror earlier that morning when she was picking up the party supplies. Rylee's swim team was called the Dolphins—along with most of the swim teams across the country—but it had also become Rylee's favorite animal and even better, the accessories looked perfect in the car.

"I can't believe you got her a car."

Maren put her phone down and turned to see her mother next to her. "Hi, Mom."

"A car?" Her mother ignored her greeting and it was all

Maren could do not to sigh. "Do you think that's a good idea? I mean, she's only—"

"Sixteen, Mom. Legally old enough to drive. Davis took her to the DMV this morning. She passed her test with flying colors. She's a licensed driver." She didn't bother telling her mom that the car had been more of a "oops, we forgot your birthday" guilt gift than anything else. "I'm glad you could make it," she said instead. "I'm sure Rylee will be thrilled to see you."

"You did this because of the baby, didn't you?"

Maren turned to stare at her with her mouth open, but closed it instead of saying something that she'd regret. It was never worth it to get into it with her mother. Especially during a family function. And definitely not at Rylee's birthday. "Why don't you go say happy birthday to Rylee, Mom. I should go check on the food." As she spoke, she glanced around to find Davis. She'd expected him to be right there with Rylee, pointing out all of the features of her new car, but he wasn't anywhere in sight.

Neither was Sabrina.

She needs to know the truth. It isn't right.

Absolutely not. Maren can't know. It would kill her if she knew the truth.

The text messages she'd read on Davis's phone flashed in her mind the way they had since she'd first seen them just over twenty-four hours ago. She'd done everything she could to put them out of her mind, explain them away as something else. Anything else. Something innocent. Maybe they were talking about her surprise party and how Sabrina had done most of the work.

But that wouldn't kill her to know. She already knew that. Or had assumed it anyway.

It had to be something else.

But what?

Maren had done her best not to let her imagination run wild. After all, speculation wasn't going to solve anything. She'd talk to Davis about it directly. Just as soon as the birthday party was over. She looked over the small crowd on the driveway, once more looking for him.

Where was he?

She scanned the crowd again.

Still, Sabrina wasn't there. And she knew she'd arrived at the party. She'd seen her with Rylee.

Alarm bells rang so loudly in her brain she couldn't even hear herself think, which was probably a good thing considering every single thing she'd been trying to keep out of her mind was about to come crashing in.

Maren only barely noticed as Rylee turned the keys in the ignition. She waved to her, and it looked as though she were trying to ask her something, but Maren couldn't focus on her daughter. She needed to find Davis.

And Sabrina.

Now.

Over the years, Maren had seen Davis embrace Sabrina a hundred times. They were all best friends. It was normal. Innocent.

Maybe it was because of the text messages. Maybe it was because of all the unanswered questions she had. But there was nothing innocent about the embrace she walked into in her kitchen.

They weren't kissing. And there was nothing sexual about the way her husband's arms were around her best friend.

But there was something very wrong about the way tears streamed down Sabrina's face while Davis spoke to her with hushed, firm words. Maren didn't even hear what he was saying. But as soon as she walked in, Sabrina's eyes locked on hers, and in that instant she knew her life was about to flip upside down in the worst possible way.

"Maren."

Davis turned. "Maren? Is Rylee——"

She silenced him with her hand. There was no way she was going to stand there and let him pretend everything was fine. Because she still didn't know what it was exactly, but what she did know was that it was definitely *not* fine.

"Tell me." Her stomach threatened to empty its contents, but somehow she managed the words. "Tell me what's going on." She looked at Davis. "Tell me what would kill me."

Davis had dropped his arms and without his support, Sabrina looked as if she might topple over. Her face was white, her eyes red and puffy. "Maren, I don't know——"

"No." Davis cut her off. "This isn't the time."

"I think it is."

He looked back to Maren. She could feel her body trying desperately to shake, but she pressed her lips into a firm line and crossed her arms in front of her so her fingernails dug into the flesh on each opposite elbow. Anything to keep her rooted, because she was not leaving that kitchen until she heard the truth.

The truth she was almost positive she already knew, just by looking at her best friend.

But she needed to hear it. She *needed* to hear the words from her husband's mouth.

"Tell me."

"Maren, I——"

"Tell me." Her voice shook as she struggled to keep from yelling. "Now."

"I'm the father of Sabrina's baby."

And just like that, for the second time in less than a month, Maren's entire world shattered. Only this time, there was no way she'd be able to keep the pieces together.

"Maren?"

The voice penetrated the fog in her head. Had she passed out? Blacked out momentarily? Maybe she was sleeping? Waking up from a bad dream?

Maren blinked. Slowly, deliberately.

No. It wasn't a dream. She was very much awake. And somehow she'd managed to stay on her feet.

"Maren." Sabrina's voice. "Please. If you would just listen…"

She shook her head. It was a nightmare all right, but it was very, very real. "No." When she finally spoke, she didn't recognize her own voice. "No," she repeated. Stronger this time. "I don't want to listen."

Her vision, momentarily blurred, came back into crystal-clear focus and her gaze landed directly on Sabrina's ballooning stomach. A wave of nausea slammed into her so hard it almost knocked her over. But no, she would not be sick. She would not react. Not like that. Not then.

"Maren, please." Davis took a step away from Sabrina's side, toward her. She almost laughed. Where *should* he be standing? "It's not what you think."

She put up a hand to stop him. She wasn't sure where he should be standing, but it was definitely not next to her.

"The baby isn't yours?"

"No." He shook his head. "I mean, yes. It is. But it's just—"

"I don't want to…" She shook her head. "No. Not now." She looked at both of them in turn. Her husband of almost twenty years, her best friend for so much longer.

Who were they? How could they have…

"It's Rylee's birthday."

Yes. The idea gave her strength. She just needed to get through the afternoon. Through Rylee's birthday and a house full of people without completely falling apart. And in order to do that, she couldn't think about whatever it was that was going on. She looked at them each one more time. Disgust and disbelief started to penetrate the confusion.

"Davis, you should be watching the grill. There are hungry teenagers to feed." She moved quickly into command mode. Most of the party guests were still on the driveway, looking at the car, but they'd be hungry soon and there was the cake to get through. "I'll get the candles." Maren moved automatically toward the drawer where she kept the party supplies, but stopped. "No," she said. "I'll get the cake. It's in the garage."

She turned to leave, but thought twice. Maren spun around again to see Sabrina and Davis still staring at her. Sabrina's face was streaked with tears. Her mascara had left black smeared blotches on her cheeks. Maren looked to Davis, who simply looked stunned as he stood there. They'd both clearly expected a different reaction from her. "What are you waiting for?" She glared at her husband. "The burgers aren't going to cook themselves."

And with that, she spun on her heel and, forcing herself not to run from the room, escaped into the foyer, where she immediately leaned up against the wall and took deep, gulping breaths.

Had that just happened? Had her life really just imploded while she stood in her kitchen on her daughter's sixteenth birthday? While she barked orders?

It had.

Another deep breath.

She squeezed her eyes shut, but only for a second. She had a cake to get, candles to light, "Happy Birthday" to sing. She had to—

"Maren?"

Her eyes snapped open. "Jessica? Hi." Her brain somehow registered the presence of her neighbor. She stood in front of her in a bright-orange blouse Maren had never seen before, a gift bag in her hand and...a man.

"This is Chad."

Chad. Chad of the car that had been parked on the street more often than not in the last few weeks.

"I came to wish Rylee happy—hey. Are you okay?"

She didn't know whether it was the concern in her friend's voice, or the strange man's handsome and way too bright of a smile that seemed to be mocking her as her life crumbled around her. But in an instant, she knew she couldn't do it. Any of it.

"You know what?" She heard herself say. "I'm actually not okay. I think I need to go lay down. Jessica, would you mind..." She waved behind her in an inadequate effort to indicate she needed her friend to handle the party and started to walk away.

"Maren?"

"Is she okay?"

On some level, Maren registered the voices behind her, but she didn't turn around. She didn't have the energy. Because every ounce she had left was channeled in putting one foot in front of the other, up the stairs and into her room, where she drew the blinds, locked the door and fell into a deep, dreamless sleep.

Rylee

THE PARTY HAD BEEN...STRANGE.

If it hadn't been for her new car, Rylee's entire sixteenth birthday would have been a total write-off. Her parents were acting super weird, and Sienna hadn't even bothered to show up.

Not that she really expected her to. But she'd hoped—no, she'd *really* hoped she would.

More than once while Rylee sat in the front seat of her new car, she'd looked around the group on the driveway, hoping to see her best friend. Getting their first cars was another one of the things they'd always talked about doing together.

About how as soon as they got wheels, they could go driving around all day with the windows down and the music cranked. They'd be able to go wherever they wanted, whenever they wanted. Together.

Rylee tried not to let it bother her that Sienna was missing the moment, but after a few minutes of sitting in the driver's seat while Brice set all the radio stations, Rylee was over it. "Do you want to get out of here?"

Brice paused, his hand over the radio dial. "Like right

now?"

"Yes." Rylee pulled the door shut and waved at the few friends who were still on the driveway. They probably wouldn't even notice if she took off for a few minutes. "Right now," she said to him. "I just need to get out of here and…" Rylee looked toward the house and her eyes locked with her grandmother's. She forced a smile, but she needn't have bothered; her grandma nodded and waved her fingers at her in a shooing motion that Rylee took as permission to take off. Not that she was looking for it. As much as her mom complained about her grandma, she just *got* Rylee. Ever since she was little, Grandma had been a safe place and Rylee could do no wrong.

Rylee blew her a kiss and turned the key in the ignition before putting the car in reverse and backing out of the drive.

The freedom of driving her very own car was more than even Rylee could have anticipated. She rolled the windows down, and let Brice pick a song on the radio, which he turned up to full blast. She drove and drove, not knowing or caring where she was going until finally the sun started to go down and she took a road that she remembered would lead to an old nature preserve her parents used to take her to for day hikes.

"What's this place?"

Once parked, they left the car in the little dirt lot and walked together down the gravel path into the trees.

"It's this old park we used to come to," Rylee said. Nostalgia washed over her as they walked and Rylee told Brice of some of the memories she had of going there when she was little. "My mom used to pack these ridiculously huge picnics," she said as Brice took her hand. "And my dad would bring a ball for us to kick. Mostly he'd end up chasing it into the trees over there." She laughed, remembering how terrible she'd been at any sport involving a ball. "We'd always have our picnic here at these tables." The old wooden tables had definitely seen better days, and were in desperate need of a coat of paint. "And then when I got older, I'd go sit by the river and watch the ducks."

She had a private clearing in the trees that had felt like her own special little hideaway where she could be alone. Looking back, her parents must have known exactly where she was. Hell, they probably could have seen her from the tables, but when she was little, it felt like a world away.

"Come on." She pulled Brice's hand and started running down the path, suddenly desperate to see if her place was still there. "I want to show you something."

It was still there. The little thicket of willows that created an almost wall around the grassy area where she'd sit, and sometimes spread out her dolls. With Brice's hand still in hers, Rylee picked her way through the shrubs so they could get into the clearing. And then, just like when she was a child, an immediate sense of peace washed over her.

She turned in a slow circle as she took in the *walls* of willows on three sides and the river rushing by on the other. "Isn't this amazing? I can't believe I'd forgotten about it."

She'd forgotten because it had been years since they'd been there. But why had they stopped going out there?

She knew exactly why. Because she'd grown up, started swimming and they'd gotten busy. Now they'd do all of those things with the new baby while Rylee was away at college. Maybe her little brother or sister would find this spot. Maybe it would give him or her the same sense of peace.

"I think *you're* amazing." Brice tugged her hand and pulled her close so her body was pressing up against his.

Instantly Rylee's thoughts turned from the past to the present and the boy who was kissing her. Everything with Brice was intense. He made her feel so...wanted. So...important.

She kissed him back and let her hands rest on his waist for a moment until he lowered her to the ground where they could sit. Only they didn't just sit.

Brice pulled her to his lap and deepened his kiss. "You are the most beautiful girl. I just can't get enough."

His voice came out in whispered pants and his words sent a thrill through her.

They'd fooled around before. A lot. But this felt different. More...special somehow.

Maybe it was because they were in her spot. Maybe it was because she was sixteen now. But Rylee felt emboldened.

She sat back and let her fingers trace the hem of her top. She'd worn it for him, and he'd noticed. When he'd first arrived at her house, it was the first thing he'd said to her, right after wishing her a happy birthday. He was so in tune with her. The only one who *got* her anymore. The only one who noticed her. And cared.

Slowly, she lifted the top up and over her head, leaving her only in her bra.

It was a warm night but the breeze coming off the river was cool. Normally she would have been chilled, but Brice's eyes watching her heated her through.

"You are so beautiful." He pulled her to him and kissed her neck before lowering his mouth to her chest. She'd never let him go so far before but it felt so good she didn't even hesitate when he reached around to her back and released the clasp of her bra.

Brice let out a small groan and she could feel him harden beneath her. The thrill of it terrified her and excited her all at once.

Were they going too far? Was it too fast?

He stroked her cheek with the back of his hand. "I love you, Rylee. You know that, right?"

No. They weren't going too fast.

She thought her heart might explode right out of her chest, and she couldn't say the words back fast enough. "I love you, too. So much."

He kissed her then and his hands were on her, holding her, touching her and it felt...wonderful. Brice shuffled back and lifted Rylee off his lap so that she was sitting next to him and he could shift his position so he was in front of her, taking off his own shirt, and then he moved so his arms were on either side of her. He cocooned her and kept her safe. He braced himself on one hand while the other slid down her body. When he reached the button of her jeans, she drew in a sharp breath.

Brice froze. "Is it...I mean, we don't have to...I just thought..."

Rylee's brain spun in a million directions. *Have to what? Is he...would I? Should I?*

"It's okay," she said quickly. "I want to."

"You do?"

She bit her bottom lip and nodded. "I do."

"Yes?"

"Yes!" She almost yelled the word. It all seemed so crazy, so...terrifying. But so exciting all at the same time.

He smiled and his hair flopped over her eye in that way and he kissed her again. "Don't worry." He pulled back a little. "I have protection."

She hadn't even thought of that. *Oh my God, was she really ready for this?* He pulled out a condom and Rylee didn't know whether she wanted to pass out or cry or kiss him. Or all of the above. Or none of the above.

But then their pants were off and then their underwear and they were kissing again and it felt good and right. She could feel him, hard and hot against her, and she just wanted to feel more. Feel his love. Feel...something.

"It might hurt a little. Are you——"

"It's okay." She bit her bottom lip and looked up into his

eyes. With the setting sun, she could barely make out the little green flecks she liked to look at when they were close. All of a sudden, she wished desperately for more light because she *needed* to see his eyes, but then it was happening.

And it hurt.

She gasped and he stopped and looked down at her in question. He would stop if she asked him to; she knew he would. All she had to do was say no. Instead, she smiled. "It's okay. I'm okay."

And then he didn't ask again; he just kept going and it wasn't okay. And she wasn't okay.

Hot tears slipped from her eyes and down her cheeks, but Brice didn't notice because his eyes were squeezed shut and his face twisted up as he thrust into her over and over. Rylee was suddenly glad for the dim light because she no longer wanted to see anything.

Her back scraped against the rocks in the grass as he moved faster and faster on top of her. Every time he grunted, Rylee swallowed back another sob. Not that he would notice. He was enjoying himself and that was good, right?

She'd wanted to feel him.

She turned her head and focused on the sound of the river. The way it flowed over the rocks.

And then with a final grunt and a shudder, it was over and Brice rolled off her. She turned and scrunched her legs up to her chest as she faced the river.

"That was..." He'd moved so he was pressed up against her back. The heat of him warmed her scratched back, and he wrapped his arm around her. "Was it...was it okay?"

She nodded, unable to speak.

"Oh good." The relief was evident in his voice and something about the insecurity of it made Rylee feel better. "I was worried it might hurt you. Did it?"

She nodded, not willing to lie.

"I'm sorry." He kissed her shoulder. "I really do love you, Rylee."

———————

It wasn't even late when Rylee pulled her new car back into the driveway, but of course the party was long over. Her friends would have all gone home when they didn't come back.

She'd dropped Brice off at home and he'd given her a hug and told her again that he loved her.

Almost like he was trying to convince himself.

She hadn't said it back.

She no longer was sure of anything.

Mostly, she felt numb, like her brain hadn't quite caught up to what her body had just experienced.

Was she supposed to feel different?

Besides a sort of a sore, achy feeling between her legs, she felt exactly the same.

Except for the numbness.

Her house was dark when she walked in the front door. That was weird. It was only nine o'clock and she hadn't even told her parents she was going out. They didn't even call to check on her.

But then again, why should they? She was sixteen, almost grown, and they obviously had a bigger problem—like her new baby brother or sister. Besides, her grandma probably told them she'd taken her car out.

Still. It would have been nice if they were even just a little bit worried.

She popped her head into the garage. *Maybe they'd gone out.*

Her mom's car was there. Her dad's was gone.

She looked across the empty space to the workshop bench where a large bakery box sat.

Her cake.

She'd been so desperate to take off in her car, she'd forgotten about her birthday cake. It seemed her parents had forgotten, too, since it was still in the garage.

Rylee took it into the kitchen and lifted the box lid.

Happy Sweet Sixteen, Rylee.

She scoffed.

There wasn't much sweet or happy about it.

She swiped a finger through the icing, smearing her name, and stuck it in her mouth.

Now, that was sweet.

She did it again, this time scooping up a little bit of cake with it. And then again. Until her hands were covered in chocolate and buttercream and she'd eaten a hole right out of the center, obliterating the words written in purple icing.

Full, and feeling more than a little sick, but not quite as numb, Rylee left the cake on the middle of the counter, washed her hands and filled a glass of water before she turned out the lights and padded upstairs.

There was no light on under her mom's bedroom door. But maybe she was still up. Rylee hesitated. She'd been pulling away from her mom—or rather, she'd been running away from her—for the last few weeks. But the desire to talk to her, to tell her what had just happened was so strong it made her want to cry.

They'd had all of those awkward talks over the years. The most recent one was only a few months ago after Rylee had come home from school where they'd had a guest speaker in talking about sexual health. She'd wanted to die of embarrassment when her mom first came and sat on her bed. "Rylee, if you have any questions about what they talked about today, you know I'm always here for you."

"I don't have any questions, Mom." She'd stared at her pillow and picked at a string that was starting to unravel.

"But if you did, Rylee...or if you were ever considering..."

Her voice was softer and something about it made Rylee look up into her eyes.

"Mom, I'd tell you." And in that moment, Rylee knew she meant it. For as much as her mother could drive her crazy sometimes or be too involved in her life, she really did love it. And she loved her mom. There was no one else she felt closer to. Not even Sienna.

"You would?" Her mom looked so happy that Rylee almost laughed. "Like when you think you might be ready, and—"

"Mom." She cut her off with a smile. "I'll tell you. I promise."

When she'd made that promise, Rylee hadn't even been dating Brice. Sex wasn't something she was even considering. At least not in a real way. A lot had changed in a few short months. A real lot. In all of the ways.

But not everything had changed. She still wanted desperately to talk to her mom. To tell her that she'd lost her virginity and it had been... More than talking, Rylee just really wanted a hug. She *needed* her mom to hold her close and stroke her hair back from her face. She wanted to feel her mom's arms around her, and know that no matter what, everything would be okay.

Rylee lifted her hand to knock on the door.

As much as she wanted all of that, she knew she couldn't have it. Things had changed. The mom she wanted to talk to and hold her was the mom of before. The one who noticed her, asked how she was doing, the one who *remembered her birthday.*

A tear streaked down her cheek. Things were different now.

She let her hand drop to her side.

Things were very different now.

Quietly, she walked down the hall to her room and locked the door before lying on the bed and crying hot tears into her pillow.

Maren

THE ONLY OTHER time Maren had gone to bed so early was five years earlier when she'd come down with a terrible case of the flu. Only unlike that time, when she could blame her vivid and often terrible dreams on the fever she was battling, this time the only thing she could blame on the dreams that plagued her was the reality she finally woke up to.

Davis was the father of Sabrina's baby.

Even in the light of a new day, it sounded terrible.

No. It sounded far worse than terrible. Her husband had slept with her best friend and not only that, she was pregnant with his child. Worse still, they'd lied about it for almost seven months. And just to put the nail in the coffin of her heart, she, too, was pregnant with his child. At forty.

Her life was a fucking soap opera.

Do they still even have soap operas?

For whatever reason, the thought made her giggle as she made her way downstairs, where her laughter stopped short.

The kitchen was remarkably tidy considering there'd been a party there the night before. A party she'd completely bailed on and left to others to take care of. But that's not what made her freeze.

The box from the bakery sat in the middle of the counter, the lid flipped back and an obvious hole from the middle, missing.

Rylee.

Maren's heart squeezed. How could she have left her daughter's party? Especially without singing "Happy Birthday"?

She was a complete failure as a mother.

A month ago, she never would have dreamed of doing that to Rylee.

Of course, a month ago she hadn't just found out she was pregnant again at forty and that her husband was also about to be the father of her best friend's baby.

The nausea hit her so fast, she sprinted to the bathroom and only barely made it before emptying the very meager contents of her stomach.

This couldn't be happening.

It had to be a really bad dream or a big practical joke or…

From the kitchen, she heard her cell phone ringing and cursed the fact that she'd taken it off silent minutes before.

Without rushing, she went back to where she'd left it and looked at the screen of her phone.

Davis.

Oh yes, it was happening all right.

She hit Ignore on her phone and automatically moved to make herself a cup of tea. While the water was boiling, the phone rang again. And then again.

She ignored it both times. It wasn't until the tea was steeping that she picked up her phone.

Maren ignored the countless texts and missed calls from Davis. There were none from Sabrina.

Good choice.

She scrolled and found her message thread with Jessica. There were three messages. The first sent the night before.

We cooked all the burgers. Teenagers eat a lot! Cleaned up for you, too. I hope everything is okay?

She owed Jessica and her new boyfriend who Maren only vaguely remembered meeting the night before. She was a good friend for taking over the party for her without so much as a word of explanation.

The next message was sent two minutes after the first.

Oh, I couldn't find Davis to tell him we were leaving. Or Rylee. Is everything okay, Maren?

Automatically, Maren went to look out the front window. Rylee's car was there. A rush of relief washed through her. Rylee must have gone out after the party. Obviously she should have known that. Should have given permission and waited up for her to be back by curfew, but...

She didn't even bother checking for Davis's car. Maren knew instinctively that he wasn't there. He wouldn't have stayed. Although it had surprised her to hear he hadn't stayed to help out with Rylee's party. Had both of them bailed on their daughter's party? If her world wasn't already in free fall, Maren would have cared about that more.

The third text message from Jessica had come in earlier that morning. Only about twenty minutes earlier.

. . .

I'm worried about you, Maren. Is everything okay??? Let me know before I panic.

Maren typed a quick response so Jessica wouldn't be compelled to call in back up.

Nothing is okay. I'll explain later. Thank you for last night.

She'd only just sat down at the table with her cup of tea when there was a knock on the back door. She didn't bother looking up. It wasn't Jessica.

"Maren. Open the door," Davis called to her through the glass. "Please."

Finally, she looked up. She worked hard to keep her gaze steady despite her racing heart, but she didn't move to open the door. He had a key.

"Maren?"

The sound of her name on his lips made her want to scream. She kept her gaze fixed straight ahead. It wasn't until she'd seen him standing outside, his hair mussed up, the stubble shadowing his chin, his eyes red and bloodshot, and generally looking like hell that Maren came up with a strategy for how she would handle the situation.

She'd stay calm.

It wasn't much of a strategy, she could admit, but it was all she had. And as much as she wished she could rewind the clock to a time before she'd seen the text messages or walked into the kitchen and seen them embracing or even…well, she wasn't sure when…she couldn't.

"Maren?" He looked as if he were going to cry. Still, she didn't look away. "I'm coming in, Maren. We need to talk."

As much as she wished that wasn't true, it was. They did need to talk.

She waited as he turned the key in the lock and stepped tentatively across the threshold into their kitchen that up until less than twenty-four hours ago had been her favorite room in their house.

"We need to talk," he said again once he stood in front of her.

"It would seem that we do." To keep her hands from shaking, she wrapped them tighter around the mug, barely noticing the heat burning her skin. "Sit down." She didn't even recognize her own voice and judging by the confused look on his face, Davis didn't either.

She had no idea what she was going to ask or how she was going to approach him. But at some point during the night, she'd had a thought. Almost a glimmer of hope that there could be an explanation for what the hell had happened. Because there *had* to be an explanation. Something more than her husband and best friend had carried out an affair. There just had to be.

"I can explain," Davis said the moment he sank into his seat across from her.

Of course he could. Because there was *an explanation.* She was right. A slight weight lifted from her chest and for half a second, Maren could breathe again.

And then he started talking.

"I didn't want to tell you, Maren. I knew it was just going to——"

"Wait." She stopped him. The weight settled back on her chest. "You didn't want to tell me? That's your explanation?"

He shook his head, and dropped his gaze. "Well, no. That's not the explanation."

"Okay, good." She almost chuckled a little. "Because I know there is one, right? I mean..." She hesitated before sharing with him the theory she'd come up with in the middle of the night. After all, it was crazy. But what part of what was going on wasn't crazy? "I get it," she said after a minute. "I don't like that you lied to me," she added. "But I guess I understand it."

His head snapped up. "You do?"

"I do." She nodded and let herself fall into the explanation that she was very quickly convincing herself was true. *It had to be.* "I mean, Sabrina decided she wanted a baby, and because she was single, obviously she needed a donor." Maren barely registered Davis's facial expressions as she spoke; she just let the words fall from her mouth, explaining the entire situation so it finally, mercifully, made sense. "And I know Sabrina probably doesn't have much in the way of a savings account and of course artificial insemination is so expensive. So, yes, Davis. I get it." She released one hand from the tea mug and pressed it palm down on the table in front of her. "You helped her out." She announced her theory and once more the weight lifted from her chest because although no, it was not an ideal situation, at least it wasn't as bad as the alternative.

"Maren, do you—"

"Understand it?" She nodded. "I guess I do. But I'm still pissed." She knew she was grasping, but it was the only possible explanation. She said as much to her husband. "I mean, that has to be what happened. Right, Davis?"

She stared straight into his green eyes. The eyes she knew so well. The eyes she'd been staring into since she was seventeen. The same eyes she'd trusted with her entire life almost as long.

And that's when she knew for sure.

The weight landed on her chest with a force that knocked whatever breath she had left straight from her lungs.

That was definitely *not* what had happened.

"I'm sorry, Maren. I can't lie to you." Davis reached out

and covered her hand with his. "It wasn't like that. The baby was obviously…well, a mistake. When she found out she was pregnant, I panicked, but she knew right away. She wanted to keep it and—"

"Of course she wanted to keep it." Just like she herself had been slapped with that choice only weeks before, Maren could never imagine Sabrina making any other decision.

Davis nodded distractedly. "Right. Of course."

"When did it happen?" She suddenly needed to know. Now that her weak theory had been blasted to bits, it became crucially important to know all of the details. "How? Do you love her?"

"No!" He shot back in his seat, but his hand didn't leave hers—a fact, she noted somewhat distractedly, she was grateful for. Somehow, the heat of his skin on hers was keeping her tethered to the moment. "I love you, Maren. Always. You've only ever been the only woman I've loved."

"But not the only one you were attracted to." It wasn't a question. Because it was fact. "Not the only one you *slept* with."

"Maren, I'm so sorry."

"When?" she asked again. "When did it happen?" She realized she could do the math herself, but it seemed important for him to tell her.

Davis shook his head. "I don't—"

"When?"

He squeezed his eyes for a second before opening them again. "You were gone with Rylee at that away meet."

"The one in California?"

She did the quick math in her head. That meet had been in September. She and Rylee had gone alone because Davis had a big account he'd been working on. It was seven months ago. The math was right.

He nodded. "That's the one. It was the anniversary of her mom's death and you know how upset she gets. I was comforting her and one thing led to another and it just kind of—"

"Her mom died in December," she interrupted.

"What?" He stared at her, and she could see the lie in his eyes. "Right," he said quickly. "She passed away right before Christmas. I remember."

"So, that couldn't have been when the baby was conceived." She spoke slowly, watching his eyes. "The baby had to be conceived in September, like you said. But I worked the late-night volunteer shift for the swim club on December tenth. Remember? The club was given an opportunity to volunteer at the casino but they needed parents to work the shift from ten to three in the morning. I volunteered." The pieces started to fall into place as she spoke, and as each piece clicked into place, she wished she could take them all back and throw the puzzle in the air. She no longer wanted to solve it. "That was the anniversary of her mom's passing. And you—"

"Maren, I'm *so* sorry. It was—"

"It happened more than once?"

Somehow that made it worse. Oh, so much worse if it had happened more than one time. If it was a *relationship*.

He nodded, but she already knew the truth.

"How many times?" Her voice was barely more than a whisper.

"I don't—"

"How long?" She took a different approach. "How long has it been going on?"

Whatever she thought he might have said, whatever explanation she could have been looking for, it never could have prepared her for the truth.

"Years." He spoke softly, but the word rang out in the empty room.

Years.

"I'm so—"

"No."

"Maren, I—"

"How could you? For *years?*" Red-hot mortification mixed with pain and humiliation and…all the feelings…raced through her. "But you don't love her?" Nothing made sense.

"It wasn't like a relationship," he said in an attempt to explain. "It was more like a familiarity."

Familiarity?

"Like a comfort when things were hard." He shook his head. "This isn't coming out right."

"Ya think?" She glared at him as she struggled to process what she was hearing. Finally, she spoke. "I'm your wife, Davis. I'm supposed to be your comfort. *Me.* You're supposed to come to *me* when things are hard."

"I know, and I do, Maren. It was just when Sabrina—"

"I don't give a *fuck* about Sabrina." She hissed the words, and realized with a disconcerting sense of horror that she meant them. "It wasn't your job to comfort her. You are *my* husband, Davis. Mine."

All at once, the world started to spin around her and she couldn't stand to be in his presence, let alone have him touching her. It was too much.

"Get out." She yanked her hand away from his. "Get out." She spat out the words, but he didn't move.

"Maren. We need to talk about this. We need to—"

She pushed back from the table so violently, the chair clattered to the tile floor behind her. "Get out!"

He stood and moved to step closer to her. She picked up an empty mug and threw it at him. She missed and it hit the wall behind him with a smash of yellow ceramic. "Get the fuck out of my house! Now!"

Davis froze and dropped his head. He was crying and that only pissed her off more. *How dare he cry. He's the one who did this to them. He's the one who destroyed them. He destroyed everything.*

Everything.

When he didn't move, she picked up another mug and pulled her arm back.

Davis looked at her, opened his mouth to say something else, and obviously thought better of it. Without another word, he turned and left.

The second the door clicked behind him, Maren slid to the floor and cried.

Rylee

RYLEE KNEW she shouldn't be eavesdropping. And to be fair, she wasn't. Not really.

She couldn't hear what it was her parents were talking about downstairs in the kitchen. Just their muffled voices. And then, the crash. And Mom yelled.

A moment later, Rylee left her place at the top of the stairs and went to look out her bedroom window just in time to see her dad driving away.

What the hell?

Her parents never fought. Unless you could count the time Dad totally forgot to pick up Grandma from the airport because Mom was volunteering. There had been yelling that time, but mostly because Mom had to deal with Grandma, who was not happy that she'd had to take an hour cab ride after a long flight back from her trip to Italy. But even that time, that was probably the worst, Dad hadn't left. The fight had ended with tears and a hug and then all three of them had piled onto the couch to watch a movie. Rylee couldn't remember which one, just that it was nice that no one was mad anymore and she didn't have that itchy feeling all through her body.

The same feeling she had now.

The same feeling that told her something was wrong.

After she watched her dad drive away, she went back to the stairs. She wanted to talk to her mom. She wanted to tell her about Brice. She hadn't been able to sleep and more than once she wanted to go crawl into her parents' bed the way she used to when she was little. She hadn't had that urge since…well, she couldn't remember when. But the night before, when she was lying in her bed, feeling desperately alone, it was all she'd wanted.

She almost went down the hall to their room, too. But something had stopped her.

The same something that had stopped her from going downstairs to her mom. Or maybe it was because she could hear her mom crying.

Mom never cried.

Rylee sat on the step and listened. It took her a few minutes before she realized she was crying, too.

Rylee didn't venture out of her bedroom again until much later. She'd mostly ignored her cell phone, not even bothering to look at social media or scroll through her favorite YouTube videos. Instead, she picked up an old paperback, *Little Women*. She must have read it a hundred times, but it seemed like a good way to spend a day when the only thing she really wanted to do was disappear.

It wasn't until the smell of roast beef slipped under her door and tickled her nostrils that Rylee realized how hungry she was. Besides, she couldn't hide forever and maybe her dad was back and whatever was going on with her parents was sorted out.

Her mom was setting the table when she walked down the stairs. Rylee's eyes flitted over the settings she'd just laid out.

Two.

"You're just in time." Her mom's voice was oddly high and not at all normal. "I made us a nice dinner because I feel so bad for missing the rest of your party last night, sweetie." She crossed the room and put one hand on Rylee's shoulder. "I just wasn't feeling good all of a sudden last night and I needed to go lay down. I hope you're not too upset."

Rylee shook her head. "It's fine," she lied. "I went out with Brice anyway. Grandma probably told you."

Her mom blinked slowly. Obviously Grandma hadn't told her. *What the hell was going on with her family?*

"Well, I hope you had fun." Her mom turned to the counter where she started lifting lids and stirring things.

"Actually, it was…" It was her chance. She could tell her mom about what had happened and… "Hey, why are there only two settings? Where's Dad?"

Somehow, it seemed easier not to talk about it.

"Oh, he had to do some work for a client." It would have been a barefaced lie if her mom had bothered to look at her while she said it. "I was thinking we'd just dish up at the counter, if that's okay? I hope you're hungry. I made a ton of food."

She *had* made a ton of food. There was roast beef, carrots, mashed potatoes with gravy, a salad, and those puffy Yorkshire pudding things that were her favorite. It seemed like a pretty extravagant dinner for just the two of them. Usually when Dad had to work over dinner, they'd make a breakfast dinner of waffles and eggs and sometimes bacon and eat in front of the TV watching one of their silly shows, like *RuPaul's Drag Race*, that the two of them loved and her dad hated.

But Rylee didn't say anything. Instead, she accepted the plate her mom handed her and held it quietly while her mom dished up way too much food on her plate, like she was six years old again. "Oh, no gravy for me." Rylee pulled her plate back as her mom moved toward it with the ladle. But she was too late; the gravy slopped onto the floor with a splash.

"Oh."

For a horrifying moment, Rylee thought her mom might cry over the spilled gravy. Or maybe it was because she didn't want any? Who knew.

"Don't worry, Mom." Rylee put her plate on the counter and grabbed the roll of paper towels to sop up the mess. "I got it. And maybe I will take a little gravy after all." *There, she'd covered everything.* She finished cleaning up the mess and went to throw the soiled paper towels in the trash, but as soon as she lifted the lid, she froze.

Right on top were the pieces of her favorite yellow mug. She lifted a piece, but before she asked, she already knew the answer. She'd heard the crash earlier.

"Mom?" She turned around, holding the piece of mug. "What happened to my mug?"

Her mom's forced smile dipped and she shook her head. "It just fell off the counter. I'm so sorry, sweetie. I know it's your favorite."

Rylee opened her mouth to protest what she knew was another lie, but her mom handed her a plate full of food, so she took it obediently and sat.

Dinner was quiet. Eerily quiet. Rylee was aware of every knife scrape on the plate and every gulp of water she took. Her mother's eyes kept drifting to the back door, as if her father were going to walk in at any moment.

Something told Rylee that wasn't going to happen.

Finally, she had enough.

"Are you going to tell me what's going on?"

Her mother almost choked on a piece of beef. She reached for her glass of water and drank slowly before Rylee asked again.

"Are you?"

"Nothing is going on, Rylee."

"Really?" She didn't mean to sound harsh or rude, but if her mom was going to continue to lie to her, she was going to go crazy.

"Don't use that tone with me," her mom said. But there was no force behind her words. "Eat your dinner."

"Not until you tell me what's going on." Rylee put her knife and fork down with a clatter. "Because something is going on. You didn't drop my mug. I heard you this morning."

Her mother's face blanched. "What did you hear?"

She could lie and tell her she'd heard everything. But then she might never know what actually was going on. "Enough." She then softened her voice. "Tell me, Mom. I'm not a kid anymore and I know something is going on. I mean, you left my party last night and then when I got home—"

"I said I was sorry, Rylee." Her mom looked as if she might cry. "And I really am. I know it's not…you know what?" Her mom put her napkin over her plate and stared at her.

Rylee sat straighter, but didn't speak.

"You aren't a child anymore," her mom continued. "And while I always want to protect you from things, you're going to find out sooner or later."

All of a sudden, Rylee didn't want to know. She wanted to backpedal and stick her fingers in her ears and sing a stupid song so she wouldn't hear what her mom was about to say. Because she knew in that second she wasn't going to like it. Not a little bit.

But she couldn't bring herself to say anything.

Her mom pushed her plate into the middle of the table and clasped her hands together as if she were bracing herself.

"Your dad won't be coming home for a little bit." Rylee's heart caught in her throat. "I've asked him to leave."

"What? Why? You can't do that, Mom. This is his—"

"Rylee." She spoke so calmly that instead of easing the panic that had begun to well up inside Rylee, it fueled it. *This couldn't be happening.* "There are some things that you don't understand. And I'm sorry that this is happening right now, but—"

"But you're having a baby, Mom." She realized how lame it sounded, but it was true. You only had babies with people you loved and you didn't kick people out who you loved, so nothing made sense. "You need to—"

"Your father is also having a baby with Sabrina."

She couldn't breathe.

The room spun around her. As much as she wanted to get up from the table and run up to her room where she could pretend she hadn't heard what she'd just heard, just the way she did when she found out her mom was pregnant, she couldn't feel her legs. Nothing felt real and for a hideous moment, Rylee thought she might even start laughing. After all, it was ludicrous. First her mom was having a baby, and now Auntie Sabrina? Well, she was always having a baby. But, it was her dad's? That meant that the baby was going to be her half-brother?

Nothing made sense.

She pressed her hands to the table in an effort to stop the spinning.

"Rylee?" Her mother's voice sounded as if she were underwater.

If her dad was the father, that meant... *Oh, gross. Oh, no. Her father had...*

"Rylee, did you hear me? Are you—"

"I had sex with Brice." She blurted out the words before she could stop herself and then everything was quiet again. All

221

of the ugly truths hung between them like angry black clouds, and then…the storm broke.

"Oh, Rylee." In a flash, her mother was next to her, crouched on the floor and pulling Rylee into her arms.

Rylee wrapped her arms around her mom's waist and let her hold her like a child, safe, even for a false minute, in her embrace.

Together, they cried.

Sabrina

SABRINA ALMOST HADN'T BOTHERED GOING BACK to her prenatal class. After all, it had been enough walking in alone the week before and she hadn't even been truly alone. This time, she would be alone. *Really* alone. But the incessant kicking of her unborn baby had been a sign. He was coming, whether she was ready or not. She owed it to her baby boy to be as prepared as she could be. Especially now that she'd made a total mess of her life. Just in time for his entrance into it.

The class had been just as bad as she'd thought it would be. Ariel spent at least five minutes fussing over her because her partner "wasn't able to join" her, and then she spent another few minutes talking to the partners about how important it was that they really show up for their partners throughout the process because it was hard enough to be pregnant and have the responsibility of bringing another life into the world, that the new mother should never be made to feel alone.

Or some bullshit like that.

Sabrina was ready to burst into tears before the actual class even began. But as soon as Ariel in her singsong voice started getting into the class material on *interventions* and *possible compli-*

cations and basically proceeded to tell the entire class of expectant mothers about every single thing that could possibly go wrong with their baby on what was supposed to be the very best day of their lives, Sabrina had enough.

There was nothing graceful or discreet about an eight-month pregnant woman getting up off the floor all by herself, but she didn't care.

"Sabrina?" Ariel floated over to where she was currently on all fours, trying to heave herself up to a standing position. "Do you need a potty break?"

With a grunt, Sabrina managed to get herself to standing and push her hair off her face. "No," was all she offered in way of an explanation before squatting to grab her bag. The blanket she'd remembered to bring could stay there, because there was no way she was going to be able to bend down far enough to retrieve it. "I just realized I needed to go."

Behind her, Sabrina heard Ariel saying something to the rest of the class about how important each and every session was, but she didn't care. The most important thing at that exact moment was that she get the hell out of there before she burst into tears. Because she was afraid that once she started, she'd never be able to stop.

Ever since the catastrophe that was Rylee's birthday, Sabrina had done a pretty good job of keeping her tears at bay. At work, she spent her day creating special projects and training a temp who would take over when she went on maternity leave. Dr. Tommy noticed the change in her, and more than once, he tried to reach out to see whether everything was okay. But she continually pushed him away and dropped the once flirty tone from her voice. Even if she had allowed herself to entertain the idea of anything happening with him, there was no way it could now. How would he react if he knew the truth about her baby? About what a terrible person she was, to completely tear apart so many lives?

It wasn't until she was home alone that she had time to remember the way Maren's face had looked when she'd walked into the kitchen and seen them standing there. In that one moment, everything they'd ever hid from Maren came to light in horrifying Technicolor. She never asked for details, but it was only a matter of time before Maren put it all together. How Sabrina and Davis had carried on a...she couldn't call it a relationship because it wasn't that. It was something else. Something both deeper and less important all at the same time.

Almost like a comfort blanket.

They turned to each other periodically over the years in moments of sadness and crisis. It was never about an *affair*. She hated that word. That was the word used to describe something illicit. A relationship with feelings and expectations and... that's not what they had. Not at all.

But how could she explain that to her best friend? Yes, it had been about love. But not romantically.

The first time it happened, she'd just flunked out of college in her first semester. She'd spent too much time partying and not enough time studying and her parents were going to kill her. She'd been beside herself and she'd needed someone to talk her off the ledge. Maren was in the middle of her own final exams so it was Davis who came to her dorm room and tried to calm her down.

He had.

And one thing led to another and they'd ended up sleeping together. Afterward, they'd been almost shell-shocked that they'd let something like that happen. After all, neither of them had ever had feelings like that for the other.

"I don't know why that happened," Davis said. "I'm sorry. It never should have—"

"But it didn't feel wrong."

"No." Davis shook his head and looked at her. "I mean, I

know it *was* wrong. But...you know I don't have feelings for you, right?"

"Oh my God." Sabrina had laughed. "I know. You were just trying to make me feel better."

They were young and stupid, and neither of them realized that what they'd done was wrong. At least not in any type of real sense. They'd been friends for so long, it had felt natural. At least that's how they'd managed to convince themselves that what they'd just done wasn't terrible.

But it was.

And it was even more terrible when a few years later, it happened again. And then again. But each time they got together, it was because something had happened. It was almost like they needed each other to feel better about whatever awful thing had happened in their lives. At the very time they should have been turning to Maren, they were secretly, quietly, completely destroying her.

On some level, Sabrina had always known it was wrong. She was hurting the one person in her life who would do anything for her. But on another level, she'd enjoyed their deception. It had given her a thrill that made her feel alive, and like the most terrible person on earth all at the same time.

More than once she'd decided to put an end to it, but then years would go by and she and Davis were nothing more than friends. So it didn't seem so necessary to come clean or to really do anything.

And then...

And now...

It was too late.

Despite the early hour, Sabrina was exhausted when she finally pulled up in front of her condo. All she wanted to do was make a cup of chamomile tea, crawl into bed, and forget exactly how much she'd messed up her life. But as she walked up the path, it was clear from the man sitting on the porch, his head dropped into his hands, that wasn't going to happen.

"What are you doing here?"

"I called."

"I know."

Sabrina stepped past Davis and unlocked the door. She didn't invite him in, but she didn't slam the door either. He followed her inside and into the kitchen.

"We need to talk."

Talk. Wasn't that what she wanted to do before? Before all their secrets and lies came bursting out in the worst possible way at the worst possible time? "That's exactly what I wanted to do, Davis." She dropped her bag and spun around to face him. "I wanted to talk to Maren. I wanted to tell her the truth so she could understand that..." She waved her hand between them. "That this isn't, wasn't, whatever she might have thought it was."

"Well, it's too late for that." He scrubbed a hand over his face, and Sabrina noticed for the first time how exhausted he looked, as if he hadn't slept in days. He probably hadn't. "She knows everything and she doesn't understand anything."

"Everything?"

"Well, not all the gory details, Sabrina," he spat at her. "I thought maybe I could spare her that at least." She recoiled from his anger, and he immediately stepped toward her with an apology. "I'm sorry," he said. "I don't mean to lash out at you. I just..."

Sabrina watched as Davis slumped into a chair at her kitchen table. Instinctively, she wanted to go to him and comfort him. But that couldn't happen. Instead, she just stood there and stared at him until he spoke again.

"We never should have said anything."

"No." She shook her head. "We had to tell her, Davis. It

was never right to keep it a secret. We couldn't bring a baby into this world under those circumstances. It isn't right."

"What about *my* baby?" He lifted his head. "Mine and Maren's baby? What about him? Or her." He shook his head again. "Fuck. What about my baby?"

For the last few days, Sabrina had felt nothing but regret and sadness, but as Davis spoke, another emotion emerged. Boiling, red-hot anger. "*Your* baby?" She slammed her fist down on the counter and ignored the sharp pain that raced up her arm. "What do you mean, *what about your baby?*" Her hands cupped her now huge stomach. "This *is* your baby, Davis." She was almost yelling, but she didn't care. "Or did you forget that with all of our lies? This baby is *your* baby. And what about *him?*"

"Oh my God, Sabrina." He was up out of his seat and standing in front of her in a flash, but she didn't want to look at him. "I'm so sorry. That's not what I meant." When she wouldn't meet his eyes, he turned, walked to the wall and punched the drywall. "Fuck."

"Davis? What the hell?" Sabrina crossed the floor and tried to take his hand in hers. "You might have broken it."

"No." He pulled it away from her grasp. "I didn't break it." He flexed the fingers.

"What were you thinking?" His aggressive outburst seemed to have broken the tension in the air and they both sat at the table. "Why did you do that?"

"Because I don't know what else to do. We've ruined everything. It's such a mess." He dropped his head for a moment before looking up again. "I'm sorry I said that about the baby. You know I…well, I don't know what I feel."

She knew what he meant. When they'd discovered she was pregnant, they'd discussed what a baby would mean, and how they would proceed. More than anything, Sabrina wanted to be a mother. Something she didn't even know about herself until that moment when two pink lines showed up on the stick. But of course there was no way Davis could claim the baby, not without destroying everyone's lives—a detail that had definitely proved to be true. So they'd lied. And they'd planned to continue to lie as long as they possibly could. Hopefully forever. It was best for everyone.

Until she'd changed her mind.

She reached across the table and took his hand, but it felt wrong so she immediately released it. "I went to prenatal class alone tonight."

After a moment, he looked up at her. "You can't expect Maren to—"

"I don't." She shook her head sadly. "But I thought maybe you could—"

"Are you serious?"

Sabrina sat back.

"My entire life just imploded, and you want me to start playing happy family with you?"

"No." She shook her head. "That's not what I'm saying at all. I just—"

Davis jumped up from his chair. "I never should have come here. It was a bad idea." He looked at her with so much distaste that, for the first time in their lives, Sabrina didn't recognize him. "All of this was a mistake. A huge mistake." With one final shake of his head, he turned and left her alone.

She heard the front door close, but still she stared straight ahead, Davis's words ringing in her ears.

Tears streamed down Sabrina's cheeks. She may have made some terrible choices—huge, life-altering *mistakes*—but she refused to believe that the life growing inside her was one of them.

Maren

"THANK you for coming with me, Jessica. I know you had to use a day off and I really—"

"It's nothing." She interrupted Maren, who had thanked her at least three times already since they'd gotten in Jessica's car. "I already told you," she continued. "I have more holiday days banked up than I know what to do with. Besides, I'm more than happy to go with you." She looked over and smiled at Maren as she easily navigated the streets. "I'm glad you asked."

Earlier that week, Maren didn't have any intention of asking Jessica to go with her to the appointment but as the days passed and she still hadn't had any real conversation with Davis, she was suddenly faced with the prospect of walking into Doctor Harrison's office for the procedure to remove her IUD and to see her baby on the ultrasound screen, while at the same time her entire life fell apart around her, and the idea seemed entirely unbearable. And what if something happened? At least if she had Jessica by her side, she might not feel completely and desperately alone.

Which wasn't entirely fair. Rylee had been like a different kid since their heart-to-heart the other night, and she'd been spending the evenings with Maren on the couch, catching up on all the past seasons of the shows they liked to watch together. She wasn't entirely back to her old self, but it probably had a lot to do with the way her own life had spun out into all different kinds of new directions, too. Never mind her parents' drama, Rylee had had sex.

The thought still made Maren's stomach clench into a tight knot, but ultimately she was happy Rylee had told her about it. Even if she hadn't wanted to discuss it any further. At least she still felt she could come to her mom. Maybe she wasn't totally failing at the parenting thing after all.

"Even so," Maren said to Jessica. "I am really thankful that you're here. I honestly don't know what I would do without you right now. And there's something else..." It had been nagging at Maren all week. Every time Jessica called to check up on her, or popped over with a tea latte or some flowers from her garden, or some other thoughtful thing she'd seen that "just reminded me of you," or most importantly, just sat with her on the couch while she cried about the way her life was falling apart, Maren couldn't help but feel a little bit guilty. "You've been such a good friend," she said quickly to Jessica. "And it made me realize that when you and Brent split up, I wasn't there for you. Not the way I should have been."

"Don't be silly."

"I'm serious, Jessica." Maren turned as much as she could so she faced her friend. "I mean it. I had no idea how...well, how shitty it felt to have your marriage fall apart and I didn't appreciate for one second what you must have been going through. I'm so, so sorry."

"Thank you." Jessica took her eyes off the road long enough to glance over at Maren. There were tears in her eyes, but she quickly blinked them away. "That means a lot. But honestly, it's okay. I think divorce is one of those things that you just can't sympathize with unless you've been there. Right? I mean, you can feel badly for someone or wish them happiness, or any number of things. But unless you've walked through the fire of hell that is the breaking of a promise for forever, you just have no idea."

Maren nodded and sat with that for a moment. *The breaking of a promise for forever.*

"But…" Jessica held up a finger. "That doesn't mean that you're going through a divorce," she said quickly. "I mean, you guys are just having a tough spot but that doesn't mean you have to end it."

Maren stared at her as if she'd never seen the woman before in her life. "Pardon me? Are you the same woman who kicked your husband out when you found another woman's panties in his jacket pocket?" That was exactly what had happened. Maren remembered listening to Jessica retell the details of the discovery over and over for at least two weeks before she moved from the disbelief stage to the red-hot anger stage of divorce. She wondered which stage she was in.

The coping with her life stage, she thought with a grunt.

"It's not the same thing." Jessica shrugged, dismissing the way she'd handled things. "It's not the same at all."

"Of course it's not the same." Maren tried not to raise her voice. "Your husband only had one affair, one time. Mine had a full relationship with my best friend for *decades* and is now the father of her child." She shook her head. "It's certainly not the same at all."

"You also have a family," Jessica pointed out. "One that's soon to be even bigger." She raised an eyebrow at Maren's barely bulging stomach. "And I don't think that's something that should necessarily be thrown away so quickly."

Maren couldn't believe what she was hearing. Whose side

was Jessica on, anyway? "Are you saying I should forgive him? Just pretend it didn't happen and that everything is exactly the same as it was a week ago, when poor, stupid, blind Maren didn't notice what was going on right under her nose?"

"No!" Jessica turned to face her slightly as she pulled up at a traffic light. "That's not what I'm saying at all, and...hell." She shook her head. "I don't know what I'm saying. Maren, I'm so sorry this is happening to you, and I really don't know what I'd do if I were in your position. But I guess what I am saying is that no matter what you decide to do, you're always going to have a child...children...with him. He's always going to be part of your life. So, at the very least, I think it's worth sitting down and discussing things with him. At least for the sake of the kids."

The light turned green and Jessica kept driving, leaving Maren to stare out the window and think. Her friend was right. She couldn't ignore the fact that there were children involved. Quite a few of them, as it turned out. She dropped her forehead against the cool glass and closed her eyes for the rest of the drive.

"Everything is looking really good, Maren."

She'd been worried, but the procedure to remove the IUD wasn't nearly as complicated as she'd built it up to be. And the doctor was happy with how everything looked. One less thing to worry about.

Doctor Harrison continued to move the wand around her stomach. "The heartbeat is right there and it looks strong. And you're measuring right on schedule. Just over three months now. Everything looks great. The procedure didn't disturb your uterus at all or the baby's placenta. I'm very pleased."

Maren released the breath she'd been holding. *The baby was fine.*

Not that she really thought something would happen, but the worry was always there. Plus with the stress of the last few days, she couldn't help but wonder whether maybe the baby had felt it too. She'd been so worried about the procedure to remove her IUD harming the baby, that she hadn't stopped to consider what her stress level could do.

No matter what happened with Davis, she vowed she'd stay calm. For her baby.

"That's so great," Maren said. "And I'm three months. That means, I'm…"

"Out of the danger zone, as they say?" Doctor Harrison smiled. "Like I said, there are always risks with a pregnancy, particularly at your age, but yes, I'd say that everything looks as healthy as it can. Beyond doing some more testing, if you're interested in ruling out any genetic defects or potential issues that are a higher risk, I think it's safe to proceed as normal with your pregnancy at this point. It's probably a good idea to take it easy for the next few days as well."

Doctor Harrison clicked a few buttons and a pulsing beat filled the room.

"Is that? Oh my God." Tears sprang to her eyes, and Maren pressed her hand to her mouth.

"The heartbeat," Doctor Harrison said. "And it sounds strong."

"Wow." Jessica shook her head with wonder. "That's so…"

"Amazing?"

"Totally."

Maren smiled and looked back to the doctor. "Can you tell the sex of the baby yet?" She hadn't decided whether she wanted to know or not but in the last few days, there'd been enough surprises. Maybe it was better if she knew and could be prepared.

"It's still pretty early," the doctor said. "But you never know. Let's just take a look."

He moved the wand a bit more and clicked a series of buttons on the ultrasound machine. "Hmmm…" A few more buttons were clicked, and the wand moved again. "I think maybe…you know what? I can't see clearly. I'm sorry, it's still too early."

"But you thought you might have seen something?" Jessica said. "Does that mean it's a boy?"

The doctor looked at her and shook his head. "It means I couldn't see clearly because it's still too soon to tell." He looked back at Maren. "But if you're still interested in knowing at your next appointment, I'm sure we'll be able to tell then." He put the ultrasound wand back on the cart and smoothly wiped Maren's stomach clean from the jelly before pulling her gown down. "And maybe Davis will be able to join us at that appointment? I'm sure he'll want to know the sex as well."

Maren nodded numbly. "I'm sure."

"Great." Doctor Harrison stood. "Do you have any more questions for me today?"

She shook her head.

"Okay, I'd like to see you back next month, just to be sure everything is going smoothly and then we can talk more about an amniocentesis, if that's something you're interested in. And, of course, we'll take another look to see if you have a little boy or a little girl in there. Take care, ladies."

"I'll let you get changed," Jessica said the moment the doctor left. "I'll be in the waiting room."

"Okay. Thanks again for coming," Maren added before Jessica slipped out with a grin. She knew her friend had been thrilled to see the baby on the ultrasound screen. Too bad they weren't able to see the sex, but at least that gave her something positive to look forward to. Lord knew, like it or not, there was going to be a lot of negative in the coming weeks.

With a sigh, Maren dressed and began to make her way out to the waiting room. While she'd been lying on the exam table, she'd come to the conclusion that Jessica was right. She *did* need to talk to Davis. She couldn't lock him out of her life forever. Even if that's what she would have preferred.

She'd call him when she got home and they could schedule something.

But then she saw him.

The moment she stepped into the waiting room, Davis jumped up from the seat he'd been sitting in.

I guess I won't have to call. The thought was so absurd, she almost laughed. Instead, she turned away from him, went to the desk and made her follow-up appointment before turning around and walking straight past him.

"Maren, wait."

She ignored him until she was down the corridor and out into the fresh air.

"Maren, we need to talk."

"I know." She spun around. "But do you really think this is the place?"

"I knew you had the appointment today, and I wanted to… well, I wanted to be there for you. For…our baby. Did everything go okay?"

She couldn't help it. She knew she should swallow it, but she couldn't. "You want to be there for *our* baby? What about your other baby, Davis? Were you at any of those prenatal appointments?" Suddenly, she didn't want the answer. If he hadn't been at any of the appointments, that meant he'd abandoned his responsibility, and that wasn't the Davis she knew. But if he *had* gone to the appointments, that meant…she couldn't even let herself think about it. "Never mind." She held up her hand. "I don't want to know. Not right now. And yes," she added almost as an afterthought. "Everything went fine."

"I'm so glad."

"I'm sure you are." It was mean, but she didn't care.

Davis shook his head, and Maren noticed for the first time how old he looked. As if he'd aged five years in the last five days. *Where had he been sleeping? The office? A hotel? Sabrina's?* Another question she didn't want answered.

"We need to talk, Maren," he said again. "I know you're angry and you have every right to be."

"Damn right I do. You're a cheating liar."

He swallowed hard. "I deserved that."

"You deserve a lot more than that."

He nodded. "Can we talk?"

She forced herself to keep her mouth shut. Jessica was right; they *did* need to talk. And it was only minutes before that she'd come to that conclusion herself. But now that it was him asking, she just wanted to say no out of spite. But that wasn't mature. And it wasn't helpful.

"Okay," she said after a moment. "But not here." She looked around for the first time, wondering where Jessica was. She hadn't seen her in the waiting room and surely she wouldn't have abandoned her here with Davis.

"Jessica said she'd wait in the car." Davis answered her unasked question and she hated that he knew her so well that he knew what she was thinking. "I asked her for a few—"

"Whatever." She interrupted him. "You can come over tonight. Rylee has a PD day tomorrow and she's going to be sleeping over at Sienna's, so we can talk in private. Come by at eight." She turned and started walking to the parking garage.

"Thank you," Davis said behind her.

The pathetic tone of his voice stopped her.

"Don't thank me." She spun around. "Don't ever thank me for talking to you. You have put me in the impossible position of trying to do what's best for my children when all I really want to do is close my eyes and hope to never see you again.

Because I don't think you understand how incredibly terrible it is to look at the man who swore to love me and cherish me for the last eighteen years and know it's all been a lie. So don't *thank* me for talking to you, because you need to be very clear on one thing. I'm not doing it for *you*."

Rylee

SHE PROBABLY SHOULDN'T HAVE LIED to her mom again and Rylee actually even felt bad about it when she told her that she was going to sleep at Sienna's. Especially considering she'd barely spoken to Sienna since the last time she had actually slept there. But her mom never would have let her go to the party if she'd told the truth. Especially not because she was going with Brice.

Her mom had been really cool and not nearly as judgey as Rylee had thought she'd be when she told her that she'd had sex. But that was probably because of the craziness that was going on with her parents. Her mom clearly didn't have the mental energy to worry about Rylee. Not when it turned out they were all living their very own HBO special event movie.

Rylee didn't even want to think about it. And the best way she knew how to avoid thinking or feeling anything was to go out with Brice and have a drink. Things had been a little bit weird between him since the night of her birthday party, but that didn't mean she didn't still like him. She was just...confused.

"Hey, beautiful," he said when he got into the front seat of her car. He leaned over and kissed her on her cheek. "You ready to have fun tonight?"

The easy lilt of his voice, and the compliments he always had for her, made her smile. "I am," she said truthfully. "I'm so ready."

"Good. Because look what I got for us." With a grin, Brice opened the shopping bag he was holding and slid out a bottle of clear liquid.

"What is that?"

"Vodka."

Rylee let her smile grow bigger as she drove away. "Perfect."

An hour later, she was already feeling better than she had in days. The alcohol was starting to warm her up and give her that all-over fuzzy feeling that took the edge off any actual feelings. Mason's basement was full of kids from school. Most she recognized; some she didn't. But Rylee didn't care because the music was pulsing and she was dancing with her eyes closed and sipping from her plastic cup.

"Hey." She snapped her eyes open when Brice joined her and wrapped his arms around her. Her instinct was to pull back, but that was ridiculous. He'd been nothing but sweet and attentive since they'd had sex. All the weirdness between them had come from her. And she didn't even know why. She forced herself to relax.

"Hey yourself."

"I was hoping we could…" Brice gestured with his head, and Rylee instinctively shook her head. If he wanted to have sex in the middle of the— "No," Brice said quickly. "That's not what I meant."

She stared at him. Had she said that out loud?

"I just thought we could maybe go sit down." Brice flipped his head back to get his hair out of his eyes. "And hang out," he continued. "We haven't really…well…"

"Okay." She slipped from his arms and took his hand so he could lead her to the giant overstuffed chair where they'd made out the last time they were in Mason's basement.

Before everything had been so messed up. When Sienna had still been talking to her. Before her family had gone crazy. Before she'd had sex. Back when everything was still okay.

Maybe everything could still be okay if she just tried harder. Rylee drank deeply until her cup was emptied. That's all she had to do. Try harder. She wrapped her arms around Brice's neck and started kissing him as he pulled her down to his lap.

Kissing him felt good. With all the weirdness, she'd forgotten that she'd actually liked just *kissing* him.

"I was beginning to think you didn't like me very much anymore," Brice said when they finally detached their lips from each other.

"Why would you think that?" Rylee lifted her cup to keep from looking at him, but it was empty. She faked a giggle and reached for his cup.

"I just thought maybe…I don't know." He shrugged and it struck Rylee that maybe Brice wasn't as confident as she'd thought. The idea struck her as funny and she couldn't stop the laugh that escaped her. "So I guess that means that you do still like me?"

She tipped the glass back. The alcohol stung the back of her throat but she swallowed hard, desperate for the fuzziness it would bring. "Why wouldn't I?" she answered with a laugh. "You keep bringing me vodka." She held out his now empty cup.

For a minute, she thought he was going to object, but then Brice flipped his hair off his forehead and lifted her off his lap. "Let's get another drink."

She couldn't think of anything that sounded better than that. Rylee knew she should feel guilty for being at the party instead of at Sienna's and she should definitely feel guilty for being out at all since her mom was so upset, but she couldn't be held responsible for her mom. She was just a kid, and not one time had anyone asked her whether *she* was okay with everything.

At least at the party, she could forget about everything for a while.

Brice handed her a newly refilled cup. She took a big gulp, but almost spat it back up. "This is so strong." She gaped at Brice as she wiped at her mouth.

He only grinned. "The way you were drinking, I thought maybe a stiffer drink would slow you down a bit."

That logic didn't make any sense, but Rylee wasn't about to disagree with the stronger drink.

She smiled as she once more tipped the glass to her mouth.

"Hey. Don't you think you're drinking a bit too much?"

Rylee lowered her cup and turned to see Sienna next to her.

"I'll be right back. I just want to go talk to Bobby."

She heard Brice behind her, but Rylee didn't bother looking. Her eyes were fixed squarely on her best friend. Or *former* best friend. She no longer knew.

"How would you know how much I've had to drink?" Rylee didn't mean to sound like a bitch, but she couldn't seem to stop herself. Just like she couldn't seem to stop the slight slur in her words. "I'm fine." She lifted the glass to her mouth again.

"I was watching, Rylee." Sienna reached out and for a second, Rylee thought she might try to take her cup away, but then she pulled her hand back and crossed her arms. "I saw how fast you drank the last one. I just—"

"Why are you even here?"

Sienna recoiled at her tone, and again, Rylee felt bad.

"I'm here with Cole," Sienna said.

"What? Are you *dating* now or something?"

"Yes." Sienna nodded. "We are. Not that you would care."

But she did care. She cared a lot. Rylee wanted to ask her friend a million questions. Did it happen after that night they'd all been here last? Had they kissed? Was it perfect?

"Sienna...I just..." Her voice slurred. As much as she wanted to ask Sienna everything and hear all of the details, and then tell her best friend how much she missed her and how badly the last few weeks had sucked, she couldn't seem to find the words. As much as the alcohol numbed the empty feeling inside, it dulled everything else, too. "Good for you," was all she could think of to say.

Tears burned at her eyes, and she didn't want Sienna to see. She spotted Brice across the room and took a few stumbling steps toward him.

"Rylee, are you okay? I really think you should slow down." Sienna sounded every bit the goody-two-shoes she'd always been, but Rylee didn't bother to reply.

Instead, she increased her pace, until she all but fell into Brice, who barely caught her in his arms. "Let's go somewhere." She thought she'd whispered, but she could vaguely hear Bobby chuckling.

"Where do you want to go, Rylee?" He had his arm around her, holding her tightly to him and she felt safe. Safe and wanted.

"Let's go have sex." She stood on her tiptoes and gave him a sloppy kiss.

Everything would be fine because Brice wanted her and he took care of her. He loved her and didn't stop talking to her. He didn't have lies and secrets and anything else more important than asking her if she was okay. Because she wasn't okay.

But she would be.

Maren

MAREN HAD FLUFFED the throw pillows at least three times in the last ten minutes, which was ridiculous because it wasn't as if Davis hadn't seen them before. And even if he did notice them, he would likely take the pillow and toss it on the floor next to the couch the way he always did anyway.

He wasn't expected to arrive for another thirty minutes, but with each second that passed, she got more and more nervous. It was ludicrous to be nervous to talk to one's own husband; she knew that. And maybe under normal circumstances, it would be ludicrous, but these weren't normal circumstances.

Not even close.

Maren had been hoping that by the time she had a sit-down conversation with Davis, she'd know more about what she was feeling, or at least how she wanted to proceed with… well, everything. She hadn't had much luck sorting out either of those things. Which would explain the nerves.

She glanced again at the clock and, in an effort to distract herself, went into the kitchen to make herself a cup of tea. She'd already had far too much tea, but it was something to do.

She almost dropped the mug from her hand when the

phone rang, shattering the silence of the kitchen. The house line almost never rang, so she moved quickly to answer it, worried that something was wrong with Rylee.

"Hello?"

"Maren. It's your mother."

Maren's shoulders slumped as she leaned against the counter. Her mother always announced herself as if Maren would somehow spontaneously stop recognizing her voice after forty years. "This isn't really a good time, Mom. I'm just—"

"Maren, I need to speak with you."

"Mom." She rubbed at her eyes. "It really isn't a good time. Davis is—"

"Your husband."

"Thank you." She tried hard not to roll her eyes. Her mom didn't know all the details of what exactly had gone on, but obviously she'd been at Rylee's birthday party when Maren had pulled her disappearing act. According to Jessica, who'd been her lifeline that night, her mother had fluttered around for a few minutes asking questions and when it was clear that both Maren and Davis were gone, she'd clucked her tongue in that way that her mom had when she obviously disapproved of one of Maren's choices, which was almost always, and had left Jessica to clean up the mess.

Something she still owed her friend for.

"I know he's my husband, Mom." She turned her attention back to her mother. The sooner she heard her out, the sooner she could get rid of her. "What is it you need to talk to me about?"

Her mom cleared her throat and once again, Maren tried and failed to refrain from rolling her eyes. "I know you're both going through a particularly difficult time right now." Maren's mouth dropped. Her mother didn't know anything. Did she? "Having a baby at your age is not going to be easy." *Oh, the baby. Of course.* Her mother didn't even know the half of how difficult things were about to be. "And I know the two of you were clearly having some sort of spat the other night. Why else would you leave your own daughter's birthday party?"

"Mom, it wasn't just—"

"My point is." She cut Maren off. "Whatever it is that's going on between you and Davis, I think it would serve both of you well to remember that you have a daughter who, despite your thoughts on the subject, is not fully grown and needs her mother and father."

Maren's heart clenched with the guilt that had been almost a constant sensation lately. She didn't need her mother to tell her that Rylee needed her. She might be letting things slide a little, but she wasn't failing completely. After all, Rylee *had* confided in her the other night. *Of course, she shouldn't have been turning to that boy in the first place.*

"I know, Mom." Maren struggled to focus on the conversation, so much as it was. "And I assure you, although I'm not sure I should have to, that Rylee is getting my full attention. She is and will always be our priority."

"Until the baby comes along."

"Mom!" Maren snapped. "Enough." She softened her voice and added, "Please. There's a lot going on. Things you don't even understand and I just can't deal with this right now, okay?" She glanced up at the clock just as she heard Davis's car pull up outside. The sound was as familiar as breathing. He was early. "I really have to go, Mom."

She was about to hang up, but hesitated as her mom added one more thing.

"Maren, just remember that I'm your mother."

"How could I forget?"

"And as your mother," she continued as if she hadn't heard Maren's sarcastic retort, "I love you and I'll always be here for you. No matter what you need. I'm here for you."

The words stunned her momentarily into silence. Not one

time in her life had her mother ever told her that she was there for her. Or if she had, it had been buried under all of the judgment she'd piled on over the years.

"Okay." Maren finally found her voice as Davis's face appeared through the glass of the kitchen door, and the kettle whistled from the stove. "I have to go." She hung up the phone without taking her eyes off her husband.

She turned the burner off on the stove before opening the door. It struck her that it was less than a week ago that Davis would never have dreamed of standing outside of his own house waiting for her to open the door. It was strange. But everything about their situation was strange.

"Come in," she said.

Davis stepped inside and shook the rain off his coat as he took it off. "It's really coming down out there."

She ignored his small talk. "I'm making a cup of tea. Would you like one?"

"Yes, please. Thank you."

Maren cringed. He was so painfully polite. How had so much changed in such a short time?

She squeezed her eyes shut for a second before pulling out two tea bags and pouring the water into the mugs. "Let's go sit in the living room." She turned and walked into the other room before he could object. It was suddenly very important to her to control the narrative. There was so much about what was happening that was completely out of her control, if she could just control this one small thing—where they sat down—she might feel better.

Davis waited for her to sit in the wingback chair and place both mugs on the coffee table before he sat across from her on the edge of the sofa. She noticed he didn't touch the throw pillow.

"You look tired."

He nodded. "Maren, there is so much I need to say."

"I know."

"I can't even begin to tell you how—"

"Please don't tell me you're sorry." She held up a hand. "I don't think I could stand hearing that one more time."

"But I really am—"

"No." She stopped him. "You might say it. You might even *believe* it. But if you were truly sorry, you never would have done this to me. To *us*. Because that's the thing, Davis. You haven't just done this to me. You've done this to all of us. To Rylee, and this baby, too. Everything is…" She couldn't finish.

Maren bit her bottom lip and looked at her feet in an effort to keep her emotions in check.

"Maren?"

"Can you tell me why, Davis?" She looked up into his eyes. She so desperately wanted to be able to look at him again and not feel disgust or pain or the overwhelming sadness that came over her every time she was in his presence now. "Just tell me why."

"I don't think there's anything I can say that will—"

"Yes. There is."

He hung his head, defeated, but Maren couldn't let him off so easily. She had so many questions. So many things she needed to know.

"I don't even know where to begin."

"Start with how long it's been going on." He looked up and shook his head slightly. "Was it just this last year, those few times, or was it…" She trailed off because she could see from his face that it wasn't just the last year. She pressed her hand to her mouth. "Oh God. It's been going on for—"

"Since college."

"College?" Maren couldn't decide whether she was going to be sick, or whether she was going to throw the mug of hot tea at him. "But, how…you married *me*. Why would you…"

"I never loved Sabrina," he said quickly. "Not like that. Not like I love you. It was never like that."

"How was it then?"

He shook his head. "I don't think I can even explain it."

"Try."

He took a deep breath. "We'd been friends for so long, that it almost seemed natural and normal," he said. "But it wasn't romantic and it wasn't like…it was never like it was with you."

"That's the stupidest thing I've ever heard."

"It's true." He sat forward on the couch and hung his arms between his legs. "I know it sounds crazy and I don't blame you for being mad. Hell, *I'm* mad. I can't believe I ever talked myself into believing that it was okay and…God, Maren. None of this was ever supposed to happen."

"You mean fucking my best friend throughout our entire marriage? Or getting caught?" She should have been shocked at the vulgar language coming out of her mouth. She almost never swore. Not like that. Of course, she'd never been faced with a cheating husband before. *Desperate times…*

"All of it. It was so wrong and I'm so ashamed, Maren. You have to believe me when I tell you how much I love you."

She wanted to answer back with a sharp retort about how he couldn't possibly love her after what he'd done, but she couldn't. Because the truth was, she knew how much he loved her. She'd felt it every single day of their marriage and despite how wrong his behavior had been, that much she knew to be true. "I know," she said softly. "I know that you love me."

"So we can—"

She cut him off before the hope in his voice permeated her. "Just because I know that doesn't mean I can be okay with this." She shook her head as the tears she'd worked so hard to keep at bay streamed down her face. "She's having your baby, Davis. Your *son*. How can any of that ever be okay?" Her hands moved automatically to her stomach. "*I'm* having your baby." The reality of exactly what it was that she was facing now, a new baby at forty—alone—without a husband by her side, slammed into her. She drew in a sharp breath and forced herself not to lose control completely. "Oh God. I can't do this. I can't do this alone."

"Maren?" He got up from his seat and knelt on the floor next to her. "You don't have to do this alone. We can make this work." His hands fluttered, like he wasn't sure he should touch her or not. "We can fix this."

She shook her head and stared at him. "How?" The urge to laugh bubbled up inside her, but she swallowed it down. "How do you propose we make this *work*, Davis? You want me to pretend that I never found out? Or maybe you want to be one big happy family? How exactly do you expect this to *work*? You'll have to excuse me because you've had some time to get used to all of this, but I'm still trying to *process*." She threw his own word back in his face.

"I'm such a fool," she said after a moment. "How could I not see this?" Hot humiliation spread through her body as she let herself think about the implications of the last few months. "And I was her labor coach, Davis." The idea repulsed her. "How could you let me go with her to those classes? To offer to be there when her baby was born? When *your* baby was born?"

As the thoughts settled into her brain, the mortification of it all made her want to vomit. "Do you even understand how twisted that is?" She glared at him, but had to look away. The sight of him made her sick. "How could you let me do it? To offer to throw a baby shower for this child?" She groaned. "My husband's bastard baby. Oh my God." She dropped her head into her hands.

"What could I say, Maren? How could I tell you not to? How could—"

"You could have *told* me!" She lifted her head in a rage. "You didn't have to make me the fool, Davis. Don't you think it's bad enough my husband had an affair with my best friend for years and I was stupid enough to believe nothing could ever happen between the two of you? I trusted you both so much and you betrayed me. But worse, you made me a fool, too. And somehow that feels even worse."

She fell into silence for a moment until another question took root in her mind. "When she got pregnant...was it...did you plan it?" Maren realized it was a question that had been in the back of her mind since all of this started. Something she needed to know, but didn't want to know. "Was it a mistake?" she demanded. "Or did you..." Her hands clapped over her mouth as if she could take the question back. But even if she could, she still needed to know the truth. Sabrina had always said she didn't want children of her own. Had she changed her mind? Or had the baby been a mistake?

It suddenly seemed imperative that she knew the truth.

"Maren, don't do this..." Davis shook his head. "It doesn't matter how it happened. It—"

"It does."

Davis dropped his head for a brief moment and rubbed his face. "It was an accident, Maren. God, do you really think that I'd want a baby at forty years—"

Maren sat straight back in the chair, her hands on her stomach.

"No! Maren! I didn't mean that. Not like—this is all so fucked up."

She nodded. "I'll say."

They sat quietly for a minute. And then another. Finally, Davis spoke. "Let me fix this, Maren. Don't shut me out. You said yourself you can't do this alone. Well, you don't have to. I'm here and I'm not going anywhere."

"I can't do this alone." Her voice was mechanical, distant as she contemplated what being a single mom to a newborn and a teenager at the same time would be like. She shook her head slowly. "I just can't." Maren turned to look at Davis, who was still kneeling next to her. He looked small, and sad. A weak, pathetic version of the man she loved. "The problem is," she said slowly. "I can't do it with you either."

"Yes," he said quickly. "You can. I'll—"

"No." She interrupted him. "You don't understand. I can't even stand the sight of you, Davis. It makes me sick to know that you're not the man I thought you were." She shook her head and stood in an effort to put distance between them. "I can't do this. I just can't."

"What does that mean?" Davis stood, but didn't make a move to cross the room. "Maren, what are you saying?"

She turned and planted her feet so she stared directly at him. "I can't do this with you, Davis. I just can't."

Her words hung in the air between them.

"You don't mean that."

Her cell phone rang before she could answer. Instinctively, she pulled it from her pocket. "It's Rylee."

"You said she was sleeping at Sienna's."

"Because she is," Maren snapped before she turned her attention to the phone. "Rylee," she said as she answered the call. "Is everything—"

"It's me, Mrs. Bennett. Sienna."

"Sienna? Is everything okay?" Next to her, Maren could see Davis come closer. She turned away from him. "Why are you calling me on Rylee's phone?" A flicker of fear sparked in her gut.

"I'm really sorry to bother you," Sienna started. In the background, Maren could hear loud music. "But I think Rylee's had too much to drink and I think she should go home."

"What?" Maren shook her head to clear it. "Drink? Rylee was drinking?" She could feel Davis next to her and more than anything, she wanted to shove him away. But he wasn't her focus at the moment. "I'll come get her," she said into the phone. "I'll be right—"

"We're not at my house." Sienna interrupted her. "There was a party at Mason Brewer's house. Do you know where—"

"I know where that is." Thankfully, Maren had driven enough carpool for school field trips that she knew where a lot of the kids lived. "I'll be right there."

She disconnected the call and spun around, almost crashing right into Davis.

"I'm going with you."

"No." She shook her head. "You're not." Maren tried to slide past him, but he caught her arm.

"Maren." He looked straight into her eyes. "She's my daughter too. I want to be there."

She shook free and moved into the kitchen, where she grabbed her purse and coat from the hook at the back door. Davis was right behind her. There wasn't time to argue. She needed to get to her daughter. "Fine," was all she said before heading to the car.

Maren

"WHY AREN'T they at Sienna's?"

"Where did they get the alcohol?"

"How did you not know she was at a party?"

Davis kept up a steady stream of questions that took on a more and more accusatory tone as the drive went on. Finally, Maren snapped. "You're not helping. I just want to get to Rylee and make sure she's okay." She focused on the road and increased the speed of the wipers. The rain was coming down so hard, it all but blacked out the streetlights, making the drive through the tree-lined streets even darker.

Her car slipped a little, reminding Maren that she should have her tires checked and possibly replaced soon. Car maintenance was something Davis usually handled, but if she was serious about going it alone, it would be one more thing on her to-do list.

She didn't let herself dwell on the reality of what that meant, focusing instead on getting to her daughter.

When she pulled up in front of the house, she noticed the girls right away, sitting on the porch, out of the rain. Maren threw the car into park and left it running as she ran up to the house, uncaring that the rain soaked her sweater through. Davis beat her by seconds.

"What's going on?" he demanded.

Maren shook her head at his boorish approach and looked to Sienna. "What happened? How did this…"

"I'm so sorry, Mrs. Bennett. I know Rylee told you she was sleeping at my house, but that wasn't true. By the time I got here, she was already pretty drunk. I tried to get her to…well, I kind of kept an eye on her and then Brice told me she'd passed out and we thought I should call you."

"Thank you, Sienna. Really." Mother's instinct told her there was more to the story, including where Brice was now, but Maren didn't press the girl. It was enough that she had Rylee now. "We'll get her home. Do you need a ride?"

"I'm good," Sienna said. "I haven't been drinking."

Maren thanked her again and turned to catch up with Davis, who'd already scooped Rylee up and was carrying her back to the car.

"Put her in the front." Maren opened the door and Davis slipped their daughter into the front seat. She reached across Rylee, to buckle her in, and stopped for a moment to look at her daughter's face. Even with the heavy eyeliner and mascara, she was still her little girl. "Oh, Rylee," she whispered. "What's going on with you?"

Rylee's eyelids fluttered open. "Mom?"

"I've got you, sweetheart. It's okay. We're going home."

Maren moved quickly into the driver's seat. Davis was already in the back, sitting in the middle of the two seats so he could see up front. She pulled out into the dark, rainy night, intent on getting her baby girl home as quickly as possible.

"Mom?"

"I'm here, Rylee." She reached over to put her hand on Rylee's leg. "You'll feel better soon," she lied. It was likely that if she'd drank too much, Rylee was definitely going to be feeling worse before she felt better. But that wasn't important to tell her.

"Mom? Where's Brice?"

"Brice?" Davis piped up from the backseat.

Maren ignored him.

"I don't know, sweetie." Maren forced herself to keep her voice as calm and soothing as she could. "Sienna called me."

"He was with me. I remember going into the bedroom and then...why are you here?"

"Bedroom?" Davis roared from the backseat. "I'll kill him!"

Her father's voice seemed to wake Rylee up. "Dad?" She shot up in her seat and tried to spin around to look at him. "Why are you here?"

"I'm your father."

Rylee sat back hard against the seat and crossed her arms. She muttered something under her breath that Maren didn't quite catch, but she got the gist of it, and couldn't help but smile to herself.

"Excuse me?" Davis pulled himself up so he was almost even with them.

"Sit back, Davis."

Maren flipped her wipers on full, but it still wasn't enough to clear her windshield. The car hydroplaned on a puddle, but she worked to straighten it.

"What did you just say?" Davis demanded of his daughter.

"She's drunk, Davis. Leave it alone." With one hand, Maren tried to push him back.

"No." He shook her off. "I heard you, Rylee, and I won't have you speaking to me like that."

Maren sighed, and tried to focus on the road. There was no point in arguing with either of them. Davis didn't get angry often, but when he did, he was almost impossible to deal with. Just like his daughter. Surely she wouldn't be any easier to deal with angry *and* drunk.

Sure enough, Rylee didn't react to her father's anger well. Once more, she tried to spin around, but the seat belt stopped her. "You have no right to tell me how to talk." Her words slurred, but there was no mistaking her anger. "Why are you even here?" She struggled with the seat belt and finally disengaged it so she could turn around completely. In a flash, she was almost sitting on her knees as she yelled at her father. "You're disgusting! You cheated on Mom and you're having a *baby* with Auntie Sabrina! You don't get to—"

"Sit down!" With one hand on the steering wheel, Maren reached over and tried to push Rylee back into the seat.

"That's enough out of you!"

Davis rose up in his seat right as Rylee lunged for him. Maren's arm was caught between them and her whole body was yanked to the side. The car veered sharply and once again began to hydroplane on the wet road. Maren pulled her arm back and tried in vain to control the car, but it began to spin and then, all at once, time sped up and slowed down.

The dark night outside flashed past the windows as the car spun around and around. The headlights lit the huge pines that lined the road in all directions. Someone was screaming. It might have been her. And then…nothing.

Rylee

IT HURT TO BREATHE.

Why did it hurt to breathe?

It was the first thought Rylee had as she started to wake up. She tried to move her hands to her chest, as if they could help her lungs fill with air, but her arms were too heavy.

Her head hurt. It was like someone was pounding a spike through the middle of her brain.

And it still hurt to breathe.

Finally, after what felt like hours, Rylee forced her eyelids to open. It was sunny and bright.

But that didn't make sense.

She'd been at the party. She'd been with Brice. She'd been drinking and…she remembered her mom. And her dad.

Her dad.

She'd yelled at him.

Why did it hurt to breathe?

A tear slipped down her cheek and onto the pillow.

A pillow.

She wasn't in the car.

"Mom?" Her voice was scratchy and it didn't sound right.

"Rylee? Sweetie? Oh thank God, you're awake."

She tried to turn her head, but it hurt. Everything hurt. "Grandma?"

"I'm here, sweetheart." Her grandmother's voice washed over her like the warm milk with honey she used to make her when she was little. "Don't try to talk. You might be a little sore."

"Where...what..."

"There was a car accident, Rylee. Everything is going to be..."

She didn't hear what else her grandma said, because all Rylee could focus on was two words. *Car accident.* She remembered. They were in the car. Her dad was there. She was yelling at him. He yelled at her. And then there was screaming. And then...

"Mom?" Her eyes opened wider, but she still couldn't turn her head. Her grandmother appeared over her. "Where's my mom? And Dad. Where's Dad?"

"It's okay, Rylee." Her grandma took her hand and squeezed. "The doctors want you to stay calm, honey. I need you to stay calm, okay?"

"No." It wasn't okay. Nothing was okay. Where were her parents? "Please?"

Grandma stroked her hand with her thumb. "Oh, Rylee."

Were they...no. She couldn't let herself think the worst. She couldn't bear it if anything happened to them.

"They're with the doctors," her grandma said. "They're... they're going to be okay."

She wanted to ask more. She wanted to ask what was wrong and why her grandma didn't sound so sure, but before she could say anything, there was another voice.

"Hello there, Rylee." A woman who looked to be about her mom's age appeared in her vision. "It's good to see you awake.

I'm Doctor Rose and I've been looking after you. Do you know where you are?"

She didn't. Not really. "The hospital?"

"That's right." The doctor's voice was light and airy, almost as if she were talking to an elementary classroom. "There was a car accident last night and you are a very lucky girl." Rylee blinked as the doctor shone a light in each of her eyes. "You weren't wearing a seat belt," the doctor continued. "You have three broken ribs, and a collapsed lung. That might be why you're finding it a little bit hard to breathe," she said, as if she'd read Rylee's mind. "That will get better and in a few days, you should be able to breathe a little easier. You're going to need surgery on your wrist," she continued. "It's pretty badly broken. We're just waiting for the surgeon."

"Why can't I move my head?"

Doctor Rose smiled. "The neck brace was just a precaution," she said. "I'll have the nurse remove it. Do you have any other questions right now?"

Did she? She had a million questions. "Where's my mom? Is she okay?" Her eyes flicked from the doctor to her grandmother. "She's pregnant and…"

Doctor Rose's smile slipped away and her lips pressed into a thin line. "Your parents are being taken care of." She glanced away and then back at Rylee. "Your mom was wearing her seat belt. She'll be…" Again, the doctor glanced away. Rylee followed her gaze to see her grandma wiping a tear off her cheek. "She'll be fine," the doctor finished.

"And the baby?"

It suddenly seemed just as important to Rylee to know if her baby brother or sister was okay as it was if her parents were okay.

"What about the baby?"

"Rylee, we need you to stay calm."

"And my dad?"

She took a sharp breath and instantly regretted it as pain slashed through her chest. Rylee ignored it. "Where's my dad?" She struggled to sit up, but flashes of pain stopped her. "Is he...oh my God. No."

"Rylee, I need you to calm down." Doctor Rose handed her clipboard to someone Rylee couldn't see and gazed down at her. "You have to stay calm. Your injuries aren't set yet."

But Rylee couldn't stay calm. What weren't they telling her about her dad? Where was he? What was going on? What about the baby? Panic filled her, and she couldn't settle on anything.

"Rylee, I'm just going to give you a little something to help you stay calm, okay?"

She tried to shake her head. She didn't want to stay calm. She wanted answers.

"Rylee." Grandma squeezed her hand again. "It's all going to be okay. Everything is going to be okay."

She wanted to scream that it wasn't going to be okay. If her parents weren't okay. *If the baby... no.*

Her last thought as she slipped again into the dark oblivion of unconsciousness was just that. Nothing was going to be okay. Ever again.

Maren

THE MOMENT MAREN opened her eyes, she wished she hadn't.

The bright lights of the hospital room greeted her and in an instant, the memories of the night before rushed back.

The fight with Davis. The rain. Picking up Rylee. The yelling. The crash. The pain.

Her hands went automatically to her stomach. She pressed, lightly and then harder. But the ache was still there.

The emptiness.

She squeezed her eyes shut in an effort to keep the tears at bay, but it was too late. Tears were already racing down her face to soak the pillow below.

The baby.

The doctor and nurse's voices echoed in her head.

"I'm sorry."

"We did everything we could."

"The impact…"

"Couldn't stop the bleeding…"

"I can't find a heartbeat."

It was the nurse who said that. She remembered. She remembered it all.

It felt like the screaming would never stop. They'd spun around and around. She'd closed her eyes. And then the crash. The sound of metal crumpling. The blast from the airbag. And then...the screaming stopped. Silence.

She must have lost consciousness. But only for a minute, because right away she was trying to unbuckle her seat belt and get to Rylee.

There was blood.

But she was breathing.

And then there were more voices. Hands reaching into the car, pulling her out into the rain.

She remembered yelling at the strangers, telling them to leave her. To go get her daughter. Her husband. To please help them.

And then she was in the ambulance.

The hospital.

There were doctors and nurses and lights. So many bright lights.

And the warmth spreading between her legs, soaking the gurney beneath her.

"The baby. I'm pregnant." She repeated the words over and over until they finally listened. And then...

"I can't find a heartbeat."

"I'm sorry."

"We did everything we could."

Reliving it, Maren's heart clenched impossibly tight. Somewhere, a sound like a wild animal keening in the distance sounded. She rolled over on her hospital bed and pulled her knees to her chest, ignoring the pain in her body as she rocked. Belatedly, she realized the sound was coming from her. *The baby was gone.* She felt the loss of it distinctly, like a stab directly to her heart.

"Mrs. Bennett? Do you have any pain?"

Maren shook her head. "No." At least not any the nurse could help her with.

"You've had quite a night." The nurse continued a steady prattle of conversation. "I just need to check your vitals again. And if you'd like, we can take you to see your daughter."

"Rylee." Maren flipped over, her body protesting the quick movement. "How is she? Where is she? Is she——"

The nurse smiled kindly. "She's fine," she said. "Your mother is with her."

Oh thank God.

Guilt flooded her despite the fact that she couldn't have done anything.

"We're taking good care of her," the nurse said, as if she'd read her mind. "You have nothing to worry about, Mrs. Bennett. Now, let me check those vitals quickly and we'll get you on your way to see her."

The nurse moved to take Maren's wrist, but she jerked it away. "My husband? Is he okay?"

"Why don't we just start with——"

"Tell me." She swallowed hard. "Please."

The nurse pressed her lips together in a smile designed to placate her. "Mrs. Bennett, really. I need to check your vitals."

There was no point fighting with the woman, when it was clear she wasn't going to tell her anything before she got her way. So Maren swallowed her questions and let the woman do her job.

It felt like forever before the nurse was finished and had a moment to wheel her down the hall and into a hospital room that looked just like the one she'd left. Only the new room had more monitors and wires and...Rylee.

She couldn't help it. Maren gasped when she saw her beautiful daughter lying broken, bruised, her eyes shut as she mercifully slept. Her baby looked impossibly tiny in the hospital bed. Maren's hand flew to her mouth.

"Rylee. Oh my…"

"She's okay, Maren." She hadn't noticed her mother until the moment she crossed the room and put her arm on her shoulder. Maren couldn't remember the last time she'd been so happy to see her.

"Thank you, Mom. For being here. So she wasn't alone."

There were tears in her mom's eyes, but she blinked them away quickly. "Of course, dear. I'm so—"

"Please don't say it," Maren stopped her. "Not yet." She couldn't let herself think about the baby again. Not yet. She needed to focus on Rylee and Davis. But first, Rylee. "How is she? They haven't told me anything."

She stood from the wheelchair, which was only a precaution and in no way a necessity. She'd been *lucky*, the nurse said. The airbag had saved her from any *real* injury.

Except one. One very major *injury.*

Again, Maren pushed thoughts of the baby from her mind. She needed to focus.

Slowly, she made her way to Rylee's bedside. She was battered and bruised, her face swollen. Her left arm was immobilized in a bulky white plaster cast; her right arm had tubes and IVs sticking from it. Maren slipped her fingers around that hand and gently squeezed. "How is—"

"Mrs. Bennett?"

Maren turned to see a woman in the doorway about her age, wearing a white coat and holding a clipboard.

Maren nodded and the woman came in.

"I'm Doctor Rose." She extended her hand. Maren nodded again, but she was not going to remove her hand from her daughter. Not for any reason. The doctor smiled in understanding. "I've been taking care of Rylee. She's a very lucky young woman."

Was she? She didn't look lucky. She looked as if she'd been through hell.

"Is she...will she..."

"She's fine," Doctor Rose said quickly. "She's suffered three broken ribs and a collapsed lung. Her wrist was very badly broken and will require surgery. In fact, the surgeon on call has just arrived and is prepping now. We'll need you to sign some forms."

"Of course." Maren nodded, but didn't take her eyes off Rylee.

"Like I said," the doctor continued. "She's very lucky as I understand she wasn't wearing her seat belt."

The memories rushed back. The way Rylee had yelled at Davis. She'd taken off her seat belt to turn around in her seat. Maren had tried to push her back, but the car swerved and... "No," Maren said. "It was all...it was a rough night and..."

The doctor nodded sympathetically. "It was also observed that Rylee's blood alcohol level was .08%."

Maren nodded. "Her father and I picked her up from a party," she explained. "She'd been drinking and her friend called us." She shook her head, and forced herself not to cry.

"I understand." Doctor Rose put her hand on Maren's shoulder. "I have teenagers of my own."

"Thank you." For the first time, Maren took her eyes off her daughter. "My husband? Is he..." She couldn't bring herself to ask.

"Why don't I get you those forms to sign for Rylee, and I'll take you to see him? Rylee will be going into surgery right away, and I'll make sure we have someone notify you the moment she's in recovery."

"Yes." She sagged with relief. "Thank you."

"I'll wait here with her."

Her mother stood next to her, waiting and watching silently. "Thank you, Mom."

"Stop." Her mom opened her arms and for the first time in years, Maren moved into her mother's embrace. "You don't have to thank me, sweetie. I'm here for you. Go. You'll be back before she wakes up."

If Maren thought that Rylee's hospital room with the extra monitors and wires was shocking, then she was completely unprepared to see Davis.

True to her word, after Maren signed consent forms for Rylee's surgery and had a brief conversation with the orthopedic surgeon about the fracture Rylee had sustained, Doctor Rose took her up to a different floor of the hospital, and the Intensive Care Unit.

"I've been briefed on your husband's condition," the doctor said as she pushed the wheelchair. "I want you to be prepared when you see him. The ICU can look a lot scarier than it is. That being said, your husband sustained a head injury and right now there is significant amount of swelling on the brain, which is why they've put him into a medically induced coma. They're hopeful the swelling will go down in a day or two, and they can wake him up. The CAT scans aren't showing any significant brain damage."

"What does that mean?" Maren looked straight ahead as they slowed in front of a door with Bennett written on the whiteboard next to it.

The doctor moved to open the door and smiled kindly. "Basically it means that the brain is very complex, and right now, assuming the swelling goes down the way they expect it to, your husband will be fine. There might be some memory…"

She stopped listening, fixated only on the one word. *Fine.*

He would be fine.

Maren released a breath she'd been holding. But the moment Doctor Rose wheeled her to Davis's bedside, that same breath caught in her throat again. *Fine? He was going to be fine?* She couldn't see how that was possible. She barely recognized the battered man who laid on the bed before her. His face had been cut and although the cuts had been cleaned and stitched, they looked angry and painful. His leg was bandaged up in a bulky plaster cast, obviously broken. But despite those visual injuries, that wasn't what struck her.

He was obviously sleeping, or unconscious, or whatever it was when someone was in a coma. It was like he was there, but at the same time, he wasn't.

"You can touch him." Doctor Rose took a step back to give her some privacy. "Obviously he can't respond. But he'll know you're here."

Maren hesitated but after a moment, reached out and slipped her hand over his. "Davis." Her voice was a whisper. She cleared it and tried again. "Davis. It's Maren." She giggled uncertainly. "But you probably knew that." She took a breath and exhaled slowly. "I'm here and you're going to be okay." She squeezed his hand a little and waited. She didn't know what she was expecting, but she watched his eyes, willing them to open. Of course they didn't, and after a moment she looked down before turning his hand over in hers.

She focused on the lines in his palm. It was a hand both so familiar, and at the same time, completely foreign. So much had happened. She was numb and unsure of what to feel.

"I need you to be okay, Davis," she said. "I mean it. I *need* you to be okay. You're not allowed to not be okay." A tear slipped down her cheek. She didn't think it was possible for her to cry any more than she had in the last few hours. Of course, she'd never almost lost her entire family before. "Rylee's okay," she told him. "Her wrist is pretty messed up, but the doctors are fixing it and she'll be just fine. I don't think she'll be healed in time for the summer swim season, but that's okay. It doesn't matter." Maren realized she was rambling, but she couldn't seem to stop herself. And she didn't know what else to say. It wasn't as though she could sit there and tell her unconscious husband that she'd lost their baby. The baby who she'd only *just* gotten used to the idea of. The baby who she still felt crippling guilt over not wanting when she'd first found out she was pregnant. The baby whose heartbeat she'd heard only days before. The baby who'd she'd just begun to think of in a real way. The baby she'd just recently started to love and look forward to, the way she should have from the beginning. The baby she'd seen on the ultrasound screen. The baby who the doctors had just told her had been a girl.

A girl.

They were going to have another baby girl.

And now they weren't.

The fresh realization crushed her like a weight.

She took a breath and forced herself to keep it together. "Wake up, Davis. You have to wake up." Maren focused on his eyes, but still they didn't move.

Was it really only yesterday that she'd yelled at him? That she'd told him she didn't want to be with him? That she couldn't stand the sight of him?

Did she really feel that way?

Tears blurred her eyes.

It was too much. She hated him. Hated what he'd done to her and to their family. But she loved him, too. So much.

She squeezed his hand one more time and turned around. "Take me downstairs, please," she said to the doctor. "Take me to my daughter."

Sabrina

SABRINA HAD BEEN in the waiting room for over an hour.

The night before, the hospital had called her to tell her that Maren, Davis, and Rylee had been involved in a car crash. Maren had her listed, along with her mother, as an emergency contact. Of course she had. Sabrina was like a sister to her. She was family.

She *had* been family.

With everything that had happened, she wasn't sure what she was anymore. Would Maren still want to see her?

After the hospital called the night before, Sabrina had rushed over, but they wouldn't let her see anyone. Maren's mom, Barbara, was there, too. They exchanged a few words, but neither of them were in the mood to chat and Sabrina didn't know how much Barbara knew about what had happened between them all.

Finally a doctor came out to speak to them both. "Ladies, my name is Doctor Rose. You are…"

"Barbara Magnus. I'm Maren's mother. How are they? What's happening?"

"Nobody is telling us anything," Sabrina jumped in.

"I am sorry about that," the doctor said. "In emergency situations, the priority is to stabilize the patient first. I know it can be unsettling to the family to not understand what's happening." She turned to Sabrina. "I'm sorry—you are a sister?"

Sabrina glanced at Barbara. Normally she would have instinctively answered yes. But she shook her head. "I'm a family friend. A *close* family friend. Family, really. I'm—"

The doctor nodded slightly. "Maren and Rylee are both stable now. Rylee has some broken bones, and a collapsed lung. But she's going to be okay. Maren is...well, I'm sorry to say that your daughter suffered a miscarriage."

"Oh." Barbara put her hand to her mouth and shook her head. "Oh, no."

Sabrina stared straight ahead. *A miscarriage? Maren had lost her baby?* Her own hands cupped her swollen belly. The enormity of the situation hit her.

"And Davis?" Sabrina needed to know. "Is he okay?"

"How is my son-in-law?" Barbara sounded so much calmer as she asked the question. "How is he?"

"His injuries were much more severe. He's stable, but he has a head injury. The extent of which we're..."

Sabrina stopped listening.

No.

A miscarriage. A head injury. This couldn't be happening. It was like a bad dream. A nightmare. The room spun, and she sank into a nearby chair.

A moment later, Barbara crouched in front of her. "Are you okay?"

Sabrina nodded. She would be.

"I think you should go home, dear," Barbara said. "There's nothing you can do and there's no point in both of us being here. Why don't you come back in the morning?" Her voice was kind and it took Sabrina a moment to reconcile that with all of the things Maren was always saying about how hard her mom was on her. The woman before her seemed nothing but concerned.

And she was right.

Sabrina shouldn't be there. For a million reasons. Not right then.

"Come back in the morning, dear."

Sabrina nodded. *Yes. That's what she'd do. The morning.*

Which was exactly what she'd done. She'd gone home, where she'd tossed and turned for a few hours before finally giving up and getting out of bed. She'd arrived at the hospital early, where she'd been waiting for visiting hours to start.

Finally, she was permitted to go up to the third floor and Maren's room. Her hand hovered over the button on the elevator before she finally pushed it. Maren may hate her for what she'd done. But a terrible thing had just happened, and as angry as Maren might be, she was going to need her. After all, they were family, and Sabrina couldn't stay away. She just couldn't.

The nurse on the ward told her Maren was being discharged right away, but still, she directed her down the corridor to a room on the right, but she hesitated in the hall. The door was open a crack, and finally, taking a breath for courage, Sabrina knocked. "Hello?" She slowly pushed the door open and peered inside.

Maren was dressed, sitting up on the bed, her legs hanging over the side. She looked up when Sabrina walked in and immediately looked down again. But she didn't tell her to leave. She'd take what she could get.

"How are you...never mind." Sabrina stopped herself. "That's a stupid thing to ask." She took a few tentative steps into the room. "Maren? I'm so sorry."

After a moment, Maren looked up again. Sabrina barely recognized her. The sparkle that was always in Maren's eyes had dimmed. Her skin had taken on a pasty, almost gray tone and the dark circles under her eyes were evidence to the way the last twenty-four hours had aged her.

Conscious of the makeup she'd put on that morning, Sabrina ducked her head.

"You're sorry?" There was no maliciousness in her voice but Sabrina cringed nonetheless.

"I am, Maren." She moved closer to her friend, wanting desperately to hug her, to try to take away some of her pain. But she knew she couldn't. She'd lost that right. "For everything."

"For everything?" Maren repeated robotically.

Sabrina nodded, aware that it was woefully inadequate.

"I lost the baby."

"I know. I'm so sorry, Maren."

She looked up. "Are you?"

"Oh my—yes! Of course I am. I don't even know what to say."

Maren looked down again. After a moment, she lifted her head. "Why are you here, Sabrina?"

"I'm an emergency contact, and...I love you, Maren. You're family."

She shook her head and it broke Sabrina's heart. "No. You're not. Not mine."

"Maren, I—"

"You should go. Davis is on the fifth floor. ICU. You should go to him."

"I don't know if—"

"He's the father of your child, Sabrina." Maren's eyes pierced her. "Go."

She nodded numbly and turned to go. Before she left, she turned around one more time. "I really am sorry, Maren. For everything. Really."

Maren only shook her head sadly and looked back at her shoes.

Still numb, Sabrina made her way to the fifth floor and Davis's room.

The nurse had tried to prepare her for the monitors and wires, but still, when she saw him lying motionless on the bed, she gasped. He looked as if he were sleeping, but at the same time, he looked...

No. She wouldn't let herself think the worst.

The nurse told her he might have some memory issues or brain damage. They wouldn't know the full effect or extent of his injuries until he woke up.

Sabrina didn't know what to feel as she stood next to him and gazed down at the man who was at once so familiar, and also a stranger to her. He'd been such an important part of her life for so long, but always on the fringe.

After a moment, she took his hand in hers. "Hi, Davis." She felt self-conscious talking aloud, but the nurse said he'd be able to hear her. "It's me, Sabrina. I guess you took quite a hit to your head." She tried to smile. "You know better," she teased. "You should have had your seat belt on. Safety first, right?"

The smile faded. "You're going to be okay." She said it more for herself than for him. She needed to believe it. "You have to be, okay?"

She let her eyes travel over him. The scrapes, bruises, and cuts. The broken leg.

"We've made quite a mess of things," she said after a minute. "I don't really know how to fix it, Davis. I don't know if I can. But I do know we're having this baby and despite the mess his parents have made, your son needs his father. I need you to be okay, Davis. Our son needs you to be okay." She let the tears slip down her cheeks unchecked. She stared at his eyes, willing them to open, but knowing they wouldn't. He wasn't going to wake up until the doctors wanted him to. Nothing she said would change that. "I love you, Davis."

She said the words for the first time, but they didn't feel right on her tongue.

Did she love him?

Yes. Of course she did. He was her friend. Had been her lover. Her confidant. Her comfort when she needed him. He was the father of her child. But as Sabrina watched him and held his hand, she realized something very important. Something she'd always kind of known.

She loved Davis. But she wasn't *in* love with him. She never had been. She'd made a terrible mistake. She'd been selfish, and childish, and hadn't stopped to think about what she was doing, and how it would affect anyone else. Not once.

"I'm so sorry, Davis." She shook her head. The best thing she could do now was walk away. Davis needed love and support if he was going to heal and properly recover. But it couldn't be from her.

"I'm so, so sorry," she whispered again and bent to kiss his bruised forehead before she slipped from the room.

There was a lot of healing to be done.

For everyone.

Maren

IT WAS three more days before Rylee's lung was healed enough that Maren could bring her home. Her wrist had been surgically set with four pins and a plate. She had strict orders to rest and regain her strength and let her ribs heal. She'd need physiotherapy in a few months when the cast came off. But it wasn't Rylee's physical injuries that Maren was worried about. Ever since she'd woken up after her surgery, Rylee had been depressed and withdrawn. Maren assumed it was just the after-effects of the anesthetic and the trauma of the accident. But even as the days went by, she couldn't get Rylee to open up about it. Not even her mom could get through to her and they'd always been so close.

"Are you sure you don't want to stay downstairs, sweetie?" Maren carried Rylee's bag into the house and helped Rylee slip her shoes off.

"I just want to go to bed, Mom. I'm tired."

"Are you sure? We could watch that—"

"I'm sure."

Maren pressed her lips together and nodded. "Okay, sweetie. Come on. I'll help you get settled."

Thankfully, Rylee let Maren fuss around her just enough to have her propped up in her bed with pillows, a glass of water on the table and a book. "Do you want your phone? Maybe you could check in with—"

"No."

Rylee looked straight ahead and Maren's heart broke. She'd been trying not to push her, but there was only so much her mother's heart could take.

Gently, she sat on the bed next to her. "Rylee, I—"

"No, Mom." She shook her head but wouldn't meet her eyes. "I don't want to talk."

"I know you don't, sweetie. But I really think you need to."

Unshed tears filled her daughter's eyes, but they didn't spill.

Maren took a breath and reached for her good hand. Rylee didn't pull away, so she squeezed gently. "Okay," she said after a moment. "I can't force you to talk, so I'm not going to push. But I need you to understand one thing, okay?"

Rylee turned a little to look at her.

"It was an accident," Maren started. And just as she expected, Rylee squeezed her eyes and looked away. "It was just a terrible accident, Rylee. I'm so sorry this happened to you, and your father and…" She left the thought unfinished. "I wish I could go back in time and change it, but I can't. All we can do is…well, all we can do is keep going."

When it became clear that Rylee wasn't going to talk, Maren leaned over and pressed a kiss to her daughter's cheek. "I'll be downstairs. Just text me if you need anything, okay?"

She paused at the door and looked back at her daughter. Rylee was hurting so badly she wished more than anything she could take all of the hurt away.

But she couldn't.

With one more look at her daughter, Maren slipped from the room. She got downstairs right in time to hear the knock at the back door.

Jessica met her eyes through the glass and let herself in. "Hey."

"Hey."

"Come here."

Jessica put the flowers and bag she was holding on the table and crossed the kitchen floor to pull Maren into a hug she didn't even realize she desperately needed.

"I'm so glad you're okay," Jessica said after a moment. "What a terrible thing. I'm so sorry."

"I know." Maren stepped back. "It is…it was…thank you for coming."

"Of course."

Maren sat at the table and let Jessica take charge in her kitchen. Her friend set to work, putting the kettle on before digging in the bag she brought. She produced a variety of groceries, including a box from the bakery downtown. *Food.* Of course they'd need to eat. Maren had spent every minute she could at the hospital, grabbing snacks from vending machines or eating whatever her mom forced upon her. She had no idea what they even had in the house.

"Here." Jessica put the bakery box full of cinnamon rolls in front of Maren, along with a mug of tea. "I know they're your favorite and I brought Rylee some too."

"I really don't know how to thank you, Jessica. This is all…" She let her head drop, suddenly exhausted.

Maren had been running on adrenaline for the last few days. Between both her husband and her daughter in the hospital, she'd only managed a few hours of sleep at night.

"Stop," Jessica said. "You'd do the exact same thing for me. Besides, the last thing you need to worry about is silly little details like food. Now, talk to me. How's Davis?"

She shook her head. "The same. Mostly. The doctors are hoping to wake him up in a few days. Then they'll know more. Right now they're hopeful."

"Good." Jessica nodded. "That's good to hear."

It was.

"And Rylee? She's home and—"

"She won't talk to me." Maren reached for a roll. "She's barely said a word since the accident. I asked her if she wanted to see her dad, but..." Maren shook her head. "I think she blames herself."

"But it was an accident."

She'd been drinking. There was yelling. There was so much hurt between them all. But yes, it was an *accident*. "I know," Maren said. "But she doesn't see it that way. She's hurting so much."

"She'll be okay. Give her time."

Jessica was so certain, Maren wished she could share some of that optimism. She pulled a corner of the roll off and put it in her mouth but she barely tasted the sugary treat.

"What about you?" Jessica looked her straight in the eye. "How are *you*, Maren?"

She shook her head. "I'm fine."

"Maren?"

"I am." She wouldn't meet her friend's gaze because they both knew she was lying. "I just want to move on and—"

"You've had a terrible loss, Maren. It's okay to feel however you feel about that."

And that was the whole problem. She couldn't talk about it, because Maren didn't know how she was supposed to feel about losing the baby.

Devastated? Yes.

Angry? Yes.

Guilty? Yes.

Relieved? Also...yes.

"Mom?"

It was almost eight o'clock and Maren had been staring blankly at the television, not really watching whatever it was on the screen when her daughter's voice broke her trance.

Immediately, she jumped up from the couch and went to Rylee. "What are you doing out of bed?" She led her to the couch. "You're supposed to be resting, Rylee. You can just text me if you need anything."

"I know." Rylee sat gingerly on the sofa and Maren put a throw cushion under her arm to keep it elevated. "But I wanted to talk to you. Is that okay?"

Maren hated the question in her daughter's eyes. "Of course." She sat next to her. Close, but not so close that her movement would jostle her. "We can always talk about anything."

Rylee nodded slightly and for a moment, Maren was afraid she'd shut down again. But then she said, "I know it's all my fault."

"The accident?"

Rylee nodded and Maren's heart broke.

"No, Rylee. It's not your fault. None of it is your fault. It was an accident."

"No, Mom." She shook her head vehemently. "It was an accident that never should have happened."

"Sweetie, that's what an accident is. Something that never should have happened."

"You don't understand, Mom. If I hadn't have been drinking, Sienna wouldn't have called you. You wouldn't have had to come get me and then…I was yelling at Dad, and I distracted you and I never should have—"

"Ssh." Maren moved closer and stroked Rylee's cheek. "Rylee, stop. It's not your fault. You can't do this to yourself."

Any one of them could direct the situation and blame

themselves for the way things ended up that night, but there was no point. She believed what she'd said. It was an accident.

"But you lost the baby, Mom."

Her words hit her in the heart.

"I know, sweetie."

"But it was my fault, Mom." Rylee sobbed. "The baby is dead because of *me*."

"No!" She sat back so she wouldn't jar Rylee's ribs. "It's not your fault, sweetie. The baby is…the baby didn't make it because sometimes that happens."

"It was the accident."

"Maybe," Maren admitted. "But sometimes babies don't make it and there's nothing we can do."

Rylee searched her mother's face for permission to believe her that it was, in fact, an accident. After a moment, she added, "But Dad. He's—"

"Going to be fine." Rylee's eyes locked on hers and more than anything else, in that moment, all Maren wanted was to take her daughter's pain away. "Rylee, please. The accident wasn't your fault. The baby…it's okay." It wasn't, but neither of them said anything.

Because on some level, both of them knew that it might not be okay right now.

But it would be.

Maren

RYLEE WAS DOING BETTER. Slowly, her injuries were starting to heal. It would be a long process, but more importantly, after their first big talk, she'd continued to open up to Maren.

They'd talked about how conflicted she felt about her relationship with Brice and how quickly it had become physical. As difficult as it was for her, Maren forced herself to listen and not offer any judgment. It made her heart ache to see how fast Rylee was growing up, but she was still such a little girl in so many ways. She still wanted to cuddle and together they binged more than one Netflix show, wrapped in blankets on the couch.

As much as Rylee was starting to open up, she still didn't want to talk about Sienna and what had gone wrong in their friendship.

"Best friends are special," she said one night as they were getting ready to start another season of *Friends*. She stroked Rylee's hair. "You should call her."

"I don't know, Mom."

"Do you want to talk about it?"

"Do you think that sometimes a friend can be so terrible that there's no coming back from it?"

She did. Sabrina's face flashed in her mind. Her best friend. The one person next to Davis who was closest to her. *Yes.* She did think that there were some things you couldn't come back from.

Rylee must have realized what she'd said and how it sounded, because she quickly added, "Sorry, Mom. I didn't mean…"

"It's fine." Maren tried for a light tone. "I'm sure whatever it was that happened between you two isn't so big that you can't get past it."

It wasn't an answer and they both knew it, but it was the best she could do.

Two days after bringing Rylee home from the hospital, Maren left her in her mother's care and went into the PlayTime offices. Eileen told her to take off as much time as she needed, but Maren was itching for something else to keep her busy. Something to take her mind off all the things she still couldn't bring herself to think about.

"Maren?" She'd only been at her desk for twenty minutes, sifting through files and notes and the messages that had stacked up, when Eileen appeared next to her desk. "I'm surprised to see you."

"I know you said I could take some time off, but I just needed to—"

"I understand." Eileen's smile was kind. "I'm the same way. Sometimes work can be a good distraction." She nodded and seemed to be waiting for Maren to say something more. When Maren didn't say anything, she continued. "I'm very sorry about the accident," she said. "But I'm happy to hear that everyone is okay. Is there any word on Davis?"

Maren nodded. "I'm actually going to go to the hospital after lunch, if that's okay?" she added quickly.

"Of course. You do what you need to do."

"The doctors said they were hoping to wake him up this afternoon and run some scans. We should know more then."

"Good. I'm really glad to hear it." She stood in silence again. "I meant it when I said you're welcome to take as much time as you need, Maren. I know this isn't an easy time for you or your family."

Maren appreciated her support more than she could express. But she'd meant it when she'd told her the work was a welcome distraction. "Maybe I could do some of this work at home?" The idea had occurred to her after speaking to the doctors the day before. They couldn't be sure what level of care Davis would need when he woke up. At least not right away. And despite everything, he was her husband. He'd have to come home.

Maren hadn't thought past the idea that Davis would wake up and come home. She hadn't thought to where he'd stay. Or what kind of care he would need when he did get home or what it would mean to her. To *them.*

Her body flushed and it was suddenly too warm.

"Maren?" Eileen came around the side of the desk. "Are you okay?"

She nodded and forced a smile. She was anything but okay, and no doubt anyone who looked at her could see it.

"I'm fine," she said. "And really, thank you so much for being so understanding about everything. I promise I won't let you down and I'll still be able to—"

"Maren." She put a hand on Maren's arm. "Really. There's no pressure. Just concentrate on taking care of your family.

And yourself," she added. "PlayTime and your job will always be here. You take as much time as you need."

For some reason Maren couldn't even begin to explain, Eileen's warmth and understanding at that moment almost broke her. In an instant, she was torn between telling her everything that had happened with her family, or just breaking down into tears. But before she could do either, her phone rang.

"It's the hospital. I'm sorry."

Eileen excused herself quickly and Maren answered.

"Davis is awake," Doctor Rose said.

"But you weren't supposed to…" She trailed off. It no longer seemed important.

"I'm sorry we didn't call earlier," Doctor Rose said. "We had an opening to run the tests and…well, the good news is, your husband is awake."

"Yes." Maren was already gathering up her files and shoving them into her bag. "And he's…"

"He's doing great. The swelling has gone down and the test results have come back. Things look very positive. He has some memory loss and some other relatively minor issues, but we can discuss all of those things when you come in." The doctor sounded happy, almost as if she were smiling, and Maren knew she should be happy, too.

And she was.

Of course she was happy that Davis was awake and that he was going to be fine. That was excellent news. But it also meant that she could no longer keep hiding. The accident had changed things, certainly. But it had erased nothing.

Rylee

_____

RYLEE ASKED her mom to wait in the waiting room for her. She needed to go in alone. Of course her mom agreed. Ever since the accident she'd been...different. More attentive. Acting as if Rylee might break at any moment.

Not that she minded. Not really. She'd enjoyed having her mom _back_. Having that closeness again that they'd once shared. Even if it was for a terrible reason.

She knew her mom had been surprised when Rylee asked her to drive her to the hospital. It wasn't like she'd been that nice to her dad before the accident. And of course, it didn't matter what her mom said; she knew she was the reason the accident happened in the first place. Thankfully, her mom hadn't made a big deal out of it, though. They just got in the car and drove.

It wasn't until they were inside the building that Rylee asked her to wait in the waiting room. She'd almost changed her mind about going in at all when she saw the way her mom looked at her. Kind of a mixture of happiness, pride, and sadness all at once.

It was too much.

But she wouldn't change her mind.

She couldn't.

Her dad had been moved to a hospital room almost exactly like the one she'd been in. She followed the nurse's instructions, and knocked on the door.

"Hello?"

No turning back now.

Rylee took a breath and stepped inside. "Hi, Dad."

"Rylee." He said her name almost like a question. "Sweetheart. I'm so happy to see you."

With all the feelings storming inside her, love won. She smiled and went to his bedside. "I'm so glad you're okay, Dad. I was so…" She couldn't stop the tears that sprang to her eyes.

"Hey." He reached for her, and she took his hand with her good arm. "I'm fine. Just a little banged up. What about you? Your mom said you're doing okay, but…" He gestured to her broken wrist. "That doesn't look okay."

She shrugged. Her wrist didn't hurt anymore. At least not much. Not like her ribs. Every time she sneezed or coughed, she wanted to scream. Of course, she kind of liked the pain, not that she was going to tell her dad that. But she deserved it. It didn't seem right that she'd walked away so easily from an accident that had caused everyone so much hurt.

"Hey," he said again. "What's going on?"

Her dad always could see through her tough act. Not that she was being very tough at the moment. In the past, she would have opened up to him and told him what the problem was. But that was before. Too much had happened.

"Talk to me, Rylee."

She shook her head.

"You know this isn't your fault, right?" Her head snapped up and he continued, as if aware he'd hit a nerve. "Your mom told me you were blaming yourself."

Of course she had.

"But it was just an accident. If anything, it's probably my fault."

His fault? Was he going to talk about the fight? About Auntie Sabrina and the baby?

She held her breath. Rylee wasn't sure she was ready to talk about it, but at the same time, she knew they had to. Their family was broken. She knew she couldn't fix it, but maybe she could understand it.

"I should have changed the tires," he said.

"The tires?" Rylee looked at him as if he'd just told her he was a circus clown. "What do you mean? That's why you think it's your fault?"

He nodded. "Your mom said it was raining and the car hydroplaned. I knew those tires should have been replaced. I just never got around to making the appointment."

Rylee shook her head. "Wait. I don't understand." She pulled her hand away. "What do you mean, Mom told you it was raining? Don't you remember?" She searched his eyes, looking for some sort of recognition but there was nothing.

After a moment, he shook his head.

"The doctors said that I might have some memory loss," he explained. "It might come back, but it might not."

He didn't remember? But she *needed* him to remember. She needed him to remember their fight and the things she'd said, because even though she'd been drunk, she remembered. She remembered how terrible she'd been to him. But she also remembered that he'd deserved it. She'd been so mad. So hurt. She wanted him to hurt, too.

Her eyes lifted to her strong dad, who looked so much weaker than she'd ever seen him, but she dropped them again. Unable to look at him. She'd wanted him to hurt. But not like that.

"What *do* you remember?"

He forced a small smile. "I remember talking to your mom and then she got a call from Sienna. We went to pick you up."

"And that's it?"

He nodded. "Do you want to fill me in?"

She shook her head. "Not right now. I was pretty mad at you and I'm sure Mom told you, I'd been drinking."

"She mentioned it." He reached for her hand again, and Rylee let him take it. "I don't remember the fight," he said. "But I know we had one. And I do remember why, Rylee."

"You do?"

She wanted so badly to be mad at him for breaking their family. For ruining everything. But she couldn't. He was her dad and despite his terrible choices, she loved him.

"I do, sweetie, and I want you to know how much I love you and how sorry I am for everything." He closed his eyes for a moment and Rylee's heart stopped.

"Dad?"

"Sorry." His eyes opened again, but she could see the exhaustion in them. "I'm still so tired, sweetie."

"Of course. I should—"

"We'll talk about everything." He squeezed her hand. "I know I can't make it right, but I hope you can forgive me."

She nodded.

"And Rylee, you need to know that this isn't your fault. I mean it. Sometimes terrible things happen."

He closed his eyes again, and a moment later, she knew he was asleep.

She pulled her hand out of his and stood for a minute, watching him. Nothing would ever be the same, that much was certain. But he was her dad and despite it all, she loved him. That much was also certain.

They were back in the car driving home before her mom asked her how she was doing.

"It was good to see him," Rylee answered truthfully. "I didn't know how I'd feel. But... I'm really glad he's going to be okay."

"Of course you are." Her mom's smile was sad, but she said, "So am I."

Rylee believed her.

She looked out the window at the other cars and wondered if any of those people had just had their worlds turned upside down. Maybe they were just going about their normal lives? But maybe they, too, had just gotten some news that would shatter everything? How was it that life could just continue on for everyone around her, while at the same time everything for her had changed?

"You okay, kiddo?"

She nodded. "Just thinking, Mom." She swallowed hard. "I think I understand now that it's not my fault. Not really."

"Oh, Rylee. I'm so glad to hear that." Her mother's voice was loaded with relief.

"I know that sometimes things just happen and maybe there would have been an accident even if you hadn't come to get me. And maybe if I hadn't been yelling at Dad you wouldn't have gone off the road. But maybe you would have. I guess we'll never know."

"No," her mom said. "We'll never know. And it really doesn't matter."

"I know," Rylee admitted. "But I still feel terrible."

"I understand that." Her mom glanced at her. "So do I. After all, I was the one driving."

Her mouth dropped open. Rylee had never considered that her mom might feel responsible for the accident. She'd lost her baby. She was a victim. She... "Mom. It wasn't *your* fault."

"And it wasn't yours."

Rylee sat back and let that soak in. *Really* soak in.

"And it wasn't Dad's fault either," she said after a moment. "I mean, the accident wasn't," she clarified and her mom nodded.

"No. It wasn't his fault either."

They rode in silence for a bit, and as the minutes ticked past and they grew closer to their neighborhood, Rylee began to finally feel lighter.

Her phone chimed with an incoming message. She was going to ignore it the way she'd been ignoring all of her messages, but then she changed her mind.

How are you? I've been thinking about you.

She didn't respond. Not right away. Instead, Rylee turned to her mom. "Can we make one more stop, please? There's someone else I need to apologize to."

Maren

SHE'D BEEN PUTTING it off long enough. Doctor Rose told her that Davis would be released from the hospital the day after tomorrow, which meant he needed a place to stay. Maren had already made the decision to bring him home. After all, despite everything that had happened, he *was* her husband. And it was his house.

Maren had also decided that the spare room was the best place for him to recover. There was an attached bathroom and although it was up the stairs, and would be tricky initially to get him settled, he'd be the most comfortable there while he recovered.

But if Davis was going to stay in the spare room, it meant she needed to go in there.

She'd been standing in front of the closed door for almost twenty minutes, but she hadn't yet been able to bring herself to turn the handle and go inside.

"Come on, Maren." She took a breath, pulled her shoulders back and put her hand on the handle. "It's only a room."

Only a room, she reminded herself as she turned the handle and stepped inside.

But it wasn't only a room. It was to be the baby's room. It had been only a few weeks ago when she'd started mentally planning the decor. Without knowing the sex of the baby, she'd thought a baby animal theme would be cute. Prints of different baby animals on the walls that were painted a light brown with chocolate and cream accents. She'd already found a crib and change table set online in dark oak. Mercifully, she hadn't ordered them yet. And really, there wasn't much in the room that would indicate what it was supposed to become.

The queen-sized bed still sat in the middle of the room, made up for guests with a bright-yellow and blue comforter she'd once thought so welcoming and cheery with the matching shams and pillows. But it wasn't the comforter or the throw pillows Maren focused on. Instead, it was the shopping bags she'd left on the bed to be put away later, once the new dresser had been ordered, and the tiny hangers purchased.

She hesitated, but she couldn't avoid it forever. The bags would have to be dealt with. She could just take them and put them straight in a donation bin. She didn't have to ever see them again. That's what she should have done. It would have been the easiest thing to do and no one would have blamed her.

But she couldn't.

She opened the first bag and pulled out the onesie that had caught her eye. There was nothing special about it. No funny expression printed on the front. No special fabrics or color or patterns even. It was newborn sized, impossibly tiny and plain white cotton.

Just like the ones she'd favored for Rylee when she was born. Maren sat on the bed and held the onesie between her hands. She remembered those days when Rylee was little. She'd been an easy baby. Always settled and content. The pregnancy had been so hard, but once she was there in her arms, it was like all of that went away. She was so perfect. They'd been perfect. The three of them against the world.

Except that hadn't been true.

The thought pierced her and tainted her memories. How much of what she remembered had been colored with the sins of Davis's actions? So much.

Too much.

She put the onesie aside and reached into the next bag, already knowing what it contained. A mint-green teddy bear. Not too big and not too tiny. It would have been the baby's first teddy bear. Just like the one she'd bought for Rylee the day she found out she was pregnant. It sat in her crib and then when she was old enough to reach for it, the bear became her *bubba* and she'd taken it everywhere. Rylee didn't want anyone to know about it, but Maren knew that *Bubba the bear* still slept under Rylee's pillow, where it was close enough for comfort, but not too close that it wasn't cool.

The new mint-green teddy would have been her baby's *bubba*.

And now she'd never hold it. Never carry it around with her, insisting she couldn't leave the house without it. There'd be no frantic searches late at night when she'd misplaced the bear and absolutely could not sleep without it. Maren would never have to *perform surgery* to repair a rip. There would be no teddy bear picnics in the living room while her little girl danced around in princess dresses and demanded they play dress-up and drink lemonade from tiny cups.

There would be none of those memories. Because her little girl was gone.

Gone before she ever had a chance.

Tears streamed down her face as she clenched the bear to her chest and let herself sob.

There was no telling how long she sat there, cradling the bear and rocking back and forth, but the tears didn't slow. A dam that she'd somehow managed to keep stopped up had burst inside her, and the pain poured from her.

Maren didn't hear the front door open, or the footsteps on the stairs or even her mother's voice until Barbara wrapped her arms around her daughter and pulled her close. "It's okay, honey." She stroked her hair and held her fast. "Let it out. It's okay."

The weight of her mother's arms around her gave her strength and comfort in a way that would have taken her off guard if her emotions weren't already so raw and exposed.

When finally her tears slowed, and her sobs settled into soft hiccups, Maren pulled away and took the tissue her mother handed her. "Thank you," she muttered before blowing her nose and wiping at her face.

"Honey, I'm so sorry. I wish I could take away your pain."

For the first time, Maren was struck by not only her mother's tender words, but her presence. The confusion must have shown on her face because Barbara smiled softly.

"It's true," she said. "I know we haven't always been close, but I'm still your mother, Maren, and I still feel your pain as if it were my own. You must understand that?"

Maren nodded. Because she did. When Rylee hurt, she felt it in her soul. It was a connection she'd never considered with her own mother.

"I wish I knew what to say to you to make it better," Barbara said. "But I don't think there is anything I could say."

Maren shook her head. "There's not. But thank you for being here," she added and meant it. For the first time in recent memory, she was thankful for her mother's presence. "It helps."

"I'm glad." Barbara reached for her hand. They sat there for a few moments without speaking, but somehow Maren pulled off her mother's strength and after a few minutes even started to feel a little bit better.

"I don't know how to do this, Mom." Maren dropped her head. "I don't know how to do any of this."

"First, you need to heal, honey. Let yourself grieve. This is a lot and your body—"

"That's not the only thing, Mom." There was no point in hiding the truth about Davis and Sabrina. As humiliating as it all was, it wouldn't be long before everyone knew about it all anyway. "The night of the accident, Davis and I were fighting."

"Fighting? About the baby?"

"Yes," Maren said. "But not my baby." She swallowed hard. "Davis and Sabrina…" She couldn't bring herself to say it. But she knew she had to. "They have been…" She swallowed again. "Sabrina is having Davis's baby."

She finally got the words out and looked to see her mom's reaction, but her mom was simply shaking her head.

"You knew?"

Barbara shrugged. "I had my suspicions but I hoped it wasn't true."

"What?"

"I'm sorry, Maren. I really did hope I was wrong. I guess… what are you going to do?"

Maren chuckled and shook her head. "The first thing I'm going to do is get this room ready for Davis."

"And then?"

More than anything, Maren wanted to be able to answer her mother's question. But she couldn't.

"I don't know, Mom. I really don't." She started to cry again, but this time it was from sadness, not grief. "I've never been on my own before. I don't know if I could do it."

"Of course you can." Her mother stood and started to gather up the shopping bags. "Maren, you are much stronger than you know. You can do anything. After all, you are my daughter. Why do you think I've always been so hard on you?"

Maren sat back, open-mouthed. There were a million ways she could sarcastically answer that question, but she settled for the truth. "I have no idea."

"Because I've always known that you're capable of so much more than you think you are. Maybe I didn't show it the way I should have, but I love you, Maren. For too long you've settled for a half version of yourself."

A half version?

"That's not true." She shook her head. "No. I tried so hard to be everything Rylee needed. And Davis, too. I wanted it all to be perfect. For our family to be perfect. There was nothing halfway about it." And there hadn't been. She'd given it her all, and she knew it. She'd done her job perfectly.

"You are an amazing mother. You always have been."

Maren blinked. She'd never heard her mother say such a thing. At least not to her.

"But that's not what I'm talking about."

"Then what are you talking about?"

Her mother put the bags down and put her hands on either side of Maren's face. "I'm talking about you, Maren. What is it that *you* want? It seems to me that you're at a crossroads and as difficult as it's going to be, it may also be a blessing. There is a lot of life out there, just waiting for you to go out and grab it."

Barbara stepped back and Maren suddenly felt untethered.

"I'm sorry I've been so hard," her mom continued. "It's just my way. But I want you to know that I'm here for you. No matter what you decide to do."

Maren nodded and her mind raced with possibilities.

"And Maren?"

She blinked and refocused on her mother.

"Never underestimate yourself."

Rylee

"DAD?" Her dad had been home from the hospital for a few days, but Rylee hadn't been able to bring herself to go visit him.

Until now.

She peeked into the room and saw him sitting up in the bed that was usually reserved for guests. He looked odd and out of place in the cheery room where her grandparents usually stayed when they came for the occasional Christmas.

"Hey, kiddo. Come in. It's good to see you. How are you feeling? You're looking good."

It had already been almost two weeks since the accident and although she felt *way* better than she had, her ribs still bothered her sometimes and she always seemed to be a bit out of breath. "I'm good." She nodded a little. "How about you? Your leg..."

His leg had been in a huge bulky cast in the hospital, but it didn't look nearly as bad now.

"It's feeling a lot better," he said. "Not nearly as bad as your wrist, I think. It's mostly my head that I still need to be cautious of. It's like having a really bad concussion. I need lots of rest."

"I'm glad you're going to be okay," she said truthfully. She wrapped her arms around her waist and stood awkwardly before her dad waved her to come closer. Slowly, she crossed the room.

"It's okay, Rylee," he said. "I'm not going to break."

"It's not that." She shook her head. "I just…I don't know what to say to you," she blurted out. "You almost died, but I'm still so mad at you and that doesn't feel right."

His smile was slow and sad. "Sweetie." He reached an arm out. "Will you come here? Please?"

She couldn't resist. As angry as she was with her dad, he was still her dad and she loved him. He patted the bed next to him and she sat. But she didn't say anything.

"I think we have a lot to talk about," he started. "Don't we?"

She nodded. "Do you remember yet? Before the accident, I mean?"

Her mom told her that he still couldn't remember all the details of the accident. Ever since that first time visiting him in the hospital, Rylee had been conflicted. What if he *hadn't* forgotten everything? Worse, what if he *had*? Because the truth was that even though she'd been drunk, she remembered exactly what she'd said and the worst part was…she wasn't entirely sure that she'd take it back if she could.

"No." His smile was sad. "I know we fought. I know we both said terrible things. But I don't remember what was said. The last thing I remember is getting in the car with your mom and then waking up in the hospital."

"You really don't remember what I said?"

He shook his head.

"Dad, I'm so—"

"Don't apologize." He cut her off. "You don't have anything to apologize for."

"But I was drunk, and I shouldn't have—"

"Rylee." He held up a finger to stop her. "Your drinking is a whole different conversation," he said. "But I think your mother has already addressed it." He grinned at the way she ducked her head because her mother had, in fact, already given her a lecture on drinking. "But alcohol or not, you said what you meant and that's okay. I always want you to talk to me about anything, okay? No matter what."

She nodded and bit her lip so she wouldn't cry.

"Now, I know we still have a lot to talk about. Ask me anything. I promise I'll answer you."

"Anything?"

He pressed his lips together and nodded. "Anything at all."

"Why?"

It was such an open-ended question that could mean a million things, but it was the only one she wanted an answer to.

"Rylee, I don't know if—"

"You said anything."

"I did and I'm going to be honest. I don't have an answer for that question because I don't know *why* I did what I did. Sabrina and I made some bad choices. Hurtful choices. And we didn't fully appreciate the magnitude of what we were doing. I know that doesn't make it any easier to understand, kiddo. But that's the truth. It was a terrible judgment call and somehow we managed to convince ourselves that it wasn't that bad. We were wrong. Terribly wrong and I wish we could take it all back."

Tears slipped down his cheeks while he spoke and he didn't try to wipe them away. Rylee had never seen her dad cry before. It was both alarming and comforting. He was hurting, too. And yes, he caused all of the hurt, but it was still there.

He reached out and slowly, she offered him her good hand.

"Sweetie, I'm sorry that you're hurting," he said. "You and your mother both. I never meant for any of this to happen."

She nodded because she could see that was true. After all, who would wish for their lives to implode?

"Are you and Mom going to get a divorce?"

"I love your mother very much."

"That's not an answer."

She already knew the answer and not because she'd asked, but because she could feel it. She thought it would hurt more than it did.

Her dad shook his head. "That's up to your mother."

She nodded. It would be divorce.

They sat in silence for a few moments before Rylee said, "I'm really mad at you, Dad. But I'm also really sad. And I don't really know what to do with that. Mom wants me to see a therapist."

"I think that's probably a good idea."

She nodded. It was.

"Are you going to marry Auntie Sabrina?"

"No." He sounded sad. "But she's always going to be in my life. We will have a son together. Your brother."

Rylee still didn't know how to feel about that either. It didn't seem fair that Auntie Sabrina got to have her baby when her mom lost hers. And Rylee still got a sibling. Everyone else got to have a baby but Mom. And that felt wrong.

"I'm going to need some time," she said after a minute, before pulling her hand from his and standing. "I think I still need to be mad."

He nodded and there was even a little bit of a smile. "I get that."

Before she turned to leave, she added, "But I won't be mad forever."

His smile was full-fledged then. "I'm glad to hear it."

Rylee smiled a little too. Her dad had done a terrible, awful thing, but he was still her dad and that wasn't going to change.

"Will you come back and visit with me again?"

She looked around and nodded. "Yup. Mom didn't even give you a TV in here. You must be pretty bored."

He chuckled. "It's okay. It gives me lots of time to think."

Before she could change her mind, she went to him and carefully, because they were both still healing, she wrapped her arms around him.

"I love you, Rylee. So much."

She let her tears drop to his shoulder as she said, "I love you, too, Dad."

Maren

EVER SINCE DAVIS had come home from the hospital, Maren had started to think of things in terms of *before* and *after*. Life *before* the accident and *after* had become vastly different. Not only in the way that it looked, but also in the way she felt inside.

Before Davis came home, Maren made her first decision for *after*. She hired a home nurse to handle his care. She might be okay with him staying in the house—for now—but she couldn't bring herself to handle his care as if nothing had happened between them.

In the weeks that followed, the house became a place of healing. As Rylee and Davis recovered from their injuries, there was obvious physical recovery taking place. But more importantly, as the days passed, something inside Maren began to heal.

Her mother's words continued to replay in her mind.

Never underestimate yourself.

There's a lot of life out there.

Grab it.

She still wasn't completely sure how she wanted to proceed,

but she became very aware that a particularly significant date was looming and almost exactly four weeks after the accident, on a warm June Saturday morning, Davis hobbled outside on his crutches and said, "Sabrina is in labor."

She'd tried to prepare herself for how it would feel to hear that news, but still the shot of pain in her chest took her off guard. She put her book down and turned to look at him.

"Rylee said she'd drive me to the hospital," Davis said, almost apologetically.

"Okay." She nodded, unsure of what else to say. The part of her that had loved both Sabrina and Davis for most of her life wanted to go with him and be with Sabrina, wanted to be there when she brought her new baby into the world. But the other, stronger part of herself, knew she couldn't do that. "Good luck." The words felt woefully inadequate, but they were all she could offer.

For a moment, Davis looked as if he wanted to say something more, but he dropped his head. When he looked up again, the moment was gone. "Thank you." He lifted his head to the sun. "It's a beautiful day." She nodded. "Maybe...well, maybe when I get back, we can..."

"You should go."

He pressed his lips together and nodded. "Right."

At some point in the night, Maren heard the door open and the now familiar thumping of Davis's crutches on the stairs as he made his way slowly and painfully upstairs. Her entire body yearned to go to him and hear about his new son. She wanted to know how Sabrina was. What the baby's name was. How much he weighed. All of the details for the baby boy who was forever linked to her in the most painful way.

But instead of slipping from her bed, Maren rolled to her

side and pulled her legs to her chest. She cried hot tears for everything she'd lost and what would no longer be. The salty tears slipped down her face and soaked the mint-green fur of the teddy bear she clutched tightly until finally, mercifully, she fell asleep.

The next morning, Maren was on her second cup of coffee by the time Davis made his way down the stairs. "Good morning."

"Morning." She tried to keep her face neutral, but was pretty sure she was failing in that department, so she picked up her mug and drank deeply. "There's coffee."

"Thanks."

They both knew he couldn't manage the mug with his crutches, so after a moment, Maren got up with a sigh, poured him a cup, and set it on the table for him. He muttered a thank-you and they sat together in awkward silence.

Finally, Davis said, "His name is James. After my father."

The air sucked from her lungs, but Maren forced herself not to react.

"He's just over eight pounds."

"Big baby," she said neutrally.

"He is." She didn't want to hear it, but she couldn't help it; the pride in Davis's voice was evident. "Sabrina did great," he continued. "There was only about four hours of labor and then...I'm sorry. You probably don't want to hear this."

But she did. It was like an exquisite form of torture, but she did want to hear it. Badly. "It's okay," she said. "That's a fast labor for a first child."

Davis nodded. "There was no time for any drugs. It happened so quickly."

Sabrina had wanted an epidural so badly. Maren felt the slightest twinge of satisfaction at that news.

"I'm glad everything went smoothly," she said after a moment. "Congratulations, Davis."

He opened his mouth as if to say something, but closed it again. He rolled the mug between his palms, but finally pushed it away. "Look, Maren. I know…well…" His face was pained, as if every word were a struggle. It probably was. "I'm just really sorry. I know this is hard."

"So hard." She raised an eyebrow and looked down into her cup. She wasn't going to let him off so easily, tell him that it was okay and that she was fine.

It wasn't. And she was decidedly not.

"We haven't really…" He hesitated. "Well, we haven't really talked about…"

"Our baby?"

They hadn't. In fact, beyond Maren letting him know she'd lost the baby, they hadn't talked about it at all. What was there to say?

Davis nodded. "I'm really sorry, Maren. I wish I could have been there for you after the accident, after…well, I wish I could have been there."

"There was nothing you could do."

"I know, but I'm sorry you had to go through that alone."

She stared at him and blinked slowly. "I'm still going through it."

"Right…I…" He scrubbed his hand over his face. "Maybe it was for the best, you know? I mean, with—"

"I know." Of course she did. She'd be lying if she said the thought hadn't crossed her mind in the weeks since the accident. After all, her life had been thrown into a tailspin; bringing a child into such a situation wasn't fair. And there was Rylee to think of. She was sixteen. And of course her career that was just taking off. Yes, there were dozens of reasons why maybe it was *for the best*.

And one reason why it wasn't.

She'd been her baby. *Her child.*

And for that one, perfect reason, losing her could never be *for the best.*

"But no," she told Davis. "No matter what, it wasn't for the best."

He nodded. "Right. I shouldn't have said that. I didn't mean it."

Maybe he did. Maybe he didn't.

It didn't matter.

"I was thinking," Davis said after a moment. "I'm going to go stay over at Sabrina's for a bit. To help with the baby," he added quickly. "I'm feeling a lot better myself and since the nurse stopped coming...well, I don't really...I think it's the best thing."

He couldn't stay there forever. Not the way things were between them. Maren knew that. She'd been expecting it. Preparing for it. But still, hearing him say the words were like another blow to her heart. She wasn't sure how much more it could take but she nodded. "Okay."

"We're not together," he said, as if that even mattered. She blinked slowly and he added, "I just wanted you to know that. We've never been...well, it's not like that. I just thought you should know."

She nodded slowly and took another sip of coffee, but it was bitter on her tongue.

They sat in silence for a few minutes before Davis spoke again. "Maren, I love you." There were tears in his eyes. "More than anything," he continued. "I wish I could change everything. I'm so sorry I hurt you." Once he started talking, the words came quickly. "You and Rylee...I love you more than anything and I want to make this right. Give me a chance to prove to you that I can change. I'll do anything. Really, Maren. *Anything.* Just say the word. Tell me what to do. Tell me how to fix this."

"Davis, I don't—"

"No." He stopped her. "Don't say no. Please don't sit there and tell me that there's nothing I can do. I won't accept that."

There were tears on his cheeks now, and she had to look away. She'd only seen him cry a handful of times before, but only in grief. This was different. But maybe not. Maybe grieving death and the end of a relationship was the same.

Because that's what it was. The end.

She knew it in her heart. On some level, she'd known it from the moment she'd discovered the truth. There was no coming back from this. No way she could forget the hurt and deception. No way she could ever look at him and not remember what he'd done. And the baby…how would she ever be able to look at his son and not see the baby they had lost?

She shook her head.

It broke her heart in so many ways, but there was no other choice.

After a moment, she looked him in the eyes. "You have to."

Rylee

RYLEE DIDN'T THINK it would ever get easier to see her dad's empty spot at the breakfast table. After the accident, things had been strange with him staying in the spare room, but it had still been easy for her to believe that everything was normal.

Well, normal-ish.

After they'd gotten over their initial weirdness, slowly things had gotten back to normal. They'd talked almost every day when he was staying there, and ever since the baby was born, there'd been lots of texting and video chats. They still had a long way to go before the damage between them was fully repaired, but it would be okay.

But now that he wasn't living at the house, it could no longer be ignored. Their family looked different now. Very different.

She had a brother. And as much as Rylee had wanted to hate Auntie Sabrina for what she did, once she met James, and held his tiny body in her arms, all of that went away.

Well, maybe not all of it.

She was still mad and there was no way she'd ever be able to look at Sabrina the same way again. But no matter what terrible decisions she and her dad had made, they were all still family. And that wasn't going to change. That's what her therapist said. And as much as Rylee didn't want to admit it right away, she was right.

It had been her mom's idea for her to start seeing a therapist and again, even though she didn't want to admit it, Rylee had to agree. Talking to Tamara had helped. A lot.

Especially because she helped convince her mom that Rylee should go back to school and finish out the year with her friends. And once the doctor changed out the cast on her wrist to something a little bit more manageable, he'd even cleared her to drive.

"You're late." Sienna slipped into the passenger seat of Rylee's car.

"Hey, you try to put makeup on with this hand." Rylee lifted her arm and laughed.

"You look great," Sienna said genuinely. "I'm really glad your mom let you come back to school. Are you nervous?"

"About school?" Rylee shook her head. "No. I'm ready for things to get back to normal." Whatever *normal* even looked like anymore.

Maybe Tamara was right and *normal* would look a little different every day for a little bit. That was okay. As long as she had a few constants to cling to. Like her mom. And Sienna. Rylee took a second to look at her best friend. *Really* look at her.

On their way back from visiting her dad in the hospital after he woke up and Sienna texted at the most perfect moment, as if she knew Rylee needed her, she'd asked her mom to stop at Sienna's house, and she was so glad she had. They'd finally had the talk they'd needed to. They'd laughed and cried, and cried some more. But after all the apologies and explanations and even more tears, they'd come out the other side. Sienna was more than her best friend; she was like her sister and Rylee was never going to take that for granted again. And she was definitely not going to screw it up because of a boy.

"Hey, do you and Brice want to come with Cole and me to the mall after school? I was going to pick up a birthday present for my brother."

Rylee didn't take her eyes off the road, but she shook her head. "Not today. I'm going to see my baby brother." Just thinking of James made her smile. He was the sweetest baby and it helped that he didn't live with her, so she didn't have to deal with any of the sleepless nights, but got to enjoy as many cuddles as she wanted.

Sometimes it made her feel guilty that she enjoyed James so much. Was she being disloyal to her mom? Or the baby who was lost? Tamara was helping her to not feel guilty about that, too. But her mom actually seemed to be doing okay with it all. She'd started smiling again and the two of them were starting to figure out what things looked like as a duo instead of a trio. They still had a ways to go, but more and more, it had started to feel right.

"That's cool." Sienna was talking about the mall and how maybe the four of them could go to a movie that weekend. "Does that sound good?"

"A movie sounds great."

Brice and Cole were waiting for them when they got to the school. Rylee's heart did a little flip the way it still did when she saw Brice. She'd worried so much about what their relationship would be like after the night of the accident. A lot of things had changed for her. And even though everyone insisted that it hadn't been her fault, she was pretty sure there'd always be at least a little part of her that took responsibility. After all, if she hadn't been drinking, it never would have happened.

But she didn't plan to drink ever again. Well, at least not until she was an adult. She'd more than learned her lesson, and when she told Brice, she'd been afraid he would break up with her. But it was a risk she was willing to take. She needed to be her own person.

He'd surprised her by not only being totally okay with her decision, but his willingness to support it. "Me either," he'd said. "We don't need it. I just really like spending time with you, Rylee." He'd kissed her and for the first time since they'd had sex, she felt a different connection with him. A real one.

"There's something else," she'd said. "I don't think I'm ready to have sex." She glanced down quickly, but then before she could chicken out, looked up again. "I mean, I know we've already done it, but…maybe we could slow down for a while?"

Again, he'd surprised her when he stroked a piece of hair back off her cheek and smiled. "Of course. Rylee, I meant it when I said I loved you. I know…we're young and…whatever." He shook his head, a little embarrassed. "But I really do care about you. I never wanted to rush you into anything."

Her heart had swelled even more and she stood on her tiptoes to kiss him softly. "Thank you."

In the days since they'd had that talk, things had only gotten even better with Brice.

"Hey there, beautiful ladies," Brice greeted them as they left the car. "Good morning, gorgeous." He kissed her softly. "I'm glad you're back. In fact, I was even thinking of going to *all* of my classes today in honor of your return."

Rylee laughed. "Wow. That is quite an honor."

He took her books from her and put his free arm around her waist as they walked into the school.

Despite everything that had happened, or maybe because of it, for the first time in a long time, Rylee felt like everything was actually going to be okay.

Sabrina

"SSH...BABY. SSH. IT'S OKAY." Sabrina rocked the infant and tucked him closer to her chest, but still the crying wouldn't stop. At barely two weeks old, James was quickly starting to become what the books and websites called a *fussy* baby.

Fussy?

Sabrina could definitely think of a few different words. But whatever it was, his constant crying was starting to make her crazy. When they'd first come home from the hospital, James had slept and fed without much trouble. She'd been completely smitten with his sweet face and tiny fingers and toes. Davis had moved onto an inflatable bed in the nursery, since the baby was sleeping in her room. Even with his broken leg, he'd been a big help. Even if it was just sitting up with her during the night feedings.

But as they settled in at home, something changed. Maybe it was her own lack of sleep. But whatever it was, James was becoming harder and harder to settle, and nursing him was starting to become an exercise in frustration.

"Please stop crying." Sabrina pleaded with the baby, whose tiny, scrunched-up face had turned a bright shade of pink.

"Have you tried changing him?" Davis came into the living room, dressed for work. The crutches were gone, replaced now by his new air boot walking cast. The cuts and bruises had all but healed and there was very little evidence left that spoke of the terrible accident he'd been in and how close she'd come to losing the father of her baby. "Maybe his diaper is—"

"Of course I changed him." Sabrina shifted the baby up on her shoulder and resumed patting his back. "I just fed him but I swear my boobs still feel like they're going to explode. I don't think I'm doing it right."

"Don't be ridiculous," Davis said. "It's breastfeeding. How could you not be doing it right?"

It was a good thing she was holding the baby, because Sabrina was fairly sure if she had a free hand, she would have hit Davis.

He'd been so supportive and helpful but when it came to breastfeeding, there was nothing he could do to help. And hearing about how natural it was, and how Maren hadn't had any trouble with Rylee, was *not* helpful.

"I've been reading online." Sabrina tried to shift James in her arms. "And I think maybe he's just not getting the latch right so he's not able to get enough milk."

"So how do you fix that?"

"If I knew that, I'd be doing it!" she snapped at him and immediately regretted it. "Sorry." She handed Davis the baby. "Take him. Please. I can't even think."

Davis took the baby and started bouncing him while he talked to him in soothing voices. Almost at once James settled, his screams fading into occasional hiccups. More than once in the past few weeks, it had taken her off guard to see how good he was with the baby. It shouldn't have surprised her, though. After all, he was a father. He'd had experience with all this before. Davis knew what he was doing. It was her who was in way over her head.

She slumped into the couch. "I'm sorry. I didn't mean to snap at you." She tipped her head back and closed her tired eyes. "I really am thankful you're here, Davis. I don't know what I was thinking."

"About what?"

"All of this." She refused to open her eyes. "I didn't realize it would be so hard. So…exhausting. I mean, I knew. But I didn't know. You know?"

He chuckled and she lifted her head to look at him. "I get it," he said. "I think I'd totally blocked out those early days with Rylee. But I promise it will pass."

She assessed him for a moment. He'd sat across from her, the baby tucked into his arms. He looked down at his son with such love in his eyes that if she let herself, Sabrina could forget for a moment that their situation was such a mess. They weren't together, and even though she'd had some completely irrational moments in the days after James was born, she knew she didn't want to make a family with Davis. Obviously they'd always be a family, but never in the traditional sense. He didn't belong with her in her condo. Not long-term anyway. And they both knew it.

Davis belonged with Maren and Rylee. That was his family.

But from everything he'd said, as much as he wanted to fix things, it didn't look as though the situation was fixable.

"How was your visit with Dr. Tommy?" Davis wiggled his eyebrows and Sabrina couldn't decide whether she wanted to hit him or roll her eyes. Ever since they'd come home from the hospital, Dr. Tommy had been insisting how much he wanted to come visit her and the baby. She'd managed to put him off for a few weeks, but finally she gave in.

He'd arrived with an oversized bouquet of flowers—and a cheese platter, of all things.

"Let's just say we have enough cheese to feed…well…I

don't know what we can feed with that much cheese." She let herself laugh. "He also told me how amazing I looked and how motherhood suited me." She shook her head. "Which is obviously bullshit. I look like a deflated balloon that hasn't slept in weeks."

"You look great." Davis shook his head. "Have you ever thought that maybe he has a thing for you?"

Of course, but…

She shrugged, but no longer brushed it off because she was absolutely sure he had *a thing* for her. Just like she had one for him. She'd been so scared he'd judge her for her terrible choices, but when Dr. Tommy had come to visit, she told him everything, suddenly filled with the need for him to know the truth. No matter what, she wasn't going to keep lying about who James's daddy was. No more.

"Well, I sure think he does," Davis said. "I mean, any man who willingly braves a new mother and all the hormones—" He cut himself off with a laugh when she glared at him. "I'm just saying," he added.

"Well, whatever. I have more important things to think about right now than dating. One little man in my life is enough." She only had eyes for James. "And he actually offered to extend my maternity leave another three weeks if I wanted it."

"Really? Paid?"

Sabrina nodded and couldn't help the grin that spread across her face. Having a full three months of paid maternity leave was a blessing she hadn't expected. But she'd take it because for the life of her she couldn't imagine going back to work on such a little amount of sleep. She didn't bother telling Davis that Dr. Tommy had also asked if he could come back and visit her and James during those three months.

And she'd said yes.

"That's pretty sweet," Davis said with a laugh before

changing the subject. "I talked to Rylee this morning," Davis said. "She wants to come by after school today and see James. Does that work for you?"

"Of course. She's welcome anytime. I'd love to see her more."

Davis flashed her a look, but didn't say anything. Sabrina knew Rylee was mad at her and it broke her heart. She'd always had such a special relationship with her. It was just one more relationship they'd both ruined with their selfishness. Thankfully, Rylee had a big heart; she might not be happy with Sabrina, but she was completely smitten with her new baby brother and had already been around to visit more than once. Maybe with time, Rylee would be able to forgive her.

Sabrina bit her bottom lip. "Did she mention anything about Maren?" She hated to ask, but she needed to know. "Did you tell her that she was welcome to come visit and I'd…" She trailed off at the look on Davis's face.

"I mentioned it," he said. "I also mentioned it to Maren when I spoke with her the other day." He shook his head. "I just don't think she's ready, Sabrina." He shifted the baby in his arms and kissed James's tiny forehead. "I think coming to visit will be too hard."

Sabrina nodded. "I understand." And she did. But it was still hard. She knew it was her fault and she deserved to be shut out and pushed away. Hell, she deserved worse than that after what she'd done. But she still missed her best friend so badly it caused a physical ache. "I get it."

Davis kissed the baby again and moved to hand him back to her. "I need to get going," he said. "I have a client in less than an hour." Davis had gone back to work on a part-time basis as he recovered from the accident. Sabrina hated that he had to leave her alone, but he didn't have any other choice. Financially, things were going to start getting tight, and as much as she'd prefer time to freeze, it wasn't an option.

She tensed the moment the baby was placed in her arms again. Maybe if she didn't move he'd keep sleeping. Just long enough for her to rest her eyes for a moment.

"You're going to be okay," Davis said. "I'll be home before you know it."

She tried to smile, but all she really wanted to do was cry.

Thankfully, James slept for almost twenty minutes, during which time Sabrina scoured the internet and the baby forums and read everything she could about latches and breastfeeding problems. So when the baby woke up and predictably started screaming again, she was equipped with slightly more information and a few new ideas to try out.

"Okay, kiddo." She placed the baby in her lap while she lifted her shirt and unsnapped her nursing bra. "We've got this." She made a number of attempts to get James to latch and finally, mercifully, he did. She could have cried from the relief of having him feed. Instead, she stroked his soft cheek and gazed into his perfect blue eyes.

She was so exhausted and equally enamored with her baby while he fed that Sabrina didn't even notice the time passing until there was a knock on the door.

"Dammit."

She'd been hoping to at least brush her hair before Rylee came by, but she'd completely lost track of time. James didn't show any signs of finishing up, and she wasn't about to disturb him, so she whisper-yelled, "Come in," and turned back to her baby.

The door opened behind her.

"Hi, Rylee," Sabrina said, careful not to raise her voice. "I'm sorry I didn't have time to clean up. Come on in."

"I'm not Rylee." The familiar voice made Sabrina's breath catch. "Can I come in?"

Maren

MAREN ALMOST TURNED BACK a dozen times.

Once she pulled up to the condo unit, it had taken her almost fifteen minutes to get out of the car and walk to the door.

She didn't know how she was going to feel or what she was going to say or…anything, really.

The only thing she knew was that in order to heal, she needed to see Sabrina and her baby. Ignoring their existence wasn't healthy and the weight of *not* visiting them weighed much too heavy on her heart.

She finally worked up the courage to knock on the door. Not one time since Sabrina had moved in had Maren ever knocked. She'd always just walked in and announced herself as if she belonged there. And she had.

But not anymore.

"Come in." She heard the voice from within, followed by a welcome to Rylee. But it was too early for Rylee, who was still at school and had told Maren she'd be visiting the baby. Maren encouraged her to get to know her baby brother, as much as it hurt her. Every time Maren thought about her daughter holding her new baby brother in her arms, it caused a physical pain in her chest. She hoped it would lessen over time, especially for Rylee's sake, because for better or worse, that was the new reality. After all, it wasn't her fault all of this happened and James was her brother. They deserved to have a relationship despite the actions of their parents.

Rylee still struggled to accept everything that happened, but she was trying. One more reason why Maren needed to do this herself.

"It's not Rylee." She walked through the door of the condo. "Can I come in?"

Sabrina's head twisted around from where she sat on the couch. She nodded. "Of course."

Maren had tried to prepare herself for seeing baby James for the first time but still, the image of Sabrina nursing her baby hit her in the gut. It was a physical pain that no doubt showed on her face, but she didn't try to hide it.

"I'm sorry it's such a mess in here." Sabrina started prattling on about the state of the house and her appearance, but Maren didn't have eyes for anything but the baby, who was starting to fall asleep at the breast. "I think he's almost done," Sabrina said. "It's been such a battle to get him to…I'm sorry, would you like a tea or cheese or—"

"Cheese? No." Maren shook her head. "I can't stay long."

They were silent for a few moments while James finished nursing. Sabrina lifted him to her shoulder and patted his back until he let out a little burp.

"He's beautiful."

Sabrina lifted her eyes to meet Maren's. "Thank you. Do you…I mean…would you…"

Maren shook her head, answering the question that she didn't have to ask. She wrapped her arms around herself in a hug. "Not right now."

"Okay, I just thought maybe…I don't know…" Sabrina

swallowed hard and sat back. "I don't know what I'm trying to say. This is just so…"

"Awkward? Completely awful? Really hard?"

Sabrina chuckled. "Yes. All of those things." The laughter died on her lips and she shook her head. "Maren, I'm so sorry that all of—"

"No." She stopped her. She didn't come for apologies. "I don't want to talk about any of that." She'd already decided the details of the past weren't important. She'd been through it all a million times. The lies, the way Sabrina had gotten so mad at the news of Maren's old pregnancy…it all made as much sense as it ever would. And talking about it wasn't going to change it. Not anymore. "I just wanted to see you and meet James." Her eyes drifted again to the sleeping baby. "He seems like he's a pretty calm baby."

That made Sabrina laugh again. "Now he is. I swear, he's been so difficult, Maren. I had no idea that breastfeeding was going to be so hard. Davis keeps saying how easy it was for you, and I just don't know what I'm doing wrong." Tears flooded her eyes.

Despite herself, Maren felt a pull to ease her former friend's distress.

"Davis is an idiot," she said instead. "Sure, breastfeeding was easy for him. He didn't have to do it."

That made the other woman laugh.

"No one tells you how hard it can be," Maren continued. "And those first few weeks were challenging, but we got through it and you will too."

"God, I hope so." She shook her head and looked down at the baby.

"Just keep to a schedule and don't forget to switch sides." Maren offered suggestions. "If one side gets too full, it makes it harder for them to latch. At least that's how it worked for Rylee."

"Thank you." Sabrina looked at her with such a potent mixture of love and sadness that something inside Maren shifted.

She moved closer. "I changed my mind. Can I hold him?"

Sabrina handed her the baby and Maren sat down on the couch with the infant, who wasn't quite asleep yet, in her arms. She wasn't sure how it would feel, but when she looked down into the eyes that were the exact same sea blue that Rylee's had been when she was born before they faded to match Davis's green ones, a flood of love and regret rushed through her. Baby James was forever linked to her as Rylee's brother and Davis's son. But she'd never have the relationship with him that she'd once thought she would. She'd never be Auntie Maren to this little boy.

Those days were gone before they began and the thought made her immeasurably sad.

"He's beautiful, Sabrina. Really."

"Thank you."

His eyes finally closed in a milk-drunk sleep and she shifted the baby against her shoulder and let herself feel the weight of him against her chest. For a moment, she closed her eyes and let herself believe that it was her baby she was holding, but only for a moment. Because it wasn't her baby in her arms. It never would be and as acutely as she felt the pain of that, Maren also felt peace.

She opened her eyes and with one more look at him, handed the baby back to Sabrina, who watched her with an unreadable expression on her face. "I should go."

"You don't have to," Sabrina said quickly. "Why don't you stay? I'll make some tea."

Maren shook her head. "No. It's time. But thank you." She stood and straightened her blouse but before she turned away, she looked at Sabrina. "You're going to be a great mom. Don't doubt your instincts."

"Thank you." Tears pooled in Sabrina's eyes, and Maren had to turn away.

"Maren?"

Slowly, she turned back. Sabrina's lip quivered and her eyes were rimmed red with a mixture of exhaustion and emotion.

"Can I..." Sabrina swallowed hard. "Can I call you sometime?"

More than anything, Maren wanted to say yes. She missed her friend and the way things used to be.

But there were some things you couldn't come back from. She pressed her lips together in a sad smile. "I don't think that's a good idea."

"I understand." Sabrina nodded. "And Maren?" she said before Maren could turn away again. "I know you don't want to hear it and I know it won't change anything. But I really am sorry. I wish I could change everything."

"Don't waste a wish." Maren shook her head. "Besides, if things were different, you wouldn't have James." She let her gaze linger on the infant for one last moment before she turned and left.

As she drove away from Sabrina's house, Maren found it easier and easier to breathe, as if a weight she didn't know she was carrying had been lifted. It had been harder than she could have imagined to look Sabrina in the eye after everything she'd done. Harder still to hold her baby, the product of her husband's deception, in her arms. But it hadn't killed her.

She'd not only survived the moment, but she felt better than she had in a long time.

The closer she got to home, the lighter she felt until finally she pulled up in front of the house she'd once loved so much. The house that was supposed to be their *forever home.* Where she and Davis would raise Rylee and then wait for grandchildren to fill the rooms once again with their laughter and love. They were going to retire there, spending their days tending the gardens in the summer, traveling to warmer climates in the winter, but always returning to their home. Together.

Maren stood on the sidewalk and looked at the white clapboard-sided house. She took in the maple tree they'd planted the summer they moved in. It was almost as tall as the house now. The gardens she'd spent so many hours watering and weeding had filled in beautifully with perennials and bright blooms.

Inside, the rooms had been full of love and memories that she'd spent the last fourteen years working for. She'd dedicated her entire life for her family. Sacrificing herself to create the perfect home. To be the best mother and wife she could be. And she'd done a damn good job.

But the whole time, there'd been an undercurrent of deception waiting to bring it all down.

Would it have mattered?

Would it have changed anything if she'd known that one day her world would implode and everything she'd worked so hard to create would shatter around them? If she could have guessed at all she never knew, would things have been any different?

Would she want it to be?

Despite the warm summer day, Maren wrapped her arms around herself and squeezed.

No.

She wouldn't have changed a thing.

It had been a good life. Not a perfect one. But it had been theirs.

No matter what Davis had done—the way he'd violated their trust—the memories of the past couldn't be changed. It had happened. It had all happened. And she didn't regret a moment of it.

Just as she wouldn't regret the decision she'd come to a few days ago.

There was no going back. Only forward. Which was why before she'd gone to visit Sabrina, Maren had made a visit to her lawyer's office.

She was forty years old.

She had the rest of her life in front of her.

She was ready.

Maren

MAREN HAD THOUGHT a lot about how she'd feel. She'd imagined almost every possible scenario. But nothing could have prepared her for how it actually felt to hold in her hands the thick envelope that contained her divorce papers.

The courier from her lawyer's office had dropped them off earlier that morning, but Maren wasn't quite ready to open them. Not that she expected there to be any surprises. She knew exactly what the papers said. She and Davis had agreed easily and amicably.

There'd been hurt on both sides. But there hadn't been any anger.

As much as she loved Davis—would always love him—there was no coming back from what he'd done. They both knew that.

In the months since the accident, Maren had grown stronger and for the first time in her life, she was standing on her own two feet. And it felt good.

It was only four in the afternoon, but Maren poured herself a glass of wine and took the envelope outside to the backyard. She sat on the patio and closed her eyes, letting herself feel the heat of the summer sun while she took in the sounds of the neighborhood, the birds chirping in the trees, the delicate scent of the rosebushes she'd planted years ago and tended carefully every summer.

When she opened her eyes, she was ready.

The document was thick, yet surprisingly thin. An entire lifetime summed up in a packet of papers. A life and a marriage divided into words and paragraphs.

She didn't bother to stop the tear that slipped down her cheek as she signed and initialed in all of the necessary places.

A thick cloud of suffocating sadness swallowed her, but only for a moment as she let herself think of all the hopes and dreams she and Davis had for their life. All of the plans they'd now never realize. But then the cloud passed, the skies cleared, and the sun once more warmed her through because with every dream that died, another was born.

Carefully, she tucked the packet of papers back into the envelope and pushed them aside in favor of her wine glass.

Maren lifted it in a silent toast to the life that was and drank deeply.

To the start of her new life. Forty was always meant to be a fresh beginning for her. Although she never could have imagined her life would take the turn it did, she was ready to embrace whatever came next.

Leaving the envelope on the patio table, Maren took her wine glass and walked around to the front yard.

She was so lost in her own thoughts that she didn't notice right away when Jessica came—her own wine glass in hand—to join her where she stood, facing her house.

"I'm not going to lie," Jessica said softly. "It feels really strange to see this."

Maren nodded, knowing exactly what her friend meant.

The blue-and-red *For Sale* sign stood in stark contrast

against the backdrop of her white house. A SOLD sticker splashed across the front.

"It's time," Maren said.

"Selfishly, I wish it wasn't." Jessica laughed. "But I get it," she said. "I really do."

Maren put her arm around her friend and they tipped their heads together. She was more and more grateful for the support Jessica had given her and the way their friendship had deepened.

She'd made the decision to sell the house the same day she'd visited her lawyer and met baby James for the first time. It was time to move on, and she couldn't do that living in their family home. Rylee had been sad initially. After all, it was the only home she'd known. But together they picked out a much smaller bungalow in a nearby neighborhood with huge windows and a lemon-yellow kitchen. They'd both rolled their eyes at the paint color, but ultimately decided to keep it. At least for a little while.

They moved in two weeks.

"I'm only going to be a few minutes away," Maren said. "Besides, you and Chad...you guys seem pretty serious."

She shrugged. "Who would have guessed, right? I guess I was more ready than I thought I was."

Jessica's smile brightened her entire face. Maren had been so wrapped up in her own drama that she'd hardly noticed her friend's transformation from a bitter divorcée, stuck in the past that hadn't gone her way, to a woman in love and full of life.

"You deserve to be happy, Jess. You really do." She turned to face her friend. "I'm so happy for you."

"Thank you." She paused for a moment. "I know this seems like a strange thing to say considering everything that's happened, but...I'm really happy for you, too, Maren."

She couldn't help it; Maren laughed a little.

"Seriously," Jessica continued. "I know it might not feel like it right now, Maren. Not entirely. But this is only the beginning."

"I will absolutely toast to that." They lifted their glasses, first to the house, and then to each other, clinking before drinking.

It was a bittersweet day, to be sure. And Maren had no idea what the future held for her. But the one thing she did know for sure was that her friend was right.

This was only the beginning.

About the Author

Elena Aitken is a USA Today Bestselling Author of more than forty romance and women's fiction novels. Living a stone's throw from the Rocky Mountains with her teenager twins, their two cats and a goofy rescue dog, Elena escapes into the mountains whenever life allows. She can often be found with her toes in the lake and a glass of wine in her hand, dreaming up her next book and working on her own happily ever after with her very own mountain man.

To learn more about Elena:
www.elenaaitken.com
elena@elenaaitken.com

Made in the USA
Coppell, TX
23 November 2020